Bedste Ønsker!
Bedst
KK Brees

Headwind

The Intrepid Adventures of OSS Agent Katrin Nissen:

Volume One

by

KK Brees

Chalet Publishers, LLC

Arizona Alabama

Author's Note

This book is a work of fiction. Names, characters, places, and incidents are used fictitiously, and any resemblance to actual persons, living or dead, and actual events is entirely coincidental.

Chalet Publishers, LLC
www.ChaletPublishers.com
chaletpublishers@cox.net

ISBN: 978-0-9840836-9-5 [pbk]
978-1-936395-03-3 [ebook]

Printed in the United States of America
First Edition

To the men, women, and children

of the Danish Resistance.

Acknowledgements

Writing historical fiction demands accuracy at the very least and I am indebted to the resources provided by Bletchley Park and the information supplied by the librarians at Oxford University, England. The Danish Consulate in San Francisco answered my numerous questions and provided excellent resources as well.

Thanks to John for his patience while I wrote and rewrote.

To the Payette Lakes Writers Group for listening to the endless first drafts of early chapters. Linda, Dixie, and Christie – you helped me get to the final page. Jane, thanks for your insights and honest critique.

To Lydia, for your unwavering support and belief in the book.

And finally, to Joyce Norman and Joy Collins, my publishers at Chalet, my thanks for giving Katrin a second glance.

Preface

What General Weygand has called the Battle of France is over. I expect that the Battle of Britain is about to begin. Upon this battle depends the survival of Christian civilization. Upon it depends our own British life, and the long continuity of our institutions and our Empire. The whole fury and might of the enemy must very soon be turned on us. Hitler knows that he will have to break us in this island or lose the war. If we can stand up to him, all Europe may be freed and the life of the world may move forward into broad, sunlit uplands.

But if we fail, then the whole world, including the United States, including all that we have known and cared for, will sink into the abyss of a new dark age made more sinister, and perhaps more protracted, by the lights of perverted science. Let us therefore brace ourselves to our duties, and so bear ourselves, that if the British Empire and its Commonwealth last for a thousand years, men will still say, 'This was their finest hour.'

Winston Churchill
Prime Minister of Great Britain 1940-1945

Chapter One

March 1940
New Haven, Connecticut

Our invitation to attend the War, delivered by Western Union shortly after breakfast, lay before us on the kitchen table, awaiting the favor of a reply. To be fair, it wasn't unexpected, although the timing could have been better. Actually, the timing could have been a great deal better. To be accurate, it wasn't an invitation but rather an Order to Report. My eyes traveled back and forth from my research notes to the telegram. I sighed and drummed my fingers on the tablecloth as I read the missive for the third time.

"Client wishes to discuss contract renewals." Stop.
"New York facility ready for your use." Stop.

"If I leave now, all this," I gestured to the stacks of three by five index cards filled with data on the desk and the books piled up in odd spots around the room, "won't mean diddly squat."

"Diddly squat?" My husband, nose buried in the business section of the *New Haven Register,* didn't bother to look up.

"That's what I said. Diddly squat." I set my coffee cup down on the saucer with more force than necessary and checked to be sure I hadn't chipped the Havilland. Damn. There it was. I sighed and ran a finger along the hairline crack that extended smack dab across the saucer from rim to rim. "I'm exchanging one maelstrom for another. Cynthia Lawton is going to pounce like a rabid tigress when I'm out of the picture." I sighed again at the thought of this bane of my academic existence, and this time John looked up from the news.

"Is this a conversation I'm involved in or just a rant I'd best be left out of?"

"It's a rant but I'm running out of steam. It's safe to emerge from cover."

"In that event, I'll offer my two cents worth." He lowered the paper. "I'm not sure tigers get rabies but I *am* sure that Cynthia is eminently adaptable. She'll start nipping at someone else's heels during your absence. Her sort thrives on conflict. Don't worry, Katrin, she'll resume where she left off with you when you return to university."

"It's nice to be able to count on something in uncertain times."

"War, death, and taxes, to embellish an old phrase. You know, it's been ten years," John said, "no, closer to fifteen, since I've worked overseas."

I nodded, waiting.

"They're going to need us all, and soon. We're just the first wave."

I knew what he meant. *They* were *us*, in a manner of speaking - British Intelligence and the American Office of Strategic Services, MI6 and the OSS.

"We're going to be pulled back into the game, like it or not." John's jaw tensed, causing a small muscle to quiver below his right ear. He glanced at the telegram and shook his head.

I gathered up the breakfast dishes and carried them to the sink, leaving John to wrestle with his own demons. He'd be leaving a law practice just as he was about to make partner.

I'd be leaving Yale just as I was about to publish and make my move for a full professorship. What would we come back to? It was a question without an answer.

I washed and rinsed the dishes and paused when my finger felt the rough edge of the saucer I'd chipped. Should I throw it away or hold onto it? It seemed like a metaphor for my life. Could I stay or should I go? There really wasn't any question about it, after all, and I'd known what my answer would be as soon as I'd scanned the telegram the first time. I shelved the saucer and dried my hands on my apron. Like a marriage, we'd signed on for better or worse, in good times and bad. This qualified as bad without any doubt. I stared out the kitchen window as snow fell in lazy, spiraling patterns to the ground and framed the window in a rickrack of ice crystals, cold and sharp. I gave an involuntary shudder and poured myself another cup of coffee.

"On into the fray and all that," I said, returning to my chair across from John. "Maybe it's 'off into the fray'. Regardless," I frowned, "Hitler's not playing games." I wrapped my hands around my coffee cup and savored the warmth. "And yet he's only one man. It doesn't seem possible he can be causing so much trouble."

"Sometimes one man is all it takes to turn the world on its ass." John's eyes grew dark. "Hitler's not going to stop with what he's gained. He wants all of Europe."

"Wanting isn't necessarily getting," I said, although I had to admit Adolf had been getting more than his share lately. He was a nasty man.

"True. But he's just getting started. Give him time. This is the beginning of a blood lust and his sights are set on England and even Africa, as farfetched as that seems. He'd probably take the moon if he could find a way to get there."

"But he can't, can he? Not the moon, of course. No one will ever get to the moon," I said. Europe was a different matter, however, although Hitler was an unlikely specimen to be the next Alexander the Great. Charlie Chaplin had mocked him in *The Little Dictator*, calling him "Der Phooey" instead of "Der Fuehrer." Also, I didn't like that little black ink smudge under Hitler's nose. It looked like dirt. He was loud, too. Always yelling. The man lacked manners.

John's voice yanked me back into the moment. "Don't underestimate him or an idea whose time has come. It's a matter of priorities."

"Not our priorities, that's for certain. He sure has an impeccable sense of timing, if his goal is to make life miserable for everyone else."

John pushed back his chair and walked to the coffee table where he studied the hand-carved wooden pipe rack that resided there. "So. There it is, nevertheless." He chose the Meerschaum and reached for his tobacco pouch.

I nodded absently, my thoughts now scattered and as difficult to rein in as the snowflakes swirling beyond the window. Things change so quickly. The world was marching to war with us in the advance battalion. How it would end only heaven knew and heaven wasn't telling. Outside, the wind grew stronger. My gentle winter scene had evaporated into a blizzard of confused snowflakes, hurtling against each other as they fell to earth. I left John to his pipe and set off to the bedroom to pack.

The old Gladstone suitcase had been my companion on more trips than I could count. I pulled it down from the closet shelf, opened it up on the bed, and the tarnished hinges groaned as I called them back into service once more. The suitcase was roomy, but I had no idea what to put in it. Where was I going? How long would I be gone? Not knowing actually made the job easier. I finally decided all I could do was pack the basics. I also decided I needed some company.

Turning on the radio, I fiddled with the knob until I brought in my favorite program, "The Romance of Helen

Trent." Helen was intrepid. She was also beautiful, competent in business, and ingenious at getting herself out of scrapes. She was my kind of gal.

Fielden Farrington, the oily announcer, was humming the theme song and reciting the familiar opening and my lips moved in silent accompaniment: "Once again, we bring you the 'Romance of Helen Trent,' who sets out to prove for herself what so many women long to prove – that because a woman is thirty-five, or more, romance in life need not be over – that romance can live in life at thirty-five and after."

Well of course it could. What idiot would think that a thirty-five year old woman was past romance? It just so happened that thirty-seven wasn't over the hill either. I was doing just fine. Farrington tended to be long-winded and generally insufferable. He finally retreated to some distant part of the studio to practice his pear-shaped tone modulation, and I sat down on the bed, my arms full of lingerie, to listen. Helen had a tough life but she was a scrapper.

In today's episode, Gil Whitney, Helen's abiding love and a brilliant and prominent attorney, was a secret government agent. I huffed at the radio. That was rather farfetched. One just didn't become a government agent overnight. I knew about these things. It took time. Years, even. And training for heaven's sakes. Why just yesterday Gil had been a corporate president and today he was a master spy. And why couldn't Gil and Helen just get down to brass tacks, tell each other they loved each other, get married, and be done with it? They could have been married and divorced six times over in the time it took them to complete a sentence.

I huffed again and jammed the lingerie into the suitcase. My new six-gore slip, guaranteed to make me look ten pounds slimmer, went on top. I slipped my hand inside my only good pair of silk stockings and promptly snagged them. Grabbing an emery board, I smoothed my nails after the fact.

It seemed that the more expensive something was the shorter its lifespan. And stockings were expensive. I tossed them in anyway.

The announcer had come back on and was interjecting his concerned voice into the proceedings once again, advising me that unsightly blackheads could spoil my otherwise flawless complexion. I reached for my compact and examined my pores. I added a bar of Palmolive soap to the suitcase.

At eleven o'clock, I was packed and Helen's daily fifteen minute sojourn into danger was over, replaced by the Jimmy Dorsey Orchestra. I took a break and went to retrieve the mail, which had cascaded through the door slot and spread out across the floor. Nestled on top of the usual bills and advertisements was an airmail envelope that bore a Danish stamp. I smiled when I recognized the monthly letter from my sister, Inge.

Turning up the volume on "Lullaby on Broadway," I sat down to read the news from home.

Inge's life revolved around her husband, Lars, and she'd enclosed a recent photograph of him resplendent in his police officer's uniform. I thought, not for the first time, that police officers the world over have a quality that identifies them, even without their uniforms. Lars was no exception. Tall and muscular, Lars had a presence about him. Maybe it was the steady gaze of his deep blue eyes or the confident way he carried himself. His uniform accentuated his calm sense of purpose and authority. It wasn't just something he put on and took off when his shift was over. It defined him. I smiled at the photo and put it to the side.

I noted with passing interest the obituary of the much-beloved Pastor Lundquist, age seventy-two. Pastor had been the victim of a traffic accident while on vacation in Copenhagen. The church was hopeful of obtaining a new minister.

And then came the final item. Inge had enclosed the

quarterly dividend from the annuity controlled by the family trust. She and I were the sole beneficiaries, now that our parents were gone. A note clipped to the check said, “Contact me!” The words were underlined with two bold strokes of a pen. I scowled. Today had been notable for brief and provocative communications. I suppose it’s good to be wanted, but a warning flag had gone up with this summons. It was a feeling more than anything, but it felt like trouble.

Chapter Two

The Danish town of Sankt Peder, on the western coast of Jutland

Anna Jensen slipped the navy blue woolen sock off the darning egg and inspected her work. She stretched the fabric and held it up to the window, squinting in the sunlight, checking for holes and knots. Satisfied it was smooth and wouldn't cause Volmer's feet to hurt, she folded it with its mate and returned her mending equipment to the workbasket on the floor beside her rocking chair. She flexed her fingers and then rubbed her hands together, her swollen knuckles aching with the cold. Her eyes were tired and blurry and her bunions were also complaining. Her hands, her eyes, her feet. Anna sighed. She tapped her toes on the hardwood floor to get her circulation moving, while she considered what to do next.

She decided that a hot cup of tea would be soothing and perhaps along with it, a nice blueberry muffin, although what she really wanted was conversation and companionship. Her face brightened as she thought of Volmer across the field down by the storage shed, repairing the fishing nets. In a few moments she was humming softly as she set about preparing a mid-morning snack for the two of them to share. She would get a bit of fresh air while she checked on how

Volmer was faring.

It was a blustery March day with the hint of spring in the wind. The air was cool but the sun was warm and Anna donned her woolen coat, knit cap, scarf, and gloves, preparing to do battle with the elements. It might be shady down by the shed and the shade would still be damp. Better to be too warm and shed her coat than be too cold and shiver. Still, spring was coming. It was in the air and she could smell it in the fresh scent of the earth. Soon the daffodils and tulips would burst into bloom and also her hyacinths. Her grape hyacinths were her favorites. She inhaled happily.

Spring was also on the ground in the form of puddles. Puddles were everywhere. It had rained steadily all day yesterday and on into the night and now there were puddles. Water in the pastures had collected in the footprints of the cattle, pooled into tiny rivulets, flowed and churned down the gullies, along the fence rows, and eventually into the sea, the northern boundary of the Jensen farm. Water all the way to Volmer.

Volmer had just tied the last knot in the fishing net and now stood looking out to sea. On calm days, the water lapped gently against the shore, and on those days when the tide was low, he could walk along the rock concourse to the lighthouse a hundred yards out, climb the narrow circular staircase, and survey his world. On stormy nights, when the waters were a fury, the lighthouse warned mariners of shallow waters and dangerous rocks and currents. In all seasons and at all times of the day or night the lighthouse stood as a lonely sentinel of hope and witness to the power of nature. Today the waters were still rough and choppy after yesterday's storm.

Volmer didn't consider himself a religious man, but the seas - undisciplined, timeless, and brutal - spoke to some secret part of his soul. He knew the rhythms of the tides that flowed as surely as the blood that coursed through his veins and he could scent the change of seasons in the salt mist. There was a reassurance in the patterns of the ocean, a reminder of the presence of God. In Volmer's mind, the ocean was the way the land should be. He loved it with a passion that had not dimmed with the years.

Meanwhile, Anna was making steady, if uneven, progress towards Volmer. She had wrapped her sore feet in soft cloth and eased them into her worn, black galoshes, and with careful steps, she picked her way around the deepest water. She carried a woven wooden basket, the handle looped over her left arm. A blue and white checked cotton towel peeked over the basket edge and swaddled a thermos of hot tea, sweetened with clover honey. There were also two spoons, two knives, two blue and white china cups wrapped in dish towels and two warmed blueberry muffins with gooseberry jam.

Anna made few concessions to her age. She didn't see it so much as vanity as maintaining an inner strength. Indeed, she prided herself on her good vision, which was fairly accurate at a distance. Her nearsightedness was another matter, which she preferred not to discuss. But now she had a bead on Volmer and was honing in on him like a mosquito.

The interplay of sunlight and shadow through the broken cloud cover created a checkerboard along Anna's path, and she stepped deliberately from sunspot to sunspot.

"Anna?"

"*Ja*, I'm coming, Volmer." Anna quickened her pace. "*Ach!* Now see what you've done, Volmer. I've stepped in a shadow." She shifted the basket handle to her other arm.

"Anna, what are you doing?"

"Nothing, Volmer. I'm coming," she said, continuing on her broken path, while Volmer rummaged through the wood pile for a plank, which he set across two boulders to provide them with a seat and a table.

Anna sloshed to the board and eased herself down. Sometimes Volmer misjudged the strength of his little tables, but this one seemed sturdy enough. She set the basket on the ground and arranged their meal on the plank while Volmer poured the tea. Anna shared her husband's love of the ocean, and they sat together in companionable silence, their unspoken thoughts casting a comfortable blanket around them as they ate.

Overhead, an Arctic tern fishing off the shore had a swarm of gulls hovering, hoping for leftovers, which reminded Anna of a bit of news. "Tomorrow is the meeting of the Ladies Guild. We're planning the reception for the new pastor," Anna began. She took a bite of muffin. The Ladies Guild of the Evangelical Lutheran Church of the Redeemer of Sankt Peder was the backbone of the town's religious, social, and political life, and Anna was a dedicated and determined member of both the Church and the Guild. It had been difficult, managing without a pastor. "I hope he is as good a man as Pastor Lundquist."

"Anna, you fret too much."

She shook her head. "I wish he hadn't died."

"He probably wishes the same thing," Volmer said, reaching for the thermos and refilling his cup.

"Volmer! Such talk! Shame on you!" She sighed. So unexpected, it was, and the week before Christmas, as well. The Children's Pageant. The Christmas Bazaar. It just gave you pause to think. One false step and it was all over. A quick and violent death under the wheels of an autobus. Pastor should have been granted a gentler end. She moved closer to Volmer, who patted her hand.

Anna considered that Pastor was, no doubt, in heaven now, beaming down upon them. She looked up and smiled at the sky. The new pastor would arrive soon, and the congregation was fortunate to have gotten a replacement, given the uncertain political climate. The ladies wanted to be sure he had a proper welcome. The Parish Council would need to vote on him, of course, but with no other prospects, that was just a formality. Once approved, it would take an act of God Himself to remove the pastor. This line of thought brought her mind back to the subject of food, since she would need to bake something for the reception. That reminded her of something else.

"We're to have supper with Inge and Lars tonight," Anna said. "She sent Greta by this morning with the invitation."

"Good."

"She didn't say why."

"Who?"

"Greta. She didn't say why. Why on a Tuesday? We have supper with them on Friday. I hope nothing is wrong. Greta didn't seem upset."

"That's good."

"Maybe Lars has gotten a promotion. They want to celebrate with us."

"Good."

"But if he's being promoted, he may be transferred. Maybe to Copenhagen." Anna looked at Volmer. "I don't want them to move to Copenhagen. But maybe there's trouble. Maybe there's illness and they need help. Surely Greta would have said something."

"I'm sure everything is fine."

"Do you know something? Do you know if something is wrong, Volmer? You would tell me if you knew something."

"Yes, Anna. Maybe she has a new recipe. Inge is a good cook. She is almost as good a cook as you." He patted Anna's hand again.

"Greta will be going to university soon. Maybe they need some help with the tuition." Anna was beginning to fret her way into a state.

"Anna?"

"*Ja*, Volmer?"

"We go to dinner. We eat and we talk. Worry when it's time and not until it's time. *Ja*?"

"*Ja,* Volmer. I will stop this worry." She frowned up at the heavens and waited for some sign of reassurance. With nothing forthcoming, she stood and gathered up the cups and saucers and replaced them in the basket, wrapping them securely for their journey home.

Volmer also stood and stretched. He did not share Anna's determination to squint through later life, and now he removed his eyeglasses and polished them with the soft tail of his flannel shirt. He held them out at arms' length, checking for spots and smudges. He gave one more rub and then replaced the wires over his ears, adjusted the fit across his nose, and surveyed the ocean with a clearer perspective. It was then that something far out on the water caught his eye, and he placed a hand on Anna's shoulder, turning her so she could see towards the horizon.

Anna thought perhaps he had spotted their son Jens out on his fishing boat, and she looked along the coast, but Volmer pointed farther out to sea. There was a flash of light, but it came and went so quickly she thought it might have been the sunlight reflecting off the lenses of Volmer's glasses. She concentrated, forcing her eyes to focus. Then she saw what Volmer was pointing towards. Just two brief lights. This time she was sure. That was odd, she thought. She waited and watched but the lights did not return. She looked at Volmer with a question in her eyes. He was frowning and rubbing his right thumb across his lips. He shook his head several times, and after a few moments, he turned and shrugged. "I think we go home now, Anna."

She nodded and fetched the basket and they set off together. On the way Volmer mulled over the incident of the flashing lights and Anna considered this as well as what to bake for the Ladies Guild meeting that afternoon. Her sweet dough could become a *stollen* or bread or even rolls. What would be best? Her mind went back and forth like one of her hens pecking across the yard.

Back home, Anna immersed herself in her baking. The fragrance of lemons and almond extract created a heady bouquet as she worked the dough for her sweet pastry. When she had kneaded it to the proper consistency, she formed it into a mound, smoothed the top of the dough, and turned it into a greased pan that she covered with a damp towel. She set the bowl to rise in the warming compartment of the old wood stove.

Anna worked with the music from the radio as background. She hummed along and occasionally sang in a light soprano, reaching, but not far enough, for the high notes. The effect was discordant, but her heart was light and she sang on and on. And Volmer quietly left the room to spare his ears and climbed the stairs to his attic retreat.

The stairs were hard on his knees, but he cherished the view from his den and the privacy it afforded. When he needed to think, Volmer sought the silence. Anna's voice could shatter glass, but thank God her range was less than two floors. He had taken this knowledge into consideration when he was selecting the location of his study. From his window facing east, he could see the distant towers of Castel Grunespan, a remnant of medieval times. His own room, while not as spacious as the Castel tower, was decidedly more comfortable and definitely warmer. The morning sun streamed in through the double hung windows. He had added a fireplace when he'd finished off this room, tapping into the old stone chimney. Sometimes he speculated whether the king's wife had sung like Anna. Judging from the expanse of the Castel, she had an even wider range.

One wall of Volmer's study was lined with bookshelves that ran from floor to ceiling. Biography and military history were Volmer's principal interests and he had an impressive collection of volumes devoted to naval campaigns. From Caesar to the Kaiser, Volmer knew why these men had succeeded and the reasons why they had ultimately failed.

He rested a hand on the back of his reading chair by the northern window, from which he had a view of his pastures and the ocean beyond. Next to the chair was his desk, an old roll top that had belonged to his grandfather. A kerosene lamp with a neatly trimmed wick sat upon the desk, and next to the lamp was his pipe collection.

Pulling his wooden swivel chair with the slatted back up to the desk, Volmer reached for his pen and a clean sheet of paper to set his thoughts in order. He listed everything he could remember about the morning's incident. What did he know? He knew the time was about ten o'clock and he had an approximate location of the source of the lights. He would need to be more precise and made a note to do some calculations. His years on the ocean had taught him dead reckoning and he was confident that by using the lighthouse as a reference point, he could approximate the source of what he believed was a signal coming from a ship out on the water. He knew the lights had flashed two times with three repetitions. He also knew the seas that morning were choppy with a stiff offshore wind.

He rose and walked to the window, where his eyes marked the unceasing shoreward march of the whitecaps on the sea. Wave after wave, a relentless and tireless surge washed ashore, retreated, and marshaled forces for yet another assault. He turned to the row of books closest to him, selected a well-worn volume, and returned to his chair.

His eyes fell upon a rough piece of wood, a small fragment from a plank, that lay next to the inkwell and he remembered another morning almost twenty-four years ago, when lights on the water had called to him.

It was after the Battle of Jutland had been fought to an indecisive end. Volmer had been tending to the fishing nets on the shore that first morning of June in 1916, when his eyes had caught a flash of sunlight reflecting off something bobbing on the water some distance out. He figured it might be flotsam from one of the damaged war vessels and watched its incoming progress on the tide. But when he made out the rounded form of a man, he dropped the nets, jumped into the dinghy, and made straight for what he hoped would be a survivor.

It was. Richard Briggs had been a radioman on The *HMS Lion*, a battle cruiser of the Royal Navy. With both arms wrapped around the plank, the British sailor had hung on for dear life and it had taken some force to pry the sailor's hands free and haul him into the dinghy. He chuckled at the tenacity of the young man, even as he was barely conscious and near death from the cold waters. Dick was delirious and nearly frozen, but his viselike grip on the wood had saved him. Volmer and Anna had cared for him and had helped him get to Sweden after he was stronger. From there he made his way home. Dick was now Sir Richard Briggs, Admiral in His Majesty's Navy. Volmer called him Richard the Lionhearted, after the name of the ship he'd served on.

Volmer replaced the piece of wood on his desk and returned to his list, reviewing what he had written. Satisfied, he turned to his shortwave radio, a gift from Dick, and one he used frequently. He sent on the report of his sighting, addressing his message to "Lion" and signing it "The Dane".

He removed his earphones, and said quietly to the room around him, "Now, we wait."

Downstairs, Anna and The Ladies Guild had consumed two pots of tea and an entire batch of snickerdoodles. The business portion of the meeting had consisted of Elsa Lindersson's seconding of the motion that they have an open house for the new minister. With that settled, and the ladies departed, Anna headed to the kitchen to clean up.

Volmer, having seen the last of the women strolling down the path, descended from the attic. "Your meeting, it goes well?" he asked, pouring himself a cup of coffee from the chipped enamelware pot that was always warming on the stove. He sat down at the kitchen table and studied the pattern on the embroidered tablecloth, noticing for the first time that everything in the kitchen was either blue or white. He wondered how long it had been that way. Anna's decorating went through phases. This must be her blue phase. He smiled.

"*Ja.*" Anna took a deep breath and was ready to deliver a word by word account but realized Volmer wasn't listening. It was clear he wanted to talk, but not about the plans for the pastor. She turned from the sink, made herself yet another cup of tea, sat down at the table, and waited.

Chapter Three

New Haven

Yesterday's snowstorm had become today's drizzle. I glowered at the gray and drizzly morning and watched raindrops combine on the windowpane. They streamed relentlessly down, just like my mood. Maybe you could have too many windows, after all. John had gone out early and when he returned he'd brought the morning paper, along with his attaché case and a parcel heavily wrapped and tied with twine.

"After breakfast," John said, tossing the case and the package on the sofa. "I'm starved."

"Agreed. Eat first, and then work." I perused the paper but *The Register* had nothing encouraging to report about the war situation in Europe. The world was in a downward spiral and spinning out of control. The Finns were ready to meet Soviet terms and surrender. President Roosevelt was still holding to a policy of neutrality, at least in his public speaking. How much longer could he keep it up? There was a pro-Nazi rally in New York City. The members of the Bund were goose-stepping their way into the news even at home. I shook my head at people's willingness to be duped. It all had to do with the arrogance of ignorance. There was no reasoning with them. Did they not know what would have happened to them if they had staged a pro-England demonstration in Berlin? Idiots.

Weather has a tangible effect on mood and the lowered barometric pressure was weighing me down, as well. The heaviness of the atmosphere penetrated even the lit confines of home, which was quickly becoming too small. I was restless. Yesterday's indecision had been replaced with a firm sense of purpose. It was time to break free.

I left the desk to John and took my crumpets, jam, and coffee to my cozy sitting area by the window to eat my breakfast and watch the city come to life. On the sidewalk below, pedestrians bundled against the early morning chill swarmed towards their office buildings like so many worker bees returning to the hive. I felt the quickening heartbeat of the city in the updrifting drone of automobile and bus traffic and popped the last bite of the crumpet into my mouth. I stacked the plates, brushed the crumbs from the table, and licked a sticky spot of strawberry jam from my thumb.

John had dumped the contents of the package onto the walnut side table. There was a worn Danish Bible, travel papers, other assorted official documents, what looked like an entire book devoted to British manor houses, maps, a set of keys, and a well-thumbed brown leather address book. "Where do we start?" I asked, looking over the array of objects and rubbing my hands together in anticipation.

"In the beginning…" intoned my husband, reaching for the Bible, which he first clasped to his chest and then opened to reveal his service pistol neatly sequestered in the hollowed out pages of Psalms, Proverbs, and some minor prophets.

"Clever."

"The voice of the Lord is powerful. The voice of the Lord strikes with flashes of lightning- Psalm 29," advised my husband.

I ignored him. When he is feeling clever, I have found it best not to encourage him. Instead, I checked the passports. I had one and he had two. This provided both enlightenment as well as confusion. John had assumed numerous identities in the course of his service to the government, but this was a first. He appeared to be a schizophrenic. No longer John Joseph Breckenridge, he was now George Chichester, Ph.D. as well as the Reverend Martin Shoneborger. I hadn't expected him to don clerical robes to fight Hitler, but sure enough, underneath the familiar, handsome face on the passport was that decidedly unfamiliar name.

"Lutheran?" I glanced up.

"And married. My wife and children live in Copenhagen. They are staying with relatives for the moment, it appears."

I considered the implications as a celestial door slammed shut. I was not to be the Reverend's wife. Service and celibacy had been wrapped up together in one tidy package. Drat. Shuffling through the papers, I found my own traveling identity. Nothing creative there. I was still me, Katrin Nissen. I'd kept my maiden name after John and I had married, and I guess the Office decided it was good enough. Why a woman would want to be absorbed by her husband's identity escaped me, but not everyone shared my views. Fortunately, John did and I loved him all the more for it. However, looking further I found that I did retain a little mystery. I was divorced. "I'm a hot item here," I said to John. "A divorcée! The boys are getting a bit frisky, don't you think?"

"I told them you were a loose woman." He waggled his eyebrows.

I rolled my eyes. I shouldn't do that. It really hurts. I rubbed my forehead and returning to the dossier, learned that I was to be a switchboard operator for a beef products company in Kolding, Denmark, filling in for the woman who had been called home to help her ailing mother. Curious to find out why on earth I was being sent there, I plowed on. There was a small map enclosed, indicating that the port of Kolding was located on the eastern coast of Jutland, the Danish mainland.

"Kolding is a strategic port location and is the largest cattle exporter in Denmark," I informed John, sounding like a tour guide, as I read through the papers. "It seems they've decided to use my own past to create a new me, or something to that effect. I'm headed back home!"

John was systematically rifling through the papers, building two neat stacks as we went along, one for him and one for me. "The keys are for you," he informed me, consulting one of the documents. "Your room in a guest home and safety deposit box. The address book is for me."

"Your parishioners?"

"In a manner of speaking." He continued, "Looks like I'll be making some pastoral calls. Or at least one of me will," he corrected himself. "You're scheduled to leave tomorrow, and I'm off on Friday." He looked up at me. "We need to be letter perfect before we leave."

And letter perfect we would be. The boys at the Office were thorough. We owed the success of our mission, not to mention our lives, to their diligent efforts.

I gathered up my travel documents and arranged them like a Vegas blackjack dealer in a fan-shaped arc across the table. This was a high stakes game, no doubt about it. There were enough *Kroner* to cover my travel expenses inside Denmark and a savings passbook with a history of modest deposits and withdrawals. There was also a baptismal certificate. I examined it closely. It was the original document. The real McCoy. I whistled. The boys were good.

According to my itinerary, I would fly on the Pan Am Clipper from New York to Lisbon, with a connection to Copenhagen. From Copenhagen I would travel by train to Kolding and report to work the next morning with no time to sleep away my fatigue from traveling. Once in Kolding my means of transportation would be bicycle. Both bicycle and lodgings would be waiting for me.

And then I found out why I was headed home. My assignment was to track beef shipments, and as a switchboard operator, handling both incoming and outgoing calls, the information would literally pass through my fingers or more accurately, my ears. Churchill was gambling that Hitler would make short work of Denmark on his way to Norway. But Hitler's army, like every other since warfare began, moved on its stomach and would need to be fed. Churchill was already fairly certain of the where portion of Hitler's invasion, but the when of his operation was yet to be discovered. That was the reason the OSS had been called to service and that was where I fit into the picture.

I looked up. "Was it Napoleon who refused to move his armies without onions?"

"You know, Katrin," came the measured response, "I really had never thought about that."

One sterling attribute of my spouse is that he never is taken aback by any of my questions. He may not answer me, but he is never surprised.

"Hmm. Just wondering." Well, Napoleon and onions, Hitler and beef. It all was part of a simple, yet effective plan. I would be on staff before Hitler's expected incursion into Denmark, a loyal company employee. And given the temporary nature of my position, should be able to move on when necessary. I spent the remainder of the morning committing names, numbers, and street addresses to memory.

About eleven-thirty, I stretched and rubbed my eyes, which were beginning to blur. A dull ache was spreading across the base of my skull as well. John was still hunched over his paperwork, muttering occasionally. Next to his high-powered Bible was a Concordance, and he was annotating its pages, transferring information in his neat hand from the address book. Finally, a satisfied grunt indicated he had completed this task. He looked up, "You ready for some lunch?"

I certainly was. My initial forays into beef shipment studies had me wanting a thick, juicy hamburger, but I was flexible. "How about Glicks?"

"Sounds good."

Ten minutes later we were seated by the front window of Meyer Glick's Fine Delicatessen, shaded by the awning that proclaimed, "*No one kicks who comes to Glicks.*"

The Kosher dill pickles were crunchy, the pastrami on rye was a specialty, and there were vats of salads, lox, gefilte fish, and a vast array of other good Jewish food. Their poppy seed rolls were crusty on the outside, melt in your mouth tender on the inside. I smacked my lips at the prospect.

We ordered and as we waited for our number to be called, I watched the world pass by outside. The day had cleared and the morning's bundled masses had shed their scarves and mufflers and were now strolling along the sidewalks, window shopping and chatting, headed to their own favorite luncheon establishments. I was enjoying the fashion show playing out just for me both inside the Deli and outside on the streets.

Hemlines, hosiery, and hairdos were my areas of interest today. Hemlines were still midcalf, although seemed to be steadily creeping up. Silk hosiery with seams up the back was still in style. The seams were supposed to give the illusion of slender calves. This didn't always work. Some calves were cows. We were just emerging from the deep, dark depths of the Depression, and many women had resorted to drawing a pencil line from back of the knee to the ankle, the price of hosiery being too dear. One needed a steady hand and a good mirror to achieve optimum results and some lines resembled ocean waves.

A new fabric called "nylon" had been exhibited at the World's Fair in New York City last year. It promised to make hosiery less expensive. I wondered. It seemed as if the makers of women's hose had determined that after one wearing, hose would catch a runner. Perhaps nylon stockings would prove more durable.

Hair was still long and softly curled, swept back and

anchored with barrettes. And foreheads were adorned with bangs. Self-consciously I patted my plaited hair. My blonde braids were too long for the current style, but I couldn't bring myself to lop them off and so I wore them wound around my head and anchored with hair pins.

Straining to check out the occupants of the side booths along the wall, I spotted one couple staring soulfully into each other's eyes, their untouched food cooling on the table. Young love in early spring. I smiled dotingly and moved on. The two men behind them were engaged in animated conversation. Hands gesturing, eyes flashing, they might have been discussing sports, politics, anything volatile. They were probably Italian or Greek, given the hand signals. It was the third couple, however, whose stony silence created a chill palpable across the room.

"Are you planning on swallowing?" John was staring at me.

I had apparently been masticating the same mouthful of food for quite some time.

"Um?" I was half listening to him.

"Swallowing. It usually occurs after chewing, in most circumstances."

"Sorry. Do you see that couple in the far booth? Look at her color. She is positively livid. She's going to pop a vein." I stopped to consider. Vein? Artery? It didn't matter. "What do you suppose could have made her so angry? She's a great deal younger than he is. I wonder."

"All I can see is her hat. How do you women manage to keep those things on your heads? It looks like a small aircraft ready to take flight."

My husband has no intuitive sense, a quality that I have cultivated in myself with gratifying results on numerous occasions. There was something disturbing about this couple. I tried again. "I can sense something is very wrong with them. Can't you feel it? And hatpins," I answered him, as an afterthought. "It takes a steady hand, if you don't want to draw blood."

No response. Just a vacant, albeit friendly, look. I returned to my meal but managed to sneak a few peeks between bites. I focused on swallowing at proper intervals. The woman, Madame X, I had decided to call her, was in her early thirties. She was blonde. In fact everything about her was blonde. Blonde hair, blonde - almost sallow-complexion with high cheekbones. Perhaps a former model? I speculated.

She was fashionably dressed in a deep yellow shantung two-piece suit with matching hat. I couldn't see her legs, but would wager she didn't have to resort to the pencil trick on what I assumed were shapely blonde legs. She could afford the real thing. She looked as if she could afford someone better than her companion. Unless he was the guy funding the ensemble, of course. I may have stared too long. She looked up and fixed me with a glare. Then her eyes narrowed. I returned to my food, but there was something about that look that rang a bell. I'd seen it before.

Chapter Four

New York City

"We'll meet in London, when the job is done." That's what John had said when we parted. I didn't trust myself to try to answer. Once the old waterworks got started, I'd be a blubbering idiot and that wouldn't do either of us any good. So I'd simply hurled myself into his arms for one more kiss. One last embrace. I held him close, breathing in his scent and praying we would both make the rendezvous. We'd meet again if I had to move heaven and earth to do it.

I had one day in New York City before the flight overseas. Now, exiting Grand Central Station, my eyes watered and my nose rebelled at the exhaust fumes from the trucks and buses that clogged the streets and mingled with the cooking odors from a dozen street vendor carts. The natives might be immune but for me it was a heady mix.

It was bedlam with motion everywhere. Traffic cops in the intersections, twisting and turning to orchestrate the traffic, waved arms and gestured with white gloved hands, all the while keeping time with staccato bleats from the silver whistles gripped in their teeth. It was a full-blown Wagnerian symphony of movement.

I'd barely stepped off the curb when I was nearly run over by a taxi, whose driver leaned out the window as he barreled by, bellowing at me to get back on the sidewalk. "That's how they make angels, lady!" And he screeched away, his arm hanging out the window, slapping the outside of the door in disgust.

I jumped back onto the sidewalk as the next cab skidded to a halt just shy of where my toes had been a second before. I laid claim to this one by jerking open the passenger door, tossing the Gladstone inside, and clambering along after it.

"Where to, lady?"

All cabbies treated women like royalty. *Lady Katrin*, I rather liked the way it sounded.

"22 Jane Street. Greenwich Village," I replied.

We were off to the races. The cabbie floored the accelerator, leaned on the horn, and the cab surged back into traffic, making a space for itself where none had existed a moment before. I gritted my teeth and held on. I was still clenching the old choppers when we screeched to a halt at our destination. What the telegram euphemistically referred to as "The New York facilities," was actually a nondescript rooming house tucked away on a back street. *The Branford Arms Residence Hotel for Women* was a shabby brownstone affair that had probably been shopworn during Garfield's administration.

"Do I take a cab to the curb?" I asked, surveying the serious amount of street I needed to traverse before I reached the safety of the sidewalk.

"Two-fifty, lady."

"Right." I sighed, paid and tipped the driver, yanked the Gladstone off the seat, and bumped up to the sidewalk without getting creamed. I turned to scowl at the driver, but he was long gone in search of a better paying fare.

The Village was nothing like the rest of Manhattan, either in design or thinking. Manhattan was laid out in a neat grid, but streets in Greenwich Village were meandering paths that dated from colonial times, when they were boundaries along tobacco farms. They'd simply paved over them and called it good. Consequently, it was easy to get lost or lose yourself on purpose here, but then that was the general idea.

While Manhattan was cosmopolitan, the Village was Bohemian. An oasis of independent thinking in the otherwise buttoned down world of Manhattan; there was a charm and vibrancy to this offbeat neighborhood, where eccentric characters and odd behavior was the norm. This, The Office had reasoned, provided an excellent setting for a safe house. All in all, I had to agree.

Key in hand and revolver in coat pocket, the first rules of safety while in transit, I climbed the three stone steps to the front door and let myself into the vestibule, well lit by high wattage lamps both inside and out. No Shadows here. No Thin Men either, I mused. Strictly females. Couple the high degree of illumination with the miniscule amount of short and neatly trimmed shrubbery, and this could just as well have been the residence of a Mafioso, instead of a sorority house for the OSS.

Locking the door behind me, I turned down the corridor to my left and found apartment number three. I paused for just a second. Threes. Three steps, third apartment on the left. A person could find patterns where none existed, if she looked hard enough. But then the opposite was also true. If she failed to see patterns developing, if she dismissed them out of hand, she might come to regret the oversight. *If* she lived to regret the oversight. I'm observant, not paranoid, and dismissed this series of coincidences as just that.

Once inside, I looked around and decided this cozy little flat was quite roomy, as closets went. My trusty Gladstone seemed out of proportion, a Gulliver in the land of the Lilliputs. It took up almost half the length of the far wall. A hatbox would have been more to scale.

The furnishings were adequate but Spartan. There was a twin bed, nightstand with lamp and telephone, small writing table, and a straight-backed chair. Beige draperies, brown corduroy bedspread, and a brown hooked rug completed the depressing monochromatic attempt at decor.

The dormitory look was relieved with the addition of art on the wall above the bed. I'd almost expected a crucifix, in keeping with the convent-like approach to interior decoration, but instead there was a watercolor scene of winter desolation with Eliza running for her life, pursued by wolves. I frowned and nudged the bottom right corner upward until the picture was level. I didn't need the not so subtle reminder I was heading into the lion's den, or rather the wolf den, to keep the metaphor straight. The Office had a macabre sense of humor. Good point, though. Wolf packs of U-boats were on patrol in Europe's waters and had even been sighted off the coast of New England.

The refrigerator was well stocked with provisions, as were the cupboards above the sink. There was also a percolator with an opened can of Maxwell House coffee next to it and a hot plate off to the side. The sideboard had a sparse selection of stronger beverages. Three bottles, one each of bottom shelf gin, bourbon, and vodka, along with an empty ice bucket with tongs and two glasses. The Office didn't want me drinking alone, it seemed.

My survey complete, I laid my coat on the bed, kicked off my shoes, and sat down in what had to be the most uncomfortable chair in the entire world. I crossed my legs and began swinging my left foot. To add interest to this activity, I then uncrossed my legs, recrossed them the opposite way and began to swing my right foot. This was not providing me with much mental stimulation. I looked around for something to do. It was going to be a long, long afternoon.

I looked through the newspaper I'd picked up at the train station. An afternoon at the movies was a possibility but there was nothing interesting playing in the matinee selections. On page two above the fold, however, a story about the World's Fair that had opened in the City last year caught my eye. It seemed promising, and since I couldn't take any American money with me overseas, it was only logical to spend it now. Thrifty, even. Yep. The Fair was a perfect way to kill a few hours before locking myself in for the night. My foot was falling asleep, I needed gifts for the family, and I was really curious to see a pair of nylon hosiery. I also needed to do something about my now naked ring finger. A divorcee doesn't wear her wedding band, and mine had been on long enough to make an impression in the skin. Some costume jewelry would do the trick nicely.

Decision made. I grabbed my coat and hat and was reaching for the doorknob just as a sharp rap came from the other side. My left hand reached into my coat pocket and closed around the revolver handle. I strained to see through the peephole but my caller had a hand slapped over the opening.

I stepped to the side of the doorjamb, just in case my visitor had less than friendly intentions. "Who is it?" I called out.

"Your next door neighbor come to borrow a cup of sugar."

"Cute, but no go. Name, please."

"It won't mean anything to you. I need to talk with you. It's important."

I frowned. We seemed to be at an impasse. One final test. "Fine. What's the password?"

"Password? There isn't any password."

"Good. Just checking." I withdrew the revolver from my pocket, unlocked the door, and stepped clear. "It's open."

The woman who entered was the same blonde dish I'd seen at Glick's delicatessen. Today, however, she wasn't looking blonde and svelte - she was looking worried. She carried a large shopping bag and her concern went up a notch when she spotted the .38 snub nosed revolver pointed in her direction. She bit her lip and cleared her throat.

"Just a precaution," I said. "Put the bag down by the door and step away from it. Now, suppose you tell me who you are and why you're here. Once we get the niceties over with, we'll see where we go from there. Okay?" I smiled politely. "Have a seat." I tipped my head in the direction of the wooden chair.

"My name is Margo Speer," she said, as she sat down and smoothed her skirt over her knees.

"You're right. It doesn't mean anything to me. Should it?"

"No." She hesitated. "We haven't been formally introduced. However, we did meet in passing at the ambassador's ball last spring in Vienna."

"Let me guess. You were with the ambassador."

She reached up to tuck a wisp of hair behind her ear. "It's what I do," she said. "We all have our areas of expertise."

I nodded. "Go ahead. Keep talking. I'm listening." Intuition told me she didn't intend any harm, and I returned the revolver to my pocket.

She nodded. "Perhaps a little vodka?" Her eyes were now fixed on the sideboard and she ran her tongue over her lips.

"Go ahead. Help yourself."

She rose and poured herself a stiff one. "You?" she asked, raising the bottle in my direction.

"No thanks. It's a bit early for me."

"It's too late." She made a wry face. "For me, that is." She threw her drink back with accustomed ease.

"All right," she said, returning her glass to the sideboard. "There is a man."

"There always is," I said.

"No," she shook her head decisively. "This one is different. He's known as Ronin."

"Strange name."

"Not so strange once you know him. He's a freelancer. He has no loyalties to either side, but they both use him for that very reason. He's also extremely dangerous because of it."

"You seem to know a great deal about him," I said.

"Yes," she gave a mirthless laugh. "He's my brother."

I decided that perhaps a small measure of bourbon would be in order, after all. With my drink in hand and Margo with her own glass refreshed, we sat on the only two available surfaces in the room. I took the edge of the bed and she returned to her chair.

"What does this have to do with me?"

She regarded me with a level gaze. "He's not currently employed by our side and he's gone incommunicado. I have reason to expect he'll surface shortly somewhere in the vicinity of where you're headed."

I pursed my lips. "And how do you come to know where I'm headed?" I asked.

She shook her head. "I can't say anything more than that. You'll have to trust me."

"Trust you? I don't even know you."

"We work for the same company."

"Apparently so does your brother from time to time and you've just told me I can't trust him."

"You're a tough cookie."

"Sometimes. Mostly I'm careful."

"Go ahead. Make the call," Margo said. "Check me out. I'll wait right here." She shifted her weight in the chair. "You think they'd spring for something that conforms a tad more to the female form."

I nodded. Picking up the receiver, I dialed the Office and waited while reception passed me along the line. When a familiar voice came on the line, I simply said, "Margo Speer." The voice then described her to a T, and tossed in an extra clue. I rang off.

"Mind standing up, turning around, and showing me the back of your right knee?"

"Not at all. Anything to move this discussion along." She raised her skirt and sure enough. There was the mole in the crease behind her right knee.

"Okay. I'm all ears," I said.

She nodded. "As I was saying, in all likelihood he will be in the vicinity when you arrive in Kolding. You will need to recognize him before he discovers who you are."

"Point taken," I said. "How will I know him? What does he look like?"

"It changes. He changes." She hesitated. "He has certain qualities, but he has one weakness, if you care to call it that. When he needs a cover, he frequently reverts to his former occupation. It's still comfortable for him, in spite of his hatred for it." She sipped her drink thoughtfully.

"Bricklayer? Pharmacist? Doctor?" Seventeen more suggestions and we'd be playing twenty questions. I opted out and waited.

"Minister," she said. He's an ordained Lutheran minister. Just remember my words. Be ready for him." She drained the last few drops of her drink and stood.

"Margo," I began, but she raised a hand and cut my words short. Questions flooded my mind, but it was obvious the answers would have to wait. I don't believe in coincidences but we seemed to be stocking up on Lutheran ministers. This made two. No, make it three - with Inge's mention of Pastor Lundquist's demise. Maybe it was two too many.

She picked up the shopping bag by the door. "Hermann will be glad to have me back. I pick a fight, go shopping, check in with the Office, and then he welcomes me with his pudgy open arms." She smiled. "It's so easy, and he's so stupid."

"They're not all that stupid," I said.

"No, they're not. My brother isn't and that's gospel. But I've got Hermann, and that's stupid enough. Good luck, Katrin. Watch your back."

"And you as well, Margo."

"I don't have to. Hermann's too busy watching my front. Oh, by the way, the shopping bag? You read that one perfectly." She reached in, extracted her own service pistol and stashed it in her pocketbook. "Just a precaution," she said, as she let herself out and walked towards the entry hall. "Nothing personal."

Nothing personal. The words rang in my head long after Margo had left. Fortunately, training had kicked in and I'd done the right thing. It had become instinct, following procedures, and I said a brief prayer of thanks. I needed a break. It was time to check out the World's Fair.

Just like the Olympics, the World's Fair was supposed to showcase the benefits of peaceful international competition, promote world peace, and in the process make a ton of money for the host country. But the world was not at peace and not cooperating all that well. New York, however, was definitely raking in the bucks, in part thanks to a well-coordinated advertising campaign. Colorful posters were everywhere. World's Fairs were exciting opportunities to see what the marvels of science had created, and what wonders would change our lives in the future. Fairs were a time of firsts.

Newsboys on every corner were hawking official guide books for two bits that promised the fairgoer "a rich and rewarding experience that you will never forget." Why not? I thought and paid my twenty-five cents to purchase "The Year's Best Seller."

I learned that the first World's Fair had been back in 1851 in Merry Olde England, when Queen Victoria reigned. The fabulous Crystal Palace was a showcase and America exhibited machinery of the Industrial Revolution.

The first Ferris wheel, invented by George Ferris, had been a major attraction of the 1893 fair, and people could look down on the Fair from the staggering height of nearly two hundred and fifty feet. The Fair also had Little Egypt, the first exotic dancer, and Cracker Jack - caramel corn with peanuts and the toy hidden deep in the box.

My guidebook informed me that the United States first

hosted a Fair in 1893, The Chicago World's Fair, also known as The Columbian Exposition, and it honored the 400th anniversary of Columbus and his discovery of the New World. It also showcased the rise of Chicago from the ashes of the Fire of 1871. Its hallmark was The White City, buildings based on classical architecture that inspired a Wellesley English teacher, Katherine Lee Bates, to write her poem "America the Beautiful." The famous line "Thine alabaster cities gleam" was inspired by the White City, and the poem was later set to music.

Mostly, however, the Chicago Fair was notable for its electricity wars. Nikola Tesla and George Westinghouse had produced an alternating current which could run for half the price of direct current, which was the domain of Thomas Edison, J.P. Morgan, and General Electric. Then, when Westinghouse won the bid to provide electricity for the Fair, General Electric banned the use of Edison's lamps in retaliation. This spurred Westinghouse to design a double-stopper bulb to sidestep Edison's product. What inspires invention? I guess there are as many reasons as there are inventors, but often it's just good old necessity. I looked up from the book and realized I was lost.

Until you have actually driven somewhere yourself, it is an indisputable fact that you won't be able to find it again without extreme difficulty. The driver knows the route, while passengers have the luxury of enjoying the scenery, watching the human parade from their windows or engaging in spirited conversation. The latter can cause the driver to become distracted. This, I have learned from personal experience, is not desirable. Especially when the driver is one's husband.

I have noted that when the steering wheel is in the other hand, so to speak, the husband does not hesitate to inform the wife about the shortcomings of her driving skills. She is expected to accept these gratefully and gracefully, as they are intended for her moral betterment and general survival. All things considered, it is usually just easier to let the husband drive.

These thoughts ran through my mind as I stood in place and pivoted through a three hundred sixty degree circle, looking for something familiar to get my bearings. It had been some years since John and I had explored this region of the City and my memory was hazy. The last time we had been here, John was driving, and I was gaping like the tourist I was. Now I was on my own, and the job of finding my way about was proving to be a challenge. I was stumbling about like a Bowery bum.

I had never been to a World's Fair, and if I didn't get the directions figured out really soon, the prospects of getting to this one weren't looking hopeful. But since God watches over fools and children, He gave me a gentle nudge, and as I stopped to coordinate my bearings with the little symbol on the map, I found myself standing in front of the subway entrance. Just like that. I hurried down the steps, read the board that indicated times and tracks for departures, and caught the next train to Flushing Meadow.

I was not the only one headed to the Fair, and I was forced to shoehorn myself into the aisle with the other standees. My closest neighbors were a Hassidic Jewish family, as evidenced by the bearded father's black hat, black coat, and white shirt. His wife wore a *tikhel* that covered her hair. The little boys, somewhere between six and eight years old and wearing the familiar side curls, stood on either side of their father. The little girl looked to be around four and was holding tightly to her mother's skirt, while she stared up at me with curious eyes. I smiled down at her and the train accelerated. There was only a moment to brace, but it probably wasn't necessary. There wasn't enough room to scratch an itch, let alone fall down. So, thus wedged, we rocketed off to see the glories and the wonders in store. After a short ride, we emerged from our subterranean capsule into the brilliant light of day.

The first sights to greet us were the symbols of the Fair,

the double emblems of the Perisphere and the Trylon, a strange juxtaposition of geometric shapes - a huge circle next to a tall, skinny pyramid or perhaps it was an obelisk. The future, at least according to the architects, would be round, fat, tall, skinny, or pointed. Take your pick. The Subway Group merged forward as a unit.

The Fair was huge and I realized I'd only see a small portion in the time I had, but the map made navigating fairly easy. Mostly the Fair was a giant advertisement extolling the virtues of consumerism and the wealth of nations.

The Westinghouse Building occupied a prominent location near the entrance, and the company was still reaping the benefits of having bested General Electric way back when. The exhibit featured a cut-away duplicate of the Time Capsule they had sealed and which was to be opened by the people of the 70th century. Westinghouse had stuffed it with samples of our modern labor-saving devices. They'd also included a key to the English language in case we'd gone the way of Latin dodo birds by that time.

Affixed to the wall were posters of a cartoon family, the Middletons. There were Mom and Dad, Bud and Babs, and Grandma Middleton and they served the function of guides for visitors to the building. The Middletons weren't like any family I had ever known. They asked each other important questions, and everyone took turns giving well-informed answers. They smiled a great deal and were the Fair's conception of Middle America - that much sought after consumer market.

I thought about conversations my parents had had over the years. Mostly my father had just grunted over his newspaper. I don't recall the man ever completing an entire sentence. My mother seemed to understand this and they got along just fine. I guess it was for the best. Mrs. Middleton would have driven my father to homicide, but then they were not Middle Americans, but Central Danes. The cultural difference was notable. My Jewish family seemed entranced by the Middletons' electrical riches. The mother was eyeballing each appliance and then eyeballing her husband. I had the feeling she was creating a shopping list.

At the Halls of Power and Electrical Living, we saw the Playground of Science, the Microvivarium, and Elekto, the Moto-Man. Elekto wandered about the premises, making electrical comments and moving in a disjointed fashion with his electrical limbs. The children loved him but Elekto was too much for me. I didn't think it would add to the comfort of home to have a machine walking around the house, doing electrical things without my knowledge. Also Elekto was very, very expensive. The little girl mimicked Elekto's style of locomotion and her father patted her head with affection.

"Jew! Halt!"

Obscenities and a barrage of vicious racial slurs filled the air. We were suddenly surrounded by six thugs wearing Bund uniforms. They jabbed at the father with small wooden clubs and one of them grabbed the mother by the shoulder and spun her around. The little girl began to cry and the father put one arm around his young sons and attempted to push the men away from his wife with the other.

I realized everyone else in our group had melted away at the approach of the gang. The situation was intolerable and escalating. I reached inside my shoulder bag and wrapped my hand around the grip of my service pistol.

"Take your hand off the lady," I said.

The raucous obscenities stopped for a moment as the leader of the gang turned to see who was speaking. When he made eye contact, he spat at me.

"*Hure!*" he snarled and raised his baton.

"I wouldn't do that, if I were you," I said calmly. "I'd hate to make a hole in this leather pocketbook, but I will if I have to. So it would be best if you stepped away from the lady and her family and went about your sordid business somewhere else. I would suggest Hell," I added as an afterthought. I stood stock still, facing him down. A flash of uncertainty crossed his eyes.

"Now," I said for emphasis, keeping my eyes on him. Lacking personal initiative, the Bund members took orders from their leaders. Nazi lovers, they followed the Party line all the way. So long as I had the leader's attention, I was safe.

He blinked first. With a defiant forward thrust of his jaw, he jerked his head to the right and peeled away from the family, his henchmen at his heels like a pack of whipped pups. They were soon lost in the throng of Fairgoers, in search of easier prey.

My adrenaline rush was dissipating and my fingers now felt cold as they relaxed their grip on the pistol. I smiled at my family. "They're cowards and they're bullies," I said, but they're outnumbered here."

The father looked at the vast empty space that had opened up around us when the gang had approached. "This time, yes," he said. "The next time, perhaps not. *A sheynem dank.* Thank you."

I nodded. The Fair had lost its appeal. It was time to leave and return to my little loveless nest in the village. An earlier comment I had made to John came back to me and I realized my priorities were now clear. Any personal wars I needed to fight at the university would keep. Cynthia Lawton had become just a minor annoyance. I was back on the subway and almost to my stop when I realized I had never found the exhibit of nylon hosiery and I still needed a ring.

Chapter Five

Sankt Peder

"Volmer?" Anna's voice was gentle.

Volmer, deep in concentration, had been arranging and rearranging the positions of the salt cellar, pepper mill, and sugar bowl on the kitchen table. First, he had created a vertical line, then a horizontal one, and he was in the process of drawing a diagonal when Anna sat down opposite him.

"Your meeting?" he asked again, absently. Releasing his grip on the pepper mill, he seemed to see it for the first time and turned it around in his hand, running his fingers across the ridges carved into the soft maple wood.

"No, Volmer," she shook her head. "The meeting can wait. What is the news?"

He replaced the pepper mill with deliberate care. "I've sent Lion a message on the wireless, Anna. England needs to know what is happening here. I expect he will reply later tonight."

Anna caught a sharp breath and looked down into her teacup. All the pain she'd felt before came flooding back over her once again. At least this time, they would not take Volmer from her. There were some blessings to be found in growing old. She reached out and touched her husband's cheek and she smiled.

But her smile was short-lived. Her sons would not be spared. Just as in the last war, Germany would harvest the young men and force them to wear the hated uniform. She gripped her teacup so tightly the heat burned her fingers.

She set the cup down quickly with unsteady hands, and some of the hot liquid sloshed into the saucer. She did not want to hear what she knew Volmer was about to tell her. In her heart, she already knew, and she suddenly felt empty, as if hope had fled.

She looked out the window at her dormant garden, just now beginning to emerge from the cold sleep of winter. Springtime should be a season of hope, she reasoned. But not this year. Not this time. Spring was fast becoming a season of despair. War was so much worse than a weed. It was a poison flower, crowding out the tender blossoms, demanding the sunlight and the water, and crowding out all that was beautiful. It destroyed everything in its path. She closed her eyes and forced herself to listen as Volmer continued.

"It is beginning again, Anna," he said. "The U-boats are once again prowling the sea lanes, scouting the coast, watching and waiting." Volmer rubbed his forehead with a calloused hand, as if he could rub away the reality. "Sankt Peder will not escape them. Our port is much too valuable for their needs."

"Their needs," Anna spat the words. "Their own selfish needs. They care nothing for anyone else or their needs." Her voice was bitter. "They caused so much hurt the last time. They took you away from me. I didn't know from one day to the next if I would ever see you again. Years – so many wasted years. And now, they come again?"

"I came home, Anna." Volmer said. "That's all that matters."

"I know, but so many did not. And now," her voice drifted off, but she came back strong. "We are neutral in this. They must respect that?" But the words rang hollow in her heart. She knew the truth.

Volmer lifted the salt cellar and set it beside the pepper mill. “Neutral? That’s poor government and it’s just another word for gutless. There was a time when Denmark was strong. Now we try to sit out the wars. We hide in our homes and pretend nothing is wrong. Where is the honor in that? There is no honor. There’s only shame. Without self-respect, there is nothing.”

“So what do we do about it, Volmer? We are just two people. Two old people, I might add, if that means anything.”

“It means a great deal, Anna. Our age can be used to our advantage. The old are often overlooked. That gives us a degree of freedom that others much younger do not have. Old, however,” he looked at his wife with a steady gaze, “does not mean powerless. We have three choices, I think. We can do nothing, which is the same as surrendering and they will run right over us. Or we can call the authorities and report what we have seen, but I wouldn’t expect much help. Their power will be short-lived, if it isn’t already compromised.” Volmer looked into Anna’s eyes, a fire burning in his own. “Or we can fight.”

“Fight the Third Reich? Volmer, you have gone mad.”

“No, I haven’t gone mad but I am definitely angry. What about you, Anna? Are you angry? Angry enough to fight?” His words were hard but his voice was tender and he looked at her with a twinkle in his eye. “I don’t think the Nazis have ever encountered someone like you before. They would be well advised to proceed with caution when you are around. “

She patted his hand and smiled in spite of her fears. “Oh, Volmer. To make jokes at such a time.”

“No better time. All we have is now.” He sat back and laced his fingers behind his neck, looking up at the ceiling while his thoughts fell into place. “So,” he continued. “What do we know? We actually know quite a bit. The signal flashes could only have come from a submarine. There were no other boats on the water. Jens and the rest of the fleet had not gone out. Remember how choppy the seas were? Too much for a small boat." Volmer paused. "Why were they there?" He raised an index finger to hammer his point home. "I think they had a passenger to unload, but they couldn't. They were signaling that they would have to make another attempt. That's what I think." He nodded his head and slapped the table for emphasis.

"The rough water was not too much for the submarine, though," Anna said.

"That's true enough, but if whoever was supposed to get off drowned instead of making it to shore, it wouldn't go well for the crew. No, I think they may have decided that success demanded prudence. Justifying a delay is much easier than justifying failure. The Nazis are not known for their kindness to those who fail in their assignments."

"I understand what you are saying, Volmer, and it does make sense. How long will they wait before they try again, do you think?"

"If I had to guess, I'd say twenty-four hours. Germans are fanatical in their adherence to the clock. It is an obsession with them. If they tried at ten o'clock this morning, they'll try at ten o'clock tomorrow morning. And the morning after, if they have to."

"We must have our own plan, then." Anna was warming to the task. "We must find out who this passenger is, where he is going, and why he is going there." She dipped her finger absently into the tea cooling in her saucer and sucked it off her finger. "Do you think it will be a he? Maybe our mystery person will be a woman." I rather like that prospect. I could handle a woman. I'm sure of it. A man, probably not. But a woman? Definitely yes."

"I don't think a woman, Anna. Ships and women do not go well together. The submarine crew would probably mutiny if a woman came on board. They have their superstitions and women are considered very bad luck to a ship."

Anna sniffed. "Bad luck. I will give them bad luck. I know these superstitions. They come from ignorance. But do you really believe that in wartime they will allow such nonsense?"

"I think especially in wartime. They will take no chances."

Anna pursed her lips as if she'd tasted something sour. "So our passenger is a man. All right. I must accept that. We still need to find out who is receiving the signal from the U-boat and what this person on the boat is supposed to do. We have many questions without any answers."

Volmer nodded. "We need help with this. I have an idea, but it requires three people."

"Lars," Anna responded with a decisive bob of her head.

"Lars." Volmer agreed. "We will talk with him tonight at supper.

"That means Greta and Inge will be there too," Volmer looked to Anna. "Do we want them involved in this?"

"They will be involved regardless, Volmer. What is coming will affect us all. You can't protect them. No one can. They have a right to be part of this."

"All right then. That will give us two more pairs of eyes. We will no doubt need them."

Anna took a sip of her tea. It was cold, but she didn't notice. Drips falling from the bottom of the cup made wet circles on the tablecloth, and she didn't care.

"Don't look so worried, Anna," Inge said. "It's a celebration!" Inge's cheeks were flushed from the heat of the kitchen and there was a smudge of flour across her forehead. She took the dinner rolls from Anna and set them on the table. "We're having leg of lamb tonight. It's Lars's favorite."

Anna shot Volmer a meaningful glance and cleared her throat.

"I'll let Lars tell you all about it himself. I don't want to spoil his good news."

Anna cleared her throat again and Inge leaned towards her. "Are you all right, Anna? "

"I'm fine," Anna replied. "Just had a little something in my throat there for a minute. It's gone now." She patted Inge on the shoulder and reached up to brush away the flour from her forehead.

"Come on into the parlor," Inge said, leading the way.

Anna gave Volmer a nudge in the ribs. "I told you," she whispered.

In the parlor, Lars was waiting in front of the fireplace. He'd struck a casual pose, with one arm resting on the mantel, but it was apparent he was anything but relaxed. Greta stood to his left, a silver tray in her outstretched hand. On the tray were four small glasses into which she had poured a bit of Volmer's homemade elderberry wine.

"Welcome to the home of Police Captain Lars Jensen," she said, beaming from ear to ear. "Papa said I could have a small glass to mark the celebration," she added, as she moved among her family, distributing the drinks.

"To my husband!" Inge raised her glass.

"To Lars!" Anna and Volmer replied in unison.

"To Papa!" Greta proclaimed. "He gets a new uniform too," she said, sipping her drink.

"That part is definitely overdue," Inge said. This one is almost in tatters.

"That's a bit of an exaggeration," said Lars, "but the best part is that I will remain in Kolding. Captain Knutson is retiring and I will move into his position. So, a toast! To an increase in income - which we definitely need with Greta knocking on the door of university - to a new uniform, and especially to home!"

The christening ceremony was followed by dinner and the conversation was animated. Volmer, with frequent input from Anna, relayed the details of yesterday's strange happenings on the water and what they might possibly be able to do about it.

Now, with supper concluded, Volmer got down to business. "If the weather is good tomorrow, they will unload their passenger. It will be up to us to keep him in our sights, follow him, and learn what we can about him and his mission. This is what I think will work."

He moved the salt cellar to a central position on the kitchen table in a replay of what he'd earlier done at home. "Here is the location of the U-boat." He set the pepper mill at a right diagonal to the salt cellar. "Here is the lighthouse." He tapped it with his index finger. "I will be watching from here."

Lars set his water glass at a left diagonal and completed the triangulation. "Here is the shore. It's a fairly open area and I will wait here," he said, pointing to a spot just east of the glass, "to see which direction he goes. Someone will be waiting for him. Of that, we can be certain. He will not be acting alone."

"Once he's ashore he is likely to move quickly. There are two options. He will either pass through Sankt Peder or else he won't go anywhere but will remain here," offered Volmer. "I know that's like saying it's either going to rain or it isn't, but it's all we have to go on at this point."

"There are so many places he could go," Anna fretted. "We cannot afford to take our eyes from him for a moment. If we lose sight of him, we may never know where he is headed."

"That's true," Volmer said. "And if he is merely using Sankt Peder to reach shore, he will connect with his contact and move out quickly. There must be a car waiting."

"I'll have that part covered," said Lars. My automobile will be parked out of sight and I'll follow at a distance.

"Good," said Volmer. "If he stays here, he'll have made arrangements to blend in. That part puzzles me. Is it possible we know this man?" Volmer asked. "Is he someone who's been away for a while and is now returning? A stranger would be noticed immediately."

"There's no way a stranger could go unnoticed," Lars said, thinking aloud. "Perhaps a relative, someone who has been away for a long time?"

"That would be wonderful and would answer at least one of our questions. Is there anybody's relative that Anna doesn't know?" Inge was laughing.

"*Ja*, for sure. She knows them all." Volmer looked at his wife with affection. Anna blushed, but it was true. She knew everyone.

"The pastor," Anna said. It had come to her so suddenly that she felt she'd had a revelation. "We're expecting a pastor. He'll be a stranger but a familiar stranger. You know what I mean. He will be the stranger who isn't one." She tilted her head and considered this idea, while Volmer looked at her, mouth agape, and Lars looked as if he'd swallowed a fly. Inge was smiling, a broad ear to ear grin and she winked at her daughter.

"*Oma*, you're wonderful," Greta said.

"How does she do it?" Lars asked.

"I don't know. I really don't know," Volmer said.

"Of course, if we don't see his face as he comes ashore we can't be sure," Anna said, "but that doesn't mean we can't still watch our new pastor closely and be very careful what we say around him until we know for certain he is who he is. Or isn't," she added as an afterthought.

And so it was agreed. Volmer to the lighthouse. Lars to the shore. And Anna, Inge, and Greta to visit Mrs. Jorgensen, who lived in the only house between the shore and the main road.

"He may be wearing a hat, after he pulls up on shore," warned Lars. "You may only catch a glimpse of his face, if that."

"It's more than we have now," Volmer said. "It will be most enlightening to see how he manages his entrance into town, should he be our new minister. He'll have to leave first without being seen before he can return by more conventional means. Pastors don’t routinely get dropped off by passing submarines. But still we will at least have a thread to follow.”

“Threads can get tangled, Volmer,” said Anna. “We must be careful.”

Chapter Six

Washington, D.C.

"We've been expecting you, sir. His lordship is in the study."

"Thank you, Bentley." John handed over his hat and coat to the ancient butler who had answered the door. "How have you been?"

"I'm keeping very well, sir. Thank you for asking. And yourself, sir?"

"Very good, as well, Bentley. Better than the weather, at any rate. It's beastly outside," John said.

Bentley examined John's sodden coat with a practiced eye. "I'll just give this a bit of a brush-up, if you don't mind, sir?"

"Thank you, Bentley. I'd appreciate it. It's raining to beat the band and the wind has picked up. I was nearly blown away coming up the walk."

"Indeed. May I show you to the study, sir?" He turned without waiting for a response and led John across the foyer, a distance of about three meters, and knocked once on the walnut paneled double doors of Sir Robert Chauncy-Wilson's study. He then opened the door to the right and announced, "Mr. Breckenridge, my lord."

A booming voice called out from a chair drawn up close

to the fireplace. “John! Come in. Come in. Have a seat by the fire and warm up. It’s frightfully damp out there. Chill you to the bone.” Sir Robert’s face was as animated as his manservant’s was stoic, and his bushy white eyebrows went bounding and leaping about his forehead with each word he spoke.

“Bob, it’s good to see you.” John crossed the room to his old friend and extended his hand in greeting. Sir Robert grasped the hand and used it, along with the arm of his chair to pull himself to standing.

“It gets a bit tricky, negotiating these complex maneuvers,” he chuckled, reaching for the cane that waited against the coffee table. “I know what will set us both to rights. No, Bentley, that’s fine. I’ll do the honours.”

“Very good, my lord. If there’s nothing else then?”

“No, Bentley. I’ll ring should I need you.” The houseman took his leave and Sir Robert busied himself at the sideboard, selecting a bottle and some crystal glassware. “Eighteen year old single malt Scotch with a splash of soda, one ice cube, and here’s to your health!” He motioned John to the companion chair in front of the fireplace. “Sit. Drink. And we’ll reminisce of old times. Cabbages and kings and all that.” He raised his glass. “Ah, John, it’s good to see you. Company has been a bit sparse around here of late.”

“And you as well. It’s been a while.” John lifted his own glass.

“Seventeen years this April, if I’m not mistaken. And I rarely am.” Sir Robert’s eyes lost their twinkle and his expression darkened. “You knew it hadn’t ended, of course. It never ends.”

“I’d hoped.”

Sir Robert shook his head. “It’s the nature of the beast, I’m afraid.” He set his glass down on the small table beside his chair and folded his arms across his chest. “I’m a bit worn about the edges, this time. Don’t expect they’ll have much use for me.”

"I wouldn't count on it, Bob. You've got the know-how and the can-do. There's no age limit on that. How are you doing, really? All healed up after that spot of bad business?"

"As good as can be expected, all things considered. The chaps at Walter Reed gave it their best go. Now it's in the hands of the Almighty."

John nodded and studied the amber liquid in his glass. "It'll be different this go round, without Charlie."

"I expect he'll be watching, nevertheless. But the space never quite closes, does it? There's always a hole." Sir Robert turned to John. "It's difficult to lose a brother but he made a good end of it. He was one of the best, for bloody sure." He raised the glass again and drank.

The warmth of the fire and the fire in his drink worked their magic, and John felt the chill leave his hands and feet. "Were you able to locate Rutledge?"

"As soon as your wire arrived I had Bentley track him down. I swear that man is part bloodhound. Put him on the scent and release the tether and he does the job. He'll be here within the hour, Rutledge, that is, and he's bringing everything you requested. He snorted at me, when I asked him if he were up to the task! Actually snorted!" Sir Robert blinked rapidly and his eyebrows worked overtime keeping up their end of the agreement. "I've always enjoyed getting a rise out of him. He's actually quite stodgy for a young fellow. Do him good to stir up the fires."

John considered the assessment of Rutledge as a young fellow. The man had to be sixty-five, if he were a day. Still, age was relative. Sir Robert was close to eighty now, but his spirit and mind were as sharp as a man half his age.

Shortly, Bentley reappeared with the somber announcement that dinner would be ready at seven o'clock and would that be satisfactory. His eyes swept the room and he frowned, having noticed a wilted petal on the sideboard's floral arrangement. "I'll ring up the florist in the morning for a fresh bouquet, my lord." He removed the spent blossom and left.

"He has exacting standards," John observed. "The flowers look fine."

"Bentley conducts his own War of the Roses. It's always red and white, Lancaster and York. He insists there's always a half dozen of each color. He'd make an excellent Democrat in your government."

"It wouldn't work," John said. "He's much too efficient. Efficiency and government are mutually exclusive entities. There's nothing the politicians love better than waste."

"Then it's all to the good. I wouldn't be nearly as productive without him." Sir Robert smiled into his glass.

As if to underscore the point, Bentley reappeared at that moment. "Mr. William Rutledge has just arrived, my lord."

"What did I tell you? He keeps me in line."

"My lord?"

"Nothing, Bentley. I believe we will be three for dinner. That will be all."

"Yes, my lord."

John watched the Butler's retreating form. "How long has Bentley worked for you? Twenty years? It's got to be at least that."

"Careful, there, John. Bentley would take extreme offense at the notion he works for me. He is 'in service.' Actually it's more like thirty years, and sometimes I question who works for whom. I take my orders from him, more often than not." Sir Robert chuckled softly, a rumbling sound like a contented tom cat. "He'll be well provided for, when I pass on. I like him eminently better than any of my relatives. Shiftless lot, the bunch of them." He scowled.

Bill Rutledge entered the room, minus the formal introduction John had received. "I told Bentley I could find you without assistance. I do believe he is upset with me." He grinned. "Stay seated, old man." Bill waved a hand in the direction of his former commanding officer. "I know my way around the bar." He winked at John and Sir Robert groaned.

"He's a barrister and enjoys his little joke, although it is the only one he knows and it has gotten quite stale over the years. As has my drink," Sir Robert added, indicating his empty glass.

"Glad to see you're back on your feed," Bill said. "You've been quite cranky without your alcohol." He winked again.

"John, this is Bill Rutledge, who has been concerned about my enforced sobriety." Sir Robert said. "Bill, this is John Breckenridge, as you have no doubt surmised. Colonel John Breckenridge to be precise, and he's the chap I told you would be stopping by to pick our brains."

"Good to meet you, John. His lordship speaks highly of you." He reached for John's glass. "Scotch, right? He added a healthy measure to John's glass, refilled Sir Robert's, and poured one for himself. "I've brought everything I believe we'll find useful," he said, distributing the drinks.

"How much do you know?" He took a seat on the sofa and spent a moment rotating his neck. This produced a series of cracks and snaps. "Touch of arthritis. The damp doesn't help." He made one more rotation.

"Not much," John admitted. "Just the basics, I'm afraid. Cryptography isn't my field."

"Right." Bill shuffled through some papers he'd taken from his briefcase. "It's quite simple, once you understand a few principles. It's an ancient science, actually, although today people think of it more as parlor games and puzzles. Secret codes and all that sort of thing." He smiled. "But it's so much more than that. Julius Caesar invented the first substitution code, you know, as a way to prevent unauthorized personnel from reading his military communications. You had to decipher the code before you could read the message. It worked like this." He took a sheet of paper and pen from Sir Robert's desk and then printed the alphabet across the page. "Give me a number under 10," he said.

"Four."

"Good. Four will be the key. We'll count off the first four letters of the alphabet – *A*, *B*, *C*, *D*, and begin our encryption with the letter *E*. That means I'll start a new alphabet directly under the *E*. So *E* becomes *A* and *F* becomes *B* and so on, in my code. This is the simplest kind of encipherment, and it's called a substitution code."

"Caesar was on to something, and the idea caught fire," Sir Robert said. "Ever since that time, military intelligence has been enciphered in one form or another. In The Great War, it took us quite some time to decipher the Germans' work. They'd gotten quite good at encryption. And the codes just get more and more difficult to crack."

"It's all mathematics," Bill explained. "But then, what isn't, eh?" he said. "Radio changed everything. Once it became widely used, the military used wireless radio, or telegraphy, to report their position and progress, or lack of same. Of course, once the chaps realized their information could just as easily be intercepted by the enemy as by their own people, they began to encrypt their data to protect it."

"We'd upped the ante a bit and gotten more sophisticated. Now we weren't talking about written communication, but wireless signals," Sir Robert said. "Early in the Great War, as far back as 1914, British radio operators organized as the Royal Navy Radio Intercept Service, feeding traffic to the Admiralty. Room 40 was the site designated for cryptanalysis and it became quite a celebrated location. But because of the limited range of signals, intercept stations had to be set up clandestinely across Europe in order to get the signals out and home again. They were called Y stations.

"Why not, eh?" Bill interjected. He smirked while John and Sir Robert exchanged pained looks.

"Why not, indeed," said Sir Robert.

"Anyway," Bill continued, the information gave the boys

at sea advance warning of where the enemy was, in time for them to either avoid engagement or prepare to attack. And the Y stations proved their worth. First, the intercepts proved that the German high command had ordered the sinking of the *Lusitania*, despite their claims to the contrary. This was a big deal. And then the prize – the Zimmerman Telegram in 1917 that brought America into the war."

"And that brings us to the heart of today's work," Sir Robert said. "Encryption has become extremely sophisticated. A German, Arthur Scherbius, invented a machine back in 1918 that used a system of rotors to encrypt messages. Very ingenious device. The codes could be changed at will, and they were nearly impossible to crack."

"So this Scherbius worked for German intelligence?" John asked.

"No! That's the corker!' said Bill. "He was just an inventor who thought he'd found the perfect answer for banks to encrypt their data! Banks! Of course, it didn't go anywhere. Too complicated, but the chaps in the military pounced on it."

"Right," Sir Robert said. "Scherbius called it *Enigma*, and it became the cornerstone of German intelligence. They've done everything since then to increase its complexity. It's given us a devil of a time, I don't mind saying. We were in a bit of a bind, as you can well see," he said. "We tried everything to get through the Jerries' newest version of *Enigma*, but weren't having much success, until we got a spot of luck from the Poles."

"There was a cadre of mathematical geniuses there," Bill explained, "and they'd broken the earlier version of *Enigma.* They'd even made a replica of the machine, but they realized that the Germans would be knocking on their door soon, so they arranged a meeting in the forest, gave us the machine, and here we are."

Sir Robert nodded. "With the machine in hand, we can crack the newest codes. Without it, the odds against us were

150 million million million to one. That's 150 million to the 3rd power, if your mind has a mathematical bent. It's not the sort of thing one broadcasts to the world. Of course, it's still difficult. That's why we have decrypters working around the clock at Bletchley. The Germans constantly change the codes. We're basically just keeping up, and haven't managed yet to forge out ahead."

"And now?" John asked. "This is fascinating stuff, but what do we do with it now?"

"Now we can use Enigma to our advantage. We press on. Once you're in place, you'll be able to feed information to the Jerries and send back intelligence to us. Just remember that whatever you send to us will be read by them. As long as the Germans don't discover what we know, we have the edge." He fixed John with a level gaze and a tight-lipped smile. God knows, we're going to need it."

Chapter Seven

En route to Denmark

People traveling by car are confident, sometimes even aggressive. Those who travel by train are usually patient and expectant. But those who travel by aircraft are nervous. You can see it in their actions. They check their pockets or their pocketbooks frequently to reassure themselves the tickets are still there. They study their tickets as if they must memorize every word on them and then pull them out again to review before the exam. I think it has to do with control. People feel a fundamental need to be in control and that is not possible with air travel, so they compensate where they can.

I found myself examining my own ticket, checking departure time, and making sure my name had been correctly spelled. *Katrin Nissen* would depart from Port Washington, New York, at 7:30 in the morning and then touch down at Shediac, New Brunswick. Next stop was Botwood, Newfoundland. From there it was across the Atlantic to Foynes, Ireland, and on to the final landing at Southampton, England, at 1:00 tomorrow afternoon Greenwich Mean Time. And all that for $355 American dollars. From London I'd catch my flight to Copenhagen. I was good to go.

John had explained the principles of aerodynamics to me in simple terms, and I think that had helped me overcome my initial fears. I'll never fully understand it, but I don't need to. All I know is there is something exhilarating about flight. The racing of both pulse and engines as the aircraft speeds down the runway, and then the glorious moment it breaks free of the pull of gravity and challenges the open air.

The Pan Am Clipper that would carry me across the Atlantic was something new in the world of aviation. At first glance the aircraft resembled a battleship outfitted with pontoons and a second glance did nothing to change that perception. Ungainly, unwieldy, and lumbering on the ground, it was powerful and mighty aloft, with a massive wingspread. Its aft section curved upwards, scorpion style. Inside, however, the *Yankee Clipper* was luxurious.

Built to compete with Britain's *Empire* class aircraft, the *Clipper* was one hell of an airplane. The Boeing 314 offered all the service of an ocean liner but covered the miles in a mere fraction of the time. There were lounges, bars, powder rooms, and dining rooms that offered fare catered by four-star hotels. The seats converted into bunks for the overnight portion of the flight, and the heavy soundproofing in the cabin walls muffled the drone of the engines. I was looking forward to a restful night in my curtained bunk.

The *Yankee Clipper* was not the *Flying Dutchman,* but it well could have been shaped in its image. Unlike its ghostly counterpart, it would touch down for refueling, like a migratory bird needing to feed. And like that same bird, it returned not by instinct, but when clouds obscured the night sky, by dead reckoning, the same tool used by mariners of old.

Once we were aloft I looked out the porthole window and watched the clouds take on the aspect of an ocean. Layers of gray and white billowed above and to the sides and swirled beneath. I could imagine Viking longboats tossing on the waves, borne aloft by swirling currents, imperiled by vortexes that loomed across the horizon. We here were the gods on Olympus, looking down on the distant earth, wagering on the outcomes of the human struggle that revealed themselves in episodes as the clouds parted before our eyes. A different perspective, indeed, from this altitude, with only an occasional bump as a distant reminder of the storms that raged beneath us.

Chapter Eight

Kolding, Denmark

I slept like a baby. That is to say I tossed, turned, and twisted all night long. The more I tried to relax and will myself to sleep, the more uncomfortable my bed became and the more awake I was. Lumps appeared in my pillow, my hip felt as if I had consigned it to a fakir's nail bed, my nightgown kept tickling my thighs and when I tried to straighten the fabric, the comforter wadded up under my chin and cut off my breathing. There was also a sprung mattress coil that kept finding the small of my back. And so the hours crept by, tortoise fashion.

Predictably, sleep arrived with the first light of dawn. I'd just dozed off when the god-awful caterwauling of the alarm clock wrenched me away from the arms of Morpheus. I grimaced and tugged the covers up over my head, stuffing my face into the now soft depths of the goose down pillow and jamming my index fingers into my ears. Sleep that had eluded me all night was now so near. The bedcovers had become the softest woven cotton. Drifting with blissful sleep so close, I tried to hold back the inevitable. But the shrill din clanged on. Damn.

Groping my way out of my little cocoon, I slapped in the direction of the nightstand and managed to hit the lamp, my eyeglasses, and the book I'd been reading, now face down and splay-spined at page eighty-seven, but I didn't connect with my tormentor. I forced my head up and my eyes open. Quite simply I had forgotten I was not home, but rather several thousand miles away in an unfamiliar bed.

Sometimes I hated myself. The offending clarion call of dawn was relentlessly blaring away on the dresser, safely out of my reach. Last night, clever me had decided on this prudent strategy to ensure I would not just shut off the alarm and go back to sleep. Sleep. Fat chance. My raveled sleeve of care was not going to be knitted up today. I hated these kinds of mornings, and I knew all I would think about throughout the day was how many more hours remained until I could go back to sleep. The countdown had begun. Bed became the goal, the quest, the Holy Grail. I made a mental note to turn the mattress before I retired for the night.

Glowering at the clock, I launched myself out of bed and derived some small level of satisfaction by silencing the noise with a healthy swack. I would need coffee, and soon, and I had some serious work to do on the sleep-deprived face with the vacant stare that greeted me in the mirror above the dresser.

I was occupying one of the two guest rooms in the Pedersen home, a sunny yellow two-story house with contrasting dark brown wood timbers and gingerbread edging. It was a tasteful house that looked good enough to eat. It fronted directly onto the cobblestone street and my window opened onto the thoroughfare, giving me an excellent view of the neighborhood.

I raised the window and leaned out to catch the salty tang of the morning air. No matter where I lived, I was always drawn back to the ocean and it would always smell like home. Low tide has always held a particular appeal for me, although John maintains the aroma reminds him of rotting fish. I tend to think of it as concentrated essence of ocean. To each his own. Now, the curtains danced and fluttered in the cool breeze. I wished I felt half as chipper as they seemed to be. Truth is, I was a bit nervous about today, my first day on the job.

I didn't doubt my ability to handle the switchboard, but learning the office routine, sorting out the names, while finding a way to successfully handle my mission had me a little tense. One thing at a time, I told myself. Of course that was probably the way to become hopelessly overwhelmed in no time at all. The only way to succeed in this mission was to handle several things at once and maintain my focus.

John's strict instructions came back to me: "Get in. Do the job. Get out. Don't get caught up in people's personal lives."

Of course, I had taken issue with that, as I hardly ever get involved. But he'd had to finish with the typical male directive, "I mean it, Katrin." Well, of course he meant well, but you never could tell what was going to come up in these situations, and sometimes it just wasn't possible to avoid getting involved. But I promised him sincerely that I would do exactly what he said. And I really meant it. Sometimes, though, things just happen. At least they did to me. I often wondered why that was.

It didn't take me long to dress. I'd selected a simple, conservative outfit for today as the best approach, at least until I had the place scoped out. My forest green and gold box-pleated woolen plaid skirt, short-sleeved gold sweater with matching cardigan, and black low-heeled pumps gave me a competent air. I considered jewelry and decided on my pearl earrings. Clipping them on my earlobes, I remembered my good gloves that I'd laid out on the dresser scarf and debated whether or not to wear them. I decided to carry them in my pocketbook in case it was too chilly traveling without them. A crisp morning breeze can feel like an Arctic blast when you're on a bicycle.

Ready for the day and what it would bring, I went downstairs to the kitchen where *Frue* Pedersen was dishing up breakfast. I filled my plate at the sideboard with herring and sweet rolls, poured a cup of coffee, and took my meal to the table, where I joined the other guest, *Frue* Christiana Andersen, an owlish woman of about seventy. She explained she was a widow with time on her hands and had chosen to devote that time to visiting her relatives and offering advice on all manner of topics. A few weeks into this project, she had decided she could only stomach her relatives in small portions and had moved in to the guest home for the duration.

Christiana, as I was invited to call her, had the roundest brown eyes I had ever seen. Liberally sprinkled with golden highlights, they resembled speckled chestnuts. Her mouth was drawn up in sort of a pucker, but one that indicated she found everything, with the possible exception of her relatives, amusing. An angular woman with large hands and a deep, booming voice, she was, she informed me, a retired schoolmistress on a pension, and while she was careful of her expenses, she considered the rent at *Frue* Pedersen's well worth the cost to give her privacy and quiet.

I smiled inwardly, since it wasn't possible to get a word in edgewise with this woman who was seeking peace and quiet. She was a constant stream of chatter. I suspected her relatives were thrilled about her decision to sleep in town. Munching away at my breakfast, I offered an occasional nod and smile and that seemed to be all that Christiana required.

Annelise Pedersen ran a comfortable guest house. The rooms were spacious, and the food was excellent. She stopped by to chat for a moment, as she refilled the coffee pot. Aside from a polite inquiry into our plans for the day, she did not snoop into her boarders' affairs. It was a quality that endeared her to tired business travelers, the British trade, and in my case, the occasional government agent. And so, fortified for the morning ahead and more than ready to leave *Frue* Andersen, I collected my boxed lunch and stowed it in the wire basket of my bicycle that was my transportation to and from work.

It's not entirely true that once you've ridden a bicycle you never forget. At least for me, it took a few stutter stops and starts and wobbles before I got my bicycle legs under me. Once astride, I didn't dare slow down, so it was full speed ahead, dodging holes in the street and bumping over stones. It didn't take me long to cover the short distance to the Schmidt & Ericksen Beef Products Processing Plant and I glided to a stop in the parking area without having broken a sweat. Positioning my bicycle in the rack, I adjusted my clothing and smoothed my hair, took up my pocketbook and lunch box, and examined my surroundings.

Schmidt & Ericksen's was situated in the industrial section of town. A no-nonsense single story structure, its L-shape covered close to half a block. A spur from the rail line ran along the back portion and ended at the shipping bay. The rear section was dedicated to the business end of processing meat, while the part that faced the street housed the office. The office was my destination. I entered the hall of beef.

The first door on my right was labeled "Main Office." As good a place to start as any, I turned the knob and walked to the front desk and encountered, according to the name plate on her desk, Helga Bruegger. Helga, a woman in her early fifties, was a hale and hearty specimen of Nordic womanhood, decked out for spring in a vivid pink floral dress. Her matching hair bow was pinned securely over her left ear, giving her the appearance of a friendly flower garden running heavily to cabbage roses.

"*Goddag,*" I began. "I am Katrin Nissen, the replacement switchboard operator." I waited while *Froken* Helga inspected me. Apparently satisfied, she bellowed her welcome.

"Of course you are!"

Yes. Well. That was a positive beginning. Helga rose and walked around her desk, hand outstretched in greeting. "I am

Helga Bruegger, the General Office Manager." She bowed slightly.

I suppressed an urge to respond, "Of course you are!" and settled for a "Pleased to meet you."

Helga had a grip like a champion arm wrestler and pumped my hand up and down with enthusiasm. I winced and several tendons and a few muscles in my hand and wrist screamed for mercy. When she released my hand, I watched it fall to my side, a temporary dead weight at the end of my arm.

"You want to see the switchboard. Of course you do!"

The ensuing tour was brief, mostly consisting of Helga slowly rotating, while she pointed out the various components of the room in question. I rotated along with her. The room was square with the front entryway leading to the street on the south side. A glassed door on the east wall led into the plant, which consisted of the cutting rooms, conveyer belts, and cold storage facilities.

Helga's desk was to the left of the entryway and extended into the central portion of the room, while the file clerk's desk was close up against the north wall, along which stretched a bank of file cabinets. Anyone needing to access the files would have to maneuver sideways past the file clerk's desk, squeezing through the narrow aisle way.

The switchboard was directly opposite Helga's desk, and so my back would be to her and hers to me. That was good. There was no wasted space and everything, with the exception of the file clerk's desk which was overflowing with unfiled papers, was neat as a pin. Judging from that desk, the person who belonged to it either spent a great deal of time at the file cabinets or not enough. I suspected it was the latter.

Helga ended the tour at the switchboard, where she pointed out a chart with names and telephone numbers propped against the console. I took notes as she explained each person's title and location in the plant. Satisfied that I would not lose my way inside the office, she returned to her desk and left me to my work. At 8:30 the switchboard sprang to life, and the rest of the morning passed in a blur. By the time the lunch whistle blew, I wasn't sure what was more tired, my arms or my eyes.

A desk drawer behind me slid open and then closed, and I turned to see Helga searching through her handbag. She extracted her compact and applied a generous portion of powder to her nose. She freshened her pink lipstick and primped for the tiny mirror, turning and twisting her head as she arranged her hairdo. Finally she gave herself two healthy spritzes from a perfume atomizer that also resided within her bag and adjusted her corsets and brassiere, wriggling like an overweight puppy against the restraints of a new leash. The reason for this complicated mini-toilette soon revealed itself with the arrival of *Herre* Waldemar Hedegaard, Plant Manager.

"*Froken* Nissen, *Herre* Hedegaard." Helga's eyes danced and shone, as she conducted the introduction. It didn't take a genius or even a master spy, for that matter, to conclude that Helga was in love with Waldemar and that he returned the favor. He was as small as Helga was large. They were Brunhilde and her diminutive Tannheuser.

One benefit of this was that Wally's eye level evened out just about at Helga's ample bosom. This anatomical disparity allowed Helga to put her arm around his shoulders, drawing him in close. He seemed to appreciate this.

"Welcome to Schmidt & Ericksen." Wally's reedy tenor floated above Helga's powerful contralto and he cut a dapper figure with his crisp white jacket and floral bow tie. My eyes fixed first on its pattern and then traveled back to Helga's attire and sure enough, the tie was the same fabric and print as Helga's frock. This was a love match made of sturdy stuff, probably broadcloth, I guessed. Definitely nothing flimsy like chiffon.

Wally was a compact man and everything about him

conveyed a sense of efficient management of resources, even to his shiny bald pate still sporting a few strands of hair, valiantly attempting to do their own work as well as that of their fallen brethren. His mustache was waxed and the ends had been lovingly coaxed into an upward arc, thus defying the current trend towards that horrid Hitler rectangle. Wally was his own man, or rather, he was Helga's man and proud of it.

"*Tak*, *Herre* Hedegaard. I am glad I was available to help out." I smiled broadly at him, as his convivial manner was contagious. With his round face, pink cheeks, and turned up nose, he was my childhood vision of Father Christmas come to life.

"Just remember the motto of Schmidt and Ericksen," Wally advised. "When in doubt, ship it out!" He emphasized this directive with a solemn nod, which caused a minor disturbance among the overtaxed hairs on his head. He then extended an index finger and made a short stab towards the ceiling.

I glanced at the ceiling to see if the motto was emblazoned there. It wasn't. Wally followed my glance and then Helga joined our little stargazing group. It was at that moment the temperature seemed to drop twenty degrees in advance of an incoming cold front.

"What's going on? Has this dump sprung a leak? I wouldn't doubt it. It's such a shithole." A striking young woman had swept into the room leaving a vapor trail of expensive perfume in her wake and had tossed her purse onto the desk next to Helga's. She draped her sweater across the back of her chair, settled a stack of movie magazines on the blotter, and finally favored us with a look. I sensed Helga's form stiffening inside her corsets and watched her arm tighten possessively across Wally's shoulders. I wondered who this ice maiden would turn out to be.

"You'd be advised to watch your language. Your vulgarity is not appropriate." Helga's eyes shot arrows straight at the newcomer.

"Oh, pardon me, *Froken* Bruegger. I must have forgotten myself. How incorrect of me." Sarcasm dripped like venom from the young woman's scarlet lips. I half expected a puddle to begin forming at her feet, which were clad in some very expensive Italian pumps.

This was getting interesting, and I was curious to see who would fire the next round in this little salvo. Wally was due, but Helga jumped in instead. "*Froken* Nissen, this is Dagmar Strasser, our file clerk." Helga made the introduction as if she were describing a communicable disease.

"Well, lah dee dah. Welcome, honey." Dagmar's eyes had started at my feet and were working their way up. She was checking me out and not being the least bit subtle about it.

I resisted the urge to smooth my hair and stand up straight. Instead, I met fire with fire and brazenly looked her up and down. She smiled. It was a dazzler. All teeth - white, sharp, pointy teeth. I wondered if she filed them at night.

"You're late," Helga said. It was an accusation more than a piece of information. "Your salary will be docked four hours."

Dagmar had already turned away, having lost interest in our little game of stare down. "I came as quickly as I could. There were matters to attend to that I couldn't put off. I'll get right at the files."

But she didn't. Dagmar made herself a cup of coffee and sat staring off into space for a good ten minutes before setting to work. She was preoccupied, that much was clear. She also didn't seem a bit concerned about Helga's wrath. I wondered if that was usual. I also wondered how she managed to keep her job with her attitude. It had to be her looks. And she was a looker, all right. Some women seemed to be blessed with all the assets and born with the knowledge of how to use them.

I had the same equipment. It was just arranged differently. She was about five foot four to my five foot eleven, so I had the height advantage. However, she didn't have one pound that wasn't pure feminine curve. I've been working at losing the same ten pounds for the past ten years. No, she had me bested in the figure department. Hands down. I flexed my fingers. They were prickly now, having revived themselves from their bout with Helga's handshake. Should be back to snuff in a few more minutes. I returned to work.

By three o'clock the board had quieted down and it seemed a good time for a short break. Dagmar was at the filing cabinets, slamming drawers and muttering to herself. Bang, slam, bang. And then an unmistakable sob. Her shoulders shook and she began to bawl, her face cradled in her hands.

"Don't get involved." I heard those words again as clearly as if John had been standing at my side. But this wasn't getting involved, I reasoned. It was just offering some support. She was upset and she was also very young. Still, I hesitated for a moment, wondering how or even if I should intrude, and as she cranked up the volume, she became impossible to ignore.

Helga was bent over her work, apparently immune, although as I looked in her direction, she raised her head and rolled her eyes. I, however, was a newcomer and hadn't had time to build up any resistance to such an emotional outpouring. I wouldn't get involved. Just offer her a handkerchief and a word or two of sympathy. What could that hurt?

As I considered the right opening words, my eyes connected with Helga's. Wide eyes, lips pressed together and a firm negative headshake was all the information I needed to abandon my Good Samaritan plan and leave Dagmar to suffer in solitude, if not silence.

I wrinkled my forehead at Helga to indicate confusion,

but Helga just put an index finger to her lips in the universal, unmistakable sign for “Don’t say a word.”

Well, she had the experience, and as the old saying goes, “Experience is the best teacher, and a fool will have no other.” As I said before, I’m a quick study. I went back to work, and ultimately, when Dagmar had slammed out of the office to, I supposed, the powder room, Helga jumped in with the answer.

“It’s men. It’s always men with her. She’ll be over it by the time she comes back. Mark my words. I’ve been watching. She was sent here by the owner, not more than three weeks ago, and if you ask me, she’s not worth what he’s paying her. I don’t know why she’s here. But that’s just me. I do my job and try to get her to do hers.”

And sure enough. When Dagmar returned, there was a hard glint in her eyes, her makeup was once again perfect, and there was nary a sign of tears. Quite a chameleon, this Dagmar Strasser. I looked at Helga, who smiled and shrugged. I shook my head and gave Dagmar one last look before writing this one off. She was one tough customer, I gave her that.

To her credit, after this interlude with the tears, she got to work and did clean up the files. At least she put them in the cabinet. Whether or not she’d actually filed them remained to be seen. Regardless, at half past four her desk was cleared off and she was out the door as soon as the whistle blew.

The upside of this was I didn’t think she’d be all that interested in me or what I did. She was the only attraction in her world and nobody else rated a second glance.

Helga, however, didn’t miss a trick. She also knew how to run the switchboard, so leaving a key open to listen in on a call when she was around wasn’t going to be an option. I’d need to be careful. The fewer explanations I had to make, the better for everyone. Especially for me.

Chapter Nine

Sankt Peder

By six-thirty the next morning, Volmer was sitting on the edge of his bed, putting on his woolen socks and having some difficulty tugging one of them over his heel. *If.* That word kept running through his mind and he paused in his efforts. *If* he hadn't decided to mend the fishing nets yesterday, and *if* Anna hadn't come with the food, and *if* they hadn't sat facing the water, they would never have seen the signals. And they would have gone on with life as usual, at least for a time. But he *had* decided and she *had* come and they *had* sat and seen and those events had brought incalculable change to their lives. And how that change would play out, time could only tell. He gave a final tug to the sock, pulled on his work boots, and laced them up. He briefly rested his hands on his knees before he rose. He lifted his coat and hat from the hooks on the back of the bedroom door and went downstairs.

In the kitchen, Anna was just back from collecting eggs. She had washed up the breakfast dishes and was now arranging the eggs in a wooden basket, frowning over a crack here or a slight discoloration there, making substitutions where she deemed necessary. She wanted to make this basket perfect, down to the last detail.

She also wanted to make herself as perfect as she could and had dabbed a spot of rouge on her cheeks and dusted powder on her nose. She couldn't deny the excitement bubbling just below the surface. Today would be a different kind of a day. She would be doing something important, and her eyes sparkled with that knowledge.

In the other Jensen household down the street, Lars was pacing the parlor floor. No matter how he worked it through, the result was the same. There was danger ahead. He clenched his jaw and took a deep breath, exhaling slowly. He had sworn an oath to protect and to serve, even at the cost of his own life. He would do whatever he could, for as long as he must, at whatever the cost. He knew this to be true, but he also loved his family and the danger that lay ahead was not one he could protect them from.

At eight o'clock Lars grabbed his car key from the dresser and set off down the curved path that wound through the woods and led to the shore. His destination was a grove of beech trees slightly inland that would provide some cover but still allow an unobstructed view of the junction where the main highway intersected with the frontage road. He'd parked his car close by in a sheltered area last night and walked the short distance home.

The skeleton branches of the beech trees were ghostlike in the stark, thin light of early morning. In another month the buds would be swollen and the trees ready to burst into leaf, obscuring the view of the shore. At least this much worked in his favor, for he could see clearly and still be out of view. He took up his position and settled in to wait.

Surveillance was one of the more mind-numbing aspects of police work and ranked near the top of the list of least favorite assignments for most officers. The ability to do absolutely nothing except watch required large amounts of patience and the physical and mental stamina to withstand excruciating boredom. Today, however, Lars was anything but bored. He was coiled up like a new rope and the tension continued to build inside him. "Come on. Come on," he whispered to himself as his eyes strained to take in as much of the coastline as he could.

At five minutes past nine, he spotted a black Mercedes V 170 pull up and park by the side of the road. The driver was a young woman, dark hair, possibly early twenties, and even from this distance he could tell she was a beauty. He'd know her for sure if he saw her again. From his angle, he couldn't make out the license plate. He might get a chance as the car pulled away, but it was a long shot.

The woman picked up a magazine and leafed through the pages, looking up from time to time with a scowl on her face that did nothing to mask her good looks. She checked her watch frequently, and after a time began drumming her nails on the steering wheel.

Waiting was the official order of the morning and now, keeping to the schedule set by Berlin, Commandant Kurt von Kessel was biding his time until he could surface and dispose of his unwelcome and highly disagreeable passenger. By the ship's clock, he had twenty-seven minutes left to endure.

Von Kessel's craft was one of fifty-seven modernized U-boats that Germany possessed at the opening of WWII. It had become his after he had answered the call last August to attend a reunion for World War I U-boat commanders. Along with his fellow veterans of the Great War, von Kessel learned this gathering was not a reunion, but a mandatory reactivation. The *Unterseebootwaffe* was to begin preparations for combat.

German submarines had wreaked havoc during the Great War, sinking millions of tons of Allied shipping and von Kessel had commanded one of those U-boats with distinction. To be blunt, that meant he and his crew had survived. When the summons came again, he knew the odds were against him. He figured he'd used up his share of good luck but it didn't matter. There was no refusing the call to duty. He and his crew were in for the duration.

Von Kessel's *unterseeboot* was state of the art and that meant it was capable of speeds in excess of twenty-six knots for short periods. With its Walter turbine propulsion system, it could use oxygen generated by hydrogen peroxide to operate the turbine when submerged. And it had another modern feature, the *schnorchel* device that had been developed by the Dutch in 1936, but which had fallen into German hands in 1940. The Germans quickly saw its advantages. The *schnorchel* was essentially a tube that delivered oxygen to the diesel engines. Oxygen allowed the engines to operate at periscope depth to recharge their batteries for underwater propulsion. It also reduced the chance of detection by Allied radar. For the past few days, von Kessel's U-boat had made use of that *schnorchel* to remain hidden from view. This morning, von Kessel was determined to surface long enough to dispatch his passenger.

Below decks, that passenger, a tall, lean man with closely trimmed blond hair confirmed the time with his watch and continued his inventory of the contents of a rectangular, waterproof box. Satisfied, he replaced the lid and buckled the canvas straps that encircled the container. He then directed his attention to several documents that lay in front of him on the scarred wooden table. Refolding them with two sharp creases, he inserted them into the left breast pocket of his jacket.

He slipped a small notebook into a pouch, zipped it closed, and secured it around his waist with an elastic strap. Donning his pea coat, he gathered up his parcel and a small weather-beaten valise that contained his clothing. Without a backward glance, he exited the room and proceeded up the narrow spiral staircase toward the main deck.

Von Kessel was already topside. The storm that had whipped the ocean into a frenzy the past several days had abated. The seas this morning were noticeably calmer and he had already given the order to begin the necessary preparations. He watched as two sailors coiled the ropes that would assist in lowering the raft into the water and turned at the sound of approaching footsteps. The weather may have cleared, but he feared another storm was about to be unleashed on the mainland.

"*Guten morgen,*" Von Kessel greeted his guest. "Once we have received acknowledgement of our signal, we will launch the raft, and you should reach shore within half an hour."

The passenger gave a brief nod in reply and looked out across the water, studying the coastline.

Von Kessel regarded the man's angular profile. He hadn't been told the man's name, and it didn't matter anyway. It was none of his concern and they'd spoken very little in the week he'd been on board. The face could have been chiseled from white granite, it was stone-hard and pale as death. There were traces of laugh lines around the corners of the man's eyes, faint tracks that must have come from a very distant past. Now the grey eyes were the color of cold, hard steel.

The contrast between the two men was notable. Von Kessel had a sailor's ruddy complexion. His eyes were a clear blue and his face was deeply creased. Born to the sea, he had a quick, intuitive grasp of command and understood the superstitions seafaring men believed. He shared his crew's forebodings regarding this passenger and had promised his men extra rations of beer when the job was done. He had every intention of joining in. He would be glad to be free of his passenger. Such men are bad luck. Von Kessel inhaled deeply. Within the hour he could report he had successfully completed the drop.

When the signal came from the shoreline in three flashes, Von Kessel gave the order to respond. Three flashes were dispatched in reply and the sailors stood at the ready as the passenger pulled his stocking cap low over his head, turned up the collar of his pea coat, and positioned himself and his belongings in the small raft. The crew offloaded him into the ocean waves, and he took on some water before stabilizing. He swore, took up the oars, got a fix on the shoreline, and began to row.

Their duty discharged, Von Kessel and his men returned to their stations, looking ahead to shore leave, and the U-boat slipped under the waves, bound once again for open waters.

The man rowed with steady, even strokes at a diagonal to the coastline, the oars slapping on the waves with military precision as the raft sliced through the water. He gained the shoreline in just over half an hour and jumped onto the beach, pulling the raft ashore behind him. Deflating it, he stashed it and the oars behind some bracken above the high tide mark. He pulled off the stocking cap and used it to wipe the salt water from his face. He tossed the cap in the vicinity of the raft, and then with suitcase and parcel in hand, followed a narrow, sandy trail to the rendezvous point. As he walked he could feel the sand working its way into his boots, and by the time he reached the dirt road where the Mercedes waited, he was cursing freely.

From his vantage point, Lars made note of the arrival of the man at thirty-seven minutes past ten. He added a brief physical description to his small notebook: Tall and lean. Blond hair. Approximately forty years of age. Sharp features.

The man reached the car and opened the back door on the passenger side and deposited his baggage on the seat. Leaning against the car, he removed first one shoe and then the other, dumping out the accumulated sand and slapping the sole of each shoe against the car to dislodge what remained, leaving a network of fine scrapes on the paint. Some of the grit had worked its way into his socks and was rasping against his toes. Annoyed, he slipped his shoes back on and climbed into the waiting automobile.

The woman started the engine, and they headed east along the main highway, towards Kolding. As she pulled away, Lars captured a partial on the license plate. He made a brief notation. Once the Mercedes was underway, he sprinted to his own car and merged onto the main road, where he began to tail the Mercedes from a safe distance.

Volmer's surveillance from the lighthouse had given him a wide perspective. From his perch high above the water, he swept the ocean surface with his binoculars until he spotted the U-boat surface. He watched a dark object move away from the submarine, and as it came closer on the water, he could make out the form of a man, laboring over the oars as he fought the wind.

Volmer puffed on his pipe and then made another sweep with his binoculars. He saw the U-boat submerge, moving out to sea. He continued watching the man's assault against the waves and the wind. When the man reached shore, Volmer climbed down the steps of the lighthouse to rendezvous with Anna at the Jorgensen home.

Anna and Marta had taken their coffee to the kitchen window, where they stood and watched for any sign of a stranger walking along the road to town. By eleven o'clock no one had shown, and Anna knew this meant the one they were waiting for must have left by automobile on the main road. Marta was still straining to see down the path and was concentrating so intensely she didn't hear Volmer arrive at the back door. His deep voice called out a greeting and Marta responded with a squeak and a jump.

"*Ach!* You startled me, Volmer." She smoothed her hair and brushed at her apron. "We are conducting espionage. I was watching the road." She pointed out the window.

"A spy must look behind as well as in front, Marta."

"Well, *ja*. There is that. There is a great deal to learn, I'm afraid. We will discuss this at the next Ladies' Aid meeting." Marta went off to find a pencil to alter the agenda to include a training session for the women. "We will study the rules of spying." She called over her shoulder, "You must help me with the list."

Anna smiled at Marta's retreating form. "What did you see, Volmer?" She went to get him a cup of coffee, as he pulled out a chair and sat down.

"The submarine, a raft, and a man rowing toward the cove. We called it!" He took a sip and leaned back in the captain's chair at the head of the table. "Lars was in the perfect position and the man rowed straight towards him. Lars signaled to me after the man had disappeared from my view. He'll follow him until he knows the man's destination. Lars will stop by after his shift is over. I'll speak with him while you and Marta," he looked in his cup, "prepare for school." He rose and put his coffee cup in the sink.

Anna crossed her eyes at him and made a dismissive gesture with her hands. "I'll be home after a bit." She giggled.

"What are you laughing about?"

"Everything. Nothing." She giggled again. "It's just that here we have the Germans and their U-boat and their very important spy and everything is top secret and everywhere people are watching them!"

Volmer kissed Anna on the cheek as he took his leave. "Say goodbye to Marta for me. I'll be home when you get there."

She nodded and took his chair to the window to sit and work on her own ideas for the Ladies Aid meeting.

Chapter Ten

Sankt Peder and Kolding, on the west coast of Jutland

"I hope you didn't scratch the car. It's new." She heard the accusing tone of her voice and caught herself too late. This was not the way she wanted this meeting to begin. She needed him to be in a good frame of mind. His moodiness could cripple her plans. The best tack was to say nothing more.

"Send the bill to Papa."

She bit her tongue and let it go. "Who are you this time?" She turned her face away from the road to look at him.

"Karl. Karl Mueller."

"Hmm. Karl, is it? I shall call you *Cruel* Karl." She ran her tongue over her lips and returned her attention to driving.

Karl watched the road ahead intently and turned from time to time to check behind them. The road was still wet in places, but traffic was light. The earth had gotten a good soaking last night and they were dodging puddles and potholes.

"Relax," she said. "You're as nervous as a cat."

"Not nervous, just cautious, Dagmar. You'd do well to be more cautious yourself. And slow down. No one would be speeding this morning, and this is hardly a car that anyone passing by wouldn't remember. It would be to the good if we didn't see another vehicle until we got to Kolding."

"Don't lecture me." Damn, this wasn't going well at all and there was no way to start over. "No one passed by while I waited. And no one followed me from town. I've been doing this for a while, you know." Too long, she thought. She was running out of time. Her looks wouldn't last forever. She stole a glimpse of her face in the rear view mirror and frowned. Was that a wrinkle in her forehead? Details. Details cluttered her mind. "I must return to work after I drop you off. I was gone a day longer than I'd planned, you know."

"It couldn't be helped." His voice mocked her. "Your service to the Fatherland is most appreciated. Besides, with papa wrapped around your little finger, one telephone call from the old man and you'll get promoted."

Her hands tightened on the steering wheel and she stepped harder on the accelerator. "I don't need papa to handle my affairs," she shot back.

"No, of course not. You handle your affairs quite well. You've always managed the bedroom ones quite nicely. You just want Papa to pay any of your bad debts and indulge you in whatever else your little heart desires."

The tears that had been building up now spilled over, and as she reached up to wipe them away, the car hit a pothole, swerved, and slipped off the dirt road, sending the left rear tire into a muddy ditch, where the wet earth sucked it in.

She slumped over the steering wheel and sobbed.

"*Verdammung!* What the hell are you doing? You stupid whore!"

"You could at least ask if I'm all right!" She sniffled and stuck out her lower lip, which trembled artfully.

He climbed out of the car and slogged around to the driver's side. "Get out! I don't give a damn if you're dead. I don't believe this. This is the best the Reich has to offer." He glared at her, murderous rage barely contained in his eyes. "Christ! We've got to get back on the road. I said get out!"

She opened the door and he yanked her out onto the muddy ground without ceremony. She scrambled to keep her footing, as he took her place at the wheel and gunned the engine. It was useless. The car was stuck fast in the mud and wasn't going anywhere. He slammed his hands on the steering wheel. "Where's the jack?"

"I don't know. Why would I know? I don't change tires." She gestured wildly. "It's somewhere." She'd stopped crying and was now sniffling and dabbing at her eyes with a handkerchief.

"You are useless." He launched himself out of the car, just as two automobiles passed by. One of them slowed, but he motioned for the driver to go on. Cursing under his breath, he found the jack in the trunk. He coaxed it under the frame and managed to raise the left tire enough to fill in the muddy slop with stones and branches. When they were finally level enough, he released the jack and eased the car into reverse. The car inched backwards, spewing rocks and gravel as it clawed its way back onto the road. When they were back on solid earth, he threw the jack back in the trunk and motioned for Dagmar to get in the passenger side.

"I'm driving," he said and those were the last words said for the rest of the journey. His mind was on the job ahead, hers was on getting him back. She needed him tonight and she needed him in her bed, if her plan had any chance of working. Her time doing two bit jobs for Papa was over. *Kaput*. She had done everything they had asked of her, sleeping with every diplomat and anybody else she was told to, just to compromise them. Just to provide the Reich with the goods to use when the time suited them. She had been well paid, it was true, but it was over. Karl would be the last one.

Karl was right, she reflected, and the knowledge he was right burned inside her. She was a whore, but she'd been a faithful whore – at least to the Party. She was good at her job, dammit, but now it was time to use her talents for her own gain.

Stealing a glance at Karl, she flipped her dark hair off her shoulders with her right hand and smoothed the Veronica Lake swoop over her left eye. She moistened her lips. She had a wide, sensuous mouth and high cheekbones that loved the camera. Her eyebrows traced a dramatic arch over cobalt blue eyes and dark, curly lashes.

She knew she was beautiful. Men watched her when she entered a room and she had learned to make the most of it. Hollywood would be no different. They would sit up and take notice when she walked in. Yes, once she was there she would write her own ticket. Gable, Cooper, Bogart - they would all stand in line to be her leading men. She'd be more famous than Lombard. Better than any of them.

She pursed her lips. This was her big chance. Karl was well connected beyond the Reich. She knew that. He moved in international circles, and it was time for her to use those connections. He could help her get what she wanted. She'd become the woman in demand. *Errand Girl for the Reich.* Hollywood would drool over what she could tell them. She had stories galore. Star quality. She had star quality. She had talent. All she needed was one break and Karl could give it to her. Tonight she would give Karl what he wanted, and tomorrow he would provide her with what she needed. It was a simple plan and her heart raced. But first he had to start speaking to her. This was a problem and she searched her mind discarding one ploy after another, until she settled on one that was sure to get his testosterone up and running. She chewed on her lip.

They reached her flat in Kolding and Karl pulled up to the curb, gathered his belongings, and left her sitting in the passenger seat. Now, however, Dagmar wasn't crying. She was planning. She let herself out of the car and into her apartment. Karl was already in the bath, washing away the residue of the submarine, the sand, the mud, and his anger.

Dagmar took a bottle of beer from the refrigerator and

reached around the doorjamb of the bathroom, dangling the bottle over the tub with a well-manicured hand. He hesitated only a moment before accepting the peace offering. She smiled. Phase one completed. This would work just fine. Men were not that difficult to manage. You just had to know what they wanted and then take your time giving it to them.

She went to her closet, chose her black lace peignoir and stripped down to her garter belt, hose, and pumps and was waiting when he came into the room. As he tied the belt of his robe around his waist, she put a hand on his and slipped the robe from his shoulders. After only a brief hesitation, he reached for her. She smiled to herself. Phase Two.

"Papa doesn't know what I want," she finished the earlier conversation, although this time her voice was husky.

"Ah, but I do." He bent down to kiss her.

"I have to go back to work," Dagmar said when he released her.

"Seems a shame."

"I'm already late. I don't suppose another hour or so would make that much difference?"

"It's up to you. Do you need to report to Papa or are you handling this one all by yourself?"

Dagmar looked at him, puzzled.

"Never mind. Just stick to what you do best."

"I'm off at five." It was an invitation.

"I leave in the morning." It was an answer.

She nodded. This was finally going her way.

He watched her dress and leave and heard the sound of her car engine roar to life and then fade in the distance. He stretched out on the bed. Shortly, he dozed.

Chapter Eleven

London, England

Drippy fog blanketed the city of London, seeping into cracks and crevices, chilling every living creature and covering all with a threadbare blanket of sodden grey. John's hat brim trapped a small reservoir of droplets which now and again dribbled off in a rivulet, as he moved his head, obscuring his vision with a miniature waterfall. If the Brits could handle their weather, he grumbled to no one in particular, they could handle anything Hitler threw at them.

Approaching the offices of the Admiralty on Whitehall, he was struck by the disturbing realization should Hitler's *Luftwaffe* indeed launch an air attack, everything vital to Britain was neatly arranged in one location in Whitehall. This was for convenience for the Brits, and that convenience would extend to a bomber's payload as well. It seemed a bit of bad planning.

Just off this one street alone were the Treasury, Ministry of Defence, Scotland Yard, Horse Guards, Cabinet Office, Prime Minister's offices and lodging, and the Admiralty. With Parliament Square at the south end and Trafalgar Square at the north, efficiency equated with vulnerability. The results of an aerial bombardment would be staggering. They were up against it for sure, he thought, and this awareness followed him into the Admiralty, where grey faded to blue inside the building as cigarette smoke hung like a heavy curtain and replaced the swirling mists of fog with an acrid dryness.

Ultimately everything revolved around the Admiralty, and more precisely, around the Lord High Admiral, himself. Winston Spencer Churchill possessed an intensity of spirit, an innate drive, and an indomitable sense of his own destiny. He was also hounded by bouts of depression, which he called his "black dog." The cur would descend upon him without warning, and at those times, he withdrew and suffered until the cloud lifted. When the dog was at bay, however, Churchill worked incessantly, slept little, and produced prodigiously. And in that, John felt himself sharing at least part of Churchill's life, as sleep would be in short supply for the time he would be in England.

If Churchill didn't use his bedroom overly much for sleeping, it got plenty of use as an office. Churchill routinely conducted meetings from his sleeping quarters, and this morning was no exception. Top secret documents and an assortment of newspapers were spread across the coverlet, and Nelson, the Admiral's cat, was spread out across them, a recumbent paperweight. A bottle of Pol Roger champagne, the Admiral's current beverage of choice for breakfast, was keeping company on the nightstand with a Cuban cigar, a Romeo y Julietta No. 2, judging from the bouquet that weighted the air. Churchill was hard at work and wasted little effort on formal greetings.

"Breckenridge."

"Sir."

That exchange completed, Churchill motioned for John to join him, disturbing a pyramidal pile of cigar ashes that had accumulated on his belly as he lay abed, scanning the morning's intelligence briefings. He ignored the ashes, or more accurately, didn't notice them, as he went off on a minor tirade. "That bloody Chamberlain is an idiot. They're all idiots!" he thundered, shaking his head and thus sending the remainder of the ashes cascading to the floor.

Churchill reached for the cigar, studied it, and readjusted his bellybando. He was quite proud of his little invention, the strip he had created to cushion his mouth against the non-business end of the cigar. He smoked as many as ten of these incendiary devices a day, and his valet collected the stubs for the gardener who used the tobacco inside to fill his pipes.

As for Chamberlain, John considered that if Churchill had been feeling magnanimous he might have remembered Chamberlain was responsible for Churchill's being where he was, having reappointed him to his old post in charge of the Admiralty. But Churchill was not in a magnanimous mood. He was frustrated and taking out his frustrations on his long-suffering staff.

The current lull in Berlin's activities had caused some to reassess the overall political situation. Some were calling the hostilities to date the "Phony War." Churchill knew better. This was just an interlude, although he was not having any success in convincing the rest of the government.

For months he'd been hammering away, attempting to convince his government of the necessity of waging a preemptive strike and securing the Norwegian coast against German attack. This would pay big dividends and reverse what was quickly becoming an untenable situation. Without hard intelligence, however, his plans had run up against stiff resistance. Still, if his middle initial hadn't stood for Spencer, it might very well have stood for stubborn, and he was nothing if not persistent He was determined to push onward, convinced he would be proven right. His track record showed that sometimes he was and sometimes he wasn't. It was the latter that his adversaries remembered at their convenience.

"Operation Wilfred," Churchill inserted the cigar between his teeth and clamped down, fixing John with that defiant bulldog stare. It was a challenge more than a statement. "We will proceed with the planning. The information we need will come, and we will be ready to move when it does. Fortune favoring the brave and all that." He removed the cigar from his mouth and waved it in the air.

John merely lifted an eyebrow. Churchill had reached a decision and neither heaven nor hell had the power to change his mind or his course. They also serve, he reasoned, who eat breakfast with the Lord High Admiral of the British Empire.

"Operation Wilfred," Churchill repeated. He'd decided on the name for the adventure after a naïve character in the popular comic strip "Pip, Squeak, and Wilfred." The plan seemed innocuous enough, but it had met with nothing but resistance and Churchill's patience was wearing thin. He was beginning to think his opponents were the true pip squeaks.

"I proposed mining the Norwegian waters last November. Last November!" Churchill bellowed. "That would have forced the ore transports to travel through the open waters of the North Sea where our boys could have picked them off." Churchill glared at John. "And do you know why that ass Chamberlain and Halifax, also an ass, I might add, refused? Of course you do. They were afraid of the reaction of your government!" He pointed a chubby finger in John's direction.

John knew better than to interject his own opinions into this monologue. Privately he thought Churchill had been correct, but Roosevelt had not been in a position to move then. He was a consummate politician and he played his constituency well. He'd promised the electorate that American boys would not fight in a foreign war and right now that position was the one he was holding to.

Churchill read John's thoughts, it seemed. "'The promise given was a necessity of the past. The word broken is a necessity of the present.' That's from *The Prince*, and I can guarantee you that Hitler is using his copy like a driver's manual. Roosevelt knows this. He'll come around as soon as he finds the winds have shifted, mark my words." Churchill paused for breath. "Let's just hope it suits him soon." Churchill was nearly beside himself, a race horse champing at the bit waiting for the gate to open and the starting pistol to fire.

He pointed to a stack of papers by the foot of the bed. The Winter War between the Soviet Union and Finland was balanced on the comforter and he frowned at the increasing bulk of the thing. "This," he pointed at the pile, "should have been enough to convince them. But no. Wait and see. Wait and see. If they'd open their goddamned eyes they'd see plenty." He jammed the cigar back in his mouth and chomped on it once again.

John thought the plan was sound, but it gambled that France would approve and needing this approval galled Churchill. This was a huge gamble, not a small wager. France feared retribution from Germany if the plan failed. Fear all around, it seemed. Fear fed on itself and grew stronger.

When FDR had said the only thing we had to fear was fear itself, he had nailed it. Now fear was rampant and appeasement was the prevailing strategy. Hitler was counting on it. And he was counting on the shipments of iron ore from Sweden to fuel his war machine. Ninety per cent of these shipments reached Germany via the ice-free Norwegian port of Narvik. This port had grown substantially since its founding close to the end of the last century and it was now the main Atlantic port for the Kiruna and Gallivare iron mines.

During the summer months the ore could be shipped to Germany from the Swedish port of Lulea on the Gulf of Bothnia, but in winter when the Gulf of Bothnia froze, most of the ore had to be brought from Narvik, which was linked by rail to Sweden.

Churchill realized that control of Narvik would mean most German imports of iron ore during the winter would stop. This would be highly advantageous to the Allies and might also help shorten the war. There was another benefit as well. If England could mine Norway's territorial waters and possibly occupy the town, the Allies might be able to secure the iron ore supplies for themselves, but Churchill's own government was still playing by the rules and felt this plan would mean a violation of Norway's neutrality and sovereignty.

"They won't listen until they're running for cover." Churchill was recalling his past errors in judgment that were largely to blame for the lack of confidence in his warning now. "They don't want to listen now, but I'll be damned if I let the Germans come ashore on my watch." A determined look spread across his face. "We will proceed with the operation regardless of the obstacles."

After a moment of silence, Churchill leveled his gaze at John. "Your wife will get the intelligence we need. She has to – it all comes down to her. And now, it is time for you to collect your men and begin their briefings. You will be prepared to leave on twenty-four hours notice, and I suspect that will be coming sooner rather than later. We must move ahead while we still have the window open. With our own people in place in Denmark before Hitler marches through, we will have the inside track. After, it will be much more difficult to gather intelligence." He reached for his champagne glass and drained its contents and then took a new cigar, clipped the end and lit up. He sat, moving the cigar about his mouth. When he spoke his voice was strong. "It's time we took Herr Hitler to school. Prepare your men, prepare yourself, and be ready to move your men into Denmark when the call comes."

"Sir." It was the only reply John needed to make. With that, the meeting came to a close, Churchill returned to his briefings, and John let himself out.

Twenty minutes later he was assessing the offerings of the motor pool and explaining to the harried clerk in charge that he didn't want the ancient vehicle that had been reserved for him. If time was of the essence, then so was speed. “I’ll take that one,” he said pointing to a Harley-Davidson WLC.”

“But sir,” the clerk protested. “This,” he said, pointing to an aged car of dubious parentage, is the vehicle reserved for your use. I have a form.”

“It’s Colonel,” John said, “and I’m taking this one. Change the bloody form.” And stashing his files in the saddle bags, he adjusted his goggles and roared out of Whitehall. His first stop was Osterley Park, training facility for the British Home Guard.

Chapter Twelve

Sankt Peder

The ladies of the Evangelical Lutheran Church of the Redeemer of Sankt Peder held their handwork meeting on the second Tuesday of the month. The women took turns hosting the gathering, with this month's meeting being held at Ilsa Jensen's. Each newborn to the community received a blanket, sweater, hat, mittens, and booties, and three new arrivals were expected this spring, so fingers flew as baby layettes grew.

The women were seated according to their needlework preference, with crochet workers clustered around the kitchen table and knitters at the coffee table in the parlor. Workbaskets and tote bags sat by each woman's feet, like faithful pups of varying breeds. Gussie, the green-eyed calico cat, had been banished from her accustomed spot behind the wood stove and evicted from the house, as she couldn't resist the allure of soft balls of baby yarn. She sat on the back doorstep, tail twitching in annoyance, contemplating revenge.

Conversations that usually centered around husbands, children, recipes, and general gossip, had taken a more serious turn today. Anna contributed her news item of the submarine sighting and its connection with the spreading

German threat. This created a flurry of response. Others had heard rumors from friends of friends. It was all so frustrating, not being able to do anything about it. But then Anna suggested that perhaps they could do something.

"What do we do best?" she asked, setting down her knitting.

"Talk!" laughed Ilse, and the rest of the women nodded.

"We listen too," said Inge. "Oh *ja*, we talk some sure, sometimes too much, but we also listen. We listen to our husbands and to our children and to the pastor, and even to strangers." She was gaining confidence as she spoke. "Sometimes people do not seem to even notice we are around. We are part of the furniture."

"That has always made me angry, said Gunda Christiansen, with pursed lips. "I do not like it."

Anna picked up her knitting. "So," she paused, "when the Germans come, why should they be any different from our own families? They will not see us at all. If we watch with our eyes and listen with our ears and talk only among ourselves…." She left the sentence unfinished and looked around at the other women.

"So, you are saying what?" Gunda eyed Anna severely.

"I'm trying to put my thought together, if you will please not rush me." Anna returned Gunda's harsh look with one of her own. "This is what I think. We can make our invisibility work for us. We will keep notes and report what we learn to those who need that information, whoever that will turn out to be."

"The Germans have had to turn in their radios. How do they know what is really going on? They don't." Inge answered her own question. "The Germans, when they come, will do the same here. Oh yes," she said over protests, "they are coming. And then how will we be able to fight them? Knowledge," she raised a finger to the heavens, to indicate a central point, "is power. If we are to fight them and defeat them, we must know what is going on and become our own radios."

Gunda was not following any of this and it was making her more and more angry. "How does a woman become a radio? That is foolishness. Foolish talk!" Gunda's thoughts moved slowly. She took everything literally, at face value, and she lacked imagination.

Anna was watching Gunda carefully. She knew Gunda's inability to think in abstract terms might become a liability and she might say the wrong thing at the wrong time to the wrong person. She frowned. They would need to be careful with her, so as not to alarm her and raise her suspicions.

Ilsa's eyes, however, were shining. "We become an army. An underground army of women. I like it!"

"We need a name." Marta was on her feet.

"Something secret," said Barbara.

"Something easy to remember. Not too complicated. We don't want to seem suspicious," Anna, always the practical one, contributed.

"Something that sounds like one thing but is really something else," said Inge.

"Gefion." Marta clapped her hands together. "In Copenhagen they have a statue of her, ploughing the fields." She looked expectantly around the room at her friends.

Anna smiled. "Marta, she is the protector of virgins! It has been quite some time since you fit that category."

"She also brings good luck and prosperity, Anna," Marta replied. "And if there were ever a time we needed luck and prosperity, it is now." Marta's cheeks were red. "And she had sons, just like you Anna! Except hers were oxen. Come to think of it, Lars has always struck me as rather big." Her voice trailed off and she looked at Anna through her eyelashes. Both women burst out laughing.

"I'm sorry to be dense here, but what does Gefion have to do with us?" Ilsa asked.

"Long before we were Christians," Marta explained, "we were pagans. We Danes were a warlike people, surrounded by other warlike tribes. Come to think of it, not that much seems to have changed. Still," Marta reflected, "as Christians we are supposed to love our neighbors. It is too bad our neighbors to the south do not share that belief."

"Gefion?" prompted Ilsa.

"*Ja*. Well, Gefion was married to King Skjold, who was a son of Odin. She lived in Leire, which of course is in Denmark, where she had a sanctuary. She created the island of Zealand by plowing the soil out of central Sweden with the help of her four sons, the Swedish oxen. As I mentioned before, one of them might have been named Lars, I am not sure." She peeked at Anna, who was shaking her head. "Anyhow," she resumed, "When Gefion created the islands, the vast holes in the ground she left behind became the lakes of Sweden."

Anna continued, "So Gefion is the creator of Zealand. A woman created part of Denmark and women will reclaim our land for the Danes." She finished on a triumphant note. "When we have information to share, we will call a meeting of the Daughters of Gefion. We will be the daughters she did not have."

"This is good." Ilsa said. "We must wear the red and white of the *Dannenbrog*, when we meet."

"We must wear these colors every day," said Inge and the other women agreed.

"Do we tell our husbands?" asked Barbara, who was a new bride.

"Of course. They are not Germans," Anna said, "but you make me think of something. The new pastor is not known to us. We should be careful around him."

"We will watch him," said Marta. "For now at least, the flock will guard the shepherd."

"I think that is a wise idea, Marta," said Anna and the rest of the women nodded in agreement.

Chapter Thirteen

Kolding

When Karl awakened the next morning, a hot cup of coffee and the morning paper were waiting for him on the nightstand. She must have arisen early this morning, Karl thought, not her usual pattern. He frowned as he considered what this might mean, if anything. They'd worked the room over pretty well. If this were a film, the pictures on the wall would be dripping lingerie or stray socks. And crooked. In films the pictures were always crooked, as if the lovers had had sex on the walls and jumped into the frames. As it was, discarded clothes carpeted the rugs and the bed sheets lay in a tangle on the floor.

Sometime during the night or maybe early this morning, he must have reached down and covered himself with the spread. He didn't remember Dagmar getting up. She must have crept out of the room like a cat. It couldn't be too late, but he couldn't see the time on the clock which was behind the coffee cup, so he sat up and moved to the edge of the bed, where he dangled his legs and rubbed his face. It was just a little past nine. He stood and stretched and went into the bathroom to wash up.

Music from the radio in the kitchen filtered down the hall and into the bedroom, along with the sounds of pots and pans clattering and the aroma of sausages frying. Dagmar was in a domestic mood. He paused mid-stroke with his double-edged razor and contemplated the feasibility of making his escape before she set in again on The Hollywood Plan. It didn't look promising. In fact, it would be a minor miracle. She had some nutty ideas, but this was a corker. Oh, she had the body for it all right, all curves and heat, but she had no sense at all, common or otherwise. He hoped she wasn't going to become a problem. He didn't need complications. Frowning, he rinsed the lather from his face and slapped on some aftershave. He'd nicked the skin by the cleft in his chin and the alcohol burned.

As it turned out, a complication was indeed brewing in the kitchen, along with the morning coffee, and the early morning sun streaming through the window was not enough to raise Dagmar's spirits or improve her sour disposition even a little. Her carefully woven web of seduction had not snared her prey last night, and Karl, that insect, had dismissed her scheme as harebrained and loony. He had had the nerve to laugh at her. Laugh! She turned and cast a dark look in the direction of the bedroom.

Still, she reflected, the sex had been good. He was a passionate lover, if not an affectionate one. If only when he looked at her - just once if there were something more than desire in his eyes, but they were stone, just like the wall he had built around himself, and he never let down his guard, never let her in. She kicked the table leg. Damn him anyway, she thought, bending over to rub her foot.

Not about to abandon the plan, she was dressed, or undressed to be more precise, to the nines this morning. Her vermilion silk robe clung to her body and the deep V-throat revealed more than it concealed. The fabric skimmed her ankles and the sash tied around her waist allowed her to display shapely legs to maximum advantage. She had spent a queen's ransom for the gown in Rome and it was the top of the line. Haute couture was an investment and she had hopes it would pay off this morning. He hadn't seen it last night. But then last night he'd only wanted sex. He hadn't even looked at her, come to think of it. She could have been anyone. Somehow the thought irritated her.

Her perfume was French, Chanel Number 2. Her makeup was perfect, her hair loose around her shoulders. She was ready now, because once Karl left this morning, God only knew when he would show up on her doorstep again. She was running out of time.

This thought pulled her eyes to the hook by the front door, where Karl had hung his jacket last night. She paused over the eggs she was scrambling. The sound of running water in the bathroom told her Karl was still occupied there. She set the spatula down on the counter and, turning to the jacket, quickly patted down the pockets until she found a bulge which proved to be an envelope. She removed it from the pocket and opened it to find his travel papers and passport inside. He wouldn't be going too far from her after all. He'd only be retracing the route they had traveled together yesterday. Interesting. She peered closely at the passport photograph and nearly laughed out loud. Karl, a Lutheran minister? How farfetched was that?

Returning the documents to the envelope, she carefully replaced them where she'd found them. Her insurance policy, perhaps, if this morning's efforts proved in vain. She returned to the eggs and sausages, and when Karl came up behind her and placed his hands on her shoulders, she turned at his touch and greeted him with a warm smile.

She studied his expression. He seemed more distant this morning. His sharply chiseled nose gave him a severe profile even at rest, and the faint scar that traveled a jagged path from the corner of his left eye down to his chin added to that hardness. His ears were set close to his head. Even his clipped haircut gave the impression of a man drawn inward. There were facets to him she knew he would never reveal. He was a mystery, but that added to his allure. She liked the feeling of walking a dangerous path when she was with him.

He poured himself a fresh cup of coffee and sat down at the table. Dagmar brought his plate of food, her fingertips brushing across the back of his neck. She bit her lip, waiting for the right moment. She made her move when he had filled his mouth with a bite of sausage.

"Last night," her voice was seductive. "You do remember last night?"

He looked across the table at her and gave her a lascivious wink, which she interpreted as a go-ahead. She needed to do this right, not too fast, keep him at ease, keep him on her side.

"I wish we could get together more often," her voice had taken on a wistful tone. "We're good together. I don't suppose you can stay another day?"

"It only takes once to catch up." He leveled his gaze at her. "We're caught up."

"You are a bastard."

"So I'm told." He continued to eat.

She played her last card. "I want you to help me. You owe me."

"I didn't realize you were charging now. Does Papa know you've branched out? Just tell me how much and I'll leave it on the bed before I go."

"You're not going to do this. Don't think you can just brush me off like that. You're going to listen to me and you're going to help me."

"Do I detect a threat?" He raised an eyebrow at her. "You're walking on thin ice, my sweet. Don't go out too far or you're likely to fall through. That wouldn't be good. For you," he added.

Dagmar gave a nervous laugh, high-pitched and thin. She pressed her lips together, desperate to control her emotions before they took over and destroyed her plan. He needed to be worked carefully. She tried a new tack. "What do you know of Leni Riefenstahl?" she asked.

Karl didn't answer.

"Leni Riefenstahl." Her tone was even. "She's the *Führer's* cinematographer. She's doing important work."

"Good for her." Karl continued to sip his coffee and finish his sausages, unsure where this new topic was heading, although he suspected it would somehow come back around to Dagmar the Film Goddess.

"She's had a fascinating life. Really." She looked at Karl to see if she might have piqued his interest. She began as a painter…"

"You don't say," Karl interrupted. "Isn't that a wonderful coincidence? Your friend and *Der Führer*. Both *artistes*. It must have been written in the stars. A match from Valhalla."

Dagmar overlooked this snipe. "She actually had plans to become a dancer. An interpretive dancer," she added, as if that bit of information made all the difference in the world.

Karl set his coffee cup down and wiped his mouth with a napkin. "So what did she interpret while she was dancing?"

"You know, you can really be so obtuse when you want to be. Interpretive dancing is liberating. It is an art form." Dagmar continued, "She injured her knee and that was the end of her career as a dancer, so she became an actress."

"So what are you saying? The theater is the last refuge for the terminally clumsy?" Karl laughed in spite of himself, envisioning a traveling troupe in wheelchairs and on crutches, interpreting to pay their expenses. "Why do you want to join such a group of misfits? Last I checked your limbs were functioning superbly."

Dagmar rejoiced. She had him with her again. She'd captured him in her net and now all she had to do was gently bring him in. "Leni wasn't a misfit. She was inspired. She went to hear *Der Führer* speak in 1932 and was so in awe of him that she offered her services as a film maker to him right then and there."

"That's not all she offered, as I understand it," Karl said.

"So you do know her. You were just stringing me along."

Dagmar favored him with a smile. "So, you see how just a little talent can be bankrolled into a major career if you know the right people?" That was well done, she thought. I've clinched the case. I've captured him.

Karl didn't reply but was watching her carefully.

"I need to go to Hollywood if I'm to have a career in film. I am a romantic lead. Here the Reich is producing film for the Reich. That doesn't do me any good. I need to showcase myself." She got up from her chair and walked to Karl, where she wrapped her arms around his neck and began to work on his left ear. He reached up and took her two hands, lifted them over his head, and spun her around to face him.

"This was finished last night. Drop it." There was a warning in his cold, grey eyes. He dropped her hands and reached for a knife to butter a piece of toast. "When we began this there would be no strings attached, remember? That means no demands. Don't change the rules in the middle of the game."

He smiled at her without warmth. "Besides, my dear. I fear your talents are decidedly horizontal." He stuffed the final piece of toast into his mouth, gave his lips a final dab with his napkin, tossed it onto his plate, and pushed his chair away from the table. Bending over her, he kissed the top of her head. He collected his jacket and bags, and stood, one hand resting on the doorknob. "I'll call you next time I'm in town. We'll have a good time. Don't raise your rates, however. That could be bad for business."

Dagmar didn't answer. She clenched her fists. Rage boiled up inside her, her cheeks burned with shame, and tears threatened to spill over. She picked up his coffee cup and hurled it against the closing door, which reopened briefly as Karl inserted his head back into the room.

"Temper. Temper." He laughed and closed the door again. She listened to his footsteps fading as he left the building.

She walked to the window and pulled aside the curtain and watched as he walked down the street and disappeared around the corner. She sighed and looked down at the broken cup and stooped to pick up the shards. A sharp edge cut her finger, and she sucked the blood off it, while considering what to do next. As she dressed for work, her thoughts were moving ahead. Something would work out. It had to. She'd find a way to make him help her.

On her way out, she grabbed her coat from the door hook by the front entrance. This reminded her of the envelope in Karl's pocket and she cocked her head. Karl didn't know it yet, but they had a date and this time they would play by her rules. This time, she would win and he would pay whatever price she demanded.

Chapter Fourteen

Kolding

Karl was a tall man and he walked with a tall man's stride, purposeful and measured, to the bus station downtown. There were few other people on the street, most having already arrived at their workplaces. Children were at school and old women with shopping lists for the meat market or the bakery were still sitting in their kitchens, finishing their coffee. A brisk wind this morning had the few pedestrians turning up their collars against the chill, but the chill didn't bother Karl. It was the dampness, the insidious dampness. That was what got to him.

"One way to Esbjerg," he informed the ticket agent at the station and then proceeded to the lavatory where he removed his knit pullover and extracted a white shirt with cleric's collar from his suitcase. He held it at arm's length. A yard or so of fabric, some stitching and buttons. Work clothes for the job. Donning this garment was somehow supposed to give him a pipeline to the Almighty? He shook his head in disgust. It was a means to manipulate the dumb sheep who couldn't think for themselves. They deserved their sorry lot in life and in the hereafter as well, if there was one. The Good Shepherd. Shit. Lambs to the slaughter was more like it. "Better to reign in hell than serve in heaven," he mumbled. He stuffed the sweater into his suitcase and joined the crowd queuing up for boarding.

The Lutheran minister now awaiting the boarding call was a visibly older man from the civilian who had entered the men's room. Karl had assumed a slightly stooped posture and he moved with a stiffness that indicated arthritic hips and knees.

Once aboard, the driver closed the doors and the bus moved away from the station, proceeding at a steady clip toward the coast, passing through beech forests and farmland, neat sections of tilled earth ready for planting. It was a distance of seventy-five miles to the west coast, and as they neared the Esbjerg station, passengers began collecting their parcels and took on an expectant air. The momentary silence as the driver shut off the engine was immediately filled with the sound of rustling clothes and shuffling feet as the passengers filed off the bus and scattered to their various destinations.

The last to exit, Pastor Karl Mueller climbed down the stairs and set his bags on the curb, wondering where his transportation to the parsonage might be. Esbjerg was the nearest big town to the village of Sankt Peder, which was close enough to walk to, had he not been carrying his luggage and the box. He had been assured he would be met, but there were no vehicles in sight. No car, no truck, not even a farm wagon. Irritated, he resisted the impulse to check his watch, and it was a good ten minutes later when he saw, about a block away, a young girl loping towards him. Since there was nothing to do but wait, he waited for her to close the distance and catch her breath.

Her arrival coincided with the appearance of an ancient livestock truck, and both driver and child hailed him as he stood in the crosshairs. The girl's voice reached him first. "Pastor!" She was sucking in huge gulps of air between words. "This is Ernst!" she gasped as she bent over, hands on her knees. She looked to be about fifteen, slim, gangly, all arms and legs. Blonde pigtails swung about her face as she bobbed her head. Her face was flushed red with exertion.

Ernst, the driver of the truck, leaned out the window and confirmed the introduction with a broad smile. He brought the vehicle to a shuddering halt and jumped down from the driver's side, hand outstretched.

"Welcome, Pastor. I am Ernst, and this," he indicated the gasping girl, "is my little niece, Margrethe."

Margrethe scrunched up her nose at Ernst. "I am not little. Call me Greta, Pastor." Her breath was coming more regularly now, and she drew herself up to her full height. She actually was quite a tall girl.

Ernst directed his attention to Karl. "I sent Greta on ahead to meet you. I had assumed she would have gotten here by now." He gave her a disapproving look and continued his narrative. "I had to repair the tire that had gone flat. We were out of patching material, so by the time I stopped at *Herre* Rasmussen's to get some, I knew I would be running late. Anyhow," he was drawing to a close, "we're all here and that's all that matters, right?"

Without waiting for an answer he gathered up the suitcase and heaved it into the back of the truck. He was preparing to do the same with the box, when Karl shot out a hand and intercepted him. "I'll keep this," he said.

Ernst shrugged and looked dubiously at the truck cab. "It's going to be a tight squeeze."

Karl had no doubt. With three of them in the cab, there was hardly enough space for breathing, let alone conversation. That was all to the good. He gave Ernst the once-over. Ernst looked to be in his early thirties and was a large man, heavyset and powerful. He was blond, no surprise there, and irritatingly cheerful.

"They're expecting us at the house. Then I'll take you to the parsonage and you can get settled," Ernst said. An easygoing man, he didn't like conflict. If the pastor wanted to carry the box, he could carry the box.

"Who are *they?"* Karl asked.

"The family," Ernst replied. Fifteen minutes later, as the windows were beginning to fog up, they arrived at a farmhouse and Ernst pulled into the drive and parked the truck by the side door. "Here we are!" He indicated the house with an expansive gesture. "We'll just leave your bag in the back." He opened the door for Greta and Karl, hoisted a sack of feed on his shoulder, and headed towards the barn.

"He'll be back, pastor," Greta said, as if Karl might have thought that was the last they would see of Ernst. "He promised mama he'd get the chicken feed when he went to town. They eat scraps too, sometimes, but to get good eggs, they need more nutrients in their diet than what they can scratch up. They call the feed chicken scratch. That's a clever name, don't you think?"

Greta was squinting up at Karl, assessing his knowledge of animal husbandry and deciding what else he might need to know, when a woman appeared on the front porch and called to them

"Greta! Bring Pastor!"

"Coming, mama!"

Greta raised the latch on the gate of the picket fence that enclosed the front yard, and they proceeded up a cobblestone walkway bordered with freshly spaded flower beds, where chickens scratched and pecked. They stepped over the family watch dog, sound asleep on the top step, and Greta stopped to pet a calico cat that had parked itself next to the dog and was involved in a cleaning ritual. Pausing with a paw raised, it accepted the pat and then resumed washing its face. "That's Gussie. She lives down the street. The dog is Wulfie," Greta said. "He lives here." The family's security system seemed to consist of tripping up potential intruders and sending them sprawling.

The woman waiting on the front porch was an older version of the girl. Of course she was blonde and tall. She had a high forehead and finely shaped nose, clear, wide set eyes the color of emeralds, and her hair was neatly plaited and coiled around her head. He imagined when she let it down it would cascade around her shoulders like spun gold.

"Pastor Mueller, we are so pleased you have arrived. I am *Frue* Jensen, Inge Jensen," she added with a radiant smile. "Please, come in." She beckoned with her hand. "I have made a light meal. You must be hungry. Would you prefer tea or coffee?"

"Beware of her light meals," warned Ernst, who had returned from the barn. "She has been cooking all morning."

Karl nodded. "Coffee would be fine, thank you," and he followed Ernst into the dining room, where four places had been laid.

"Come Greta, help me bring the food," Inge called over her shoulder to her daughter.

"Coming, mama." Greta pulled herself away from what she knew would be an interesting conversation between Pastor Mueller and Ernst. Men always had the more interesting conversations. All women ever talked about were recipes and problems with children and husbands. Men, on the other hand, talked about places she wanted to visit, important topics like politics and what was happening in the world outside. Of course they sometimes talked about machinery, which she found dull, and sports which interested her some. She sighed. Women always had to bring food to the men and clean for the men and they never got to talk with the men. She stamped her foot, expelled a heart wrenching sigh and reluctantly disappeared into the kitchen.

"Why wasn't I born a man, mama?"

Inge looked up from the kitchen table where she was assembling the open-faced sandwiches, and handed her daughter the knife to slice the cake. "You were born the most beautiful daughter because that is what I asked for." Inge's answer made Greta's birth seem as if God had simply filled an order she had placed.

"Oh, mama!"

"You have still a lot to learn, my dearest one. Men only think they run the world. Oh, they talk and plan, but when matters come to a decision, it is the women who advise and the women who see that their men do the right thing. It really is quite a responsibility. And it helps," she added, "when you love the man more than life itself."

"Does papa always listen to you?" Greta was working this idea over in her mind. "I mean does he always do what you want?"

"More than that, honey, he does what's right." Inge deposited a plate of sandwiches in Greta's outstretched hands.

"Well, I still don't see how it works. And I would still rather be a man." Greta's lower lip was beginning to quiver.

"You will understand in good time. Patience." Inge set down the coffee pot and put her hands on her daughter's shoulders. "Patience is a virtue. Possess it if you can. Found seldom in a woman, but never in a man." She turned her daughter towards the door and gave her a light push. "Now go!" She laughed at the retreating form.

Greta carried the burden of her gender, along with the plate of sandwiches, into the dining room, where Ernst and Pastor Mueller were, as she had predicted, deep in a political conversation. She circumvented the table and approached them from the rear, hoping to pick up their discussion.

"…threat grows stronger daily." Ernst was speaking, his color reddening, and the vein that stood out along his right temple when he was agitated was not only visible, Greta noted with interest, it was pulsating. It really looked rather alarming.

"Denmark has said it will remain neutral, so it has nothing to fear. Germany will respect that neutrality and no harm will come to Denmark." Karl responded in an even tone.

"Of course, how foolish of me. The Germans, they are our friends. They have all the *lebensraum* they want. What happens when they decide they want more? What makes you think they will stop? Why would they stop?"

"We must have faith." Karl was making himself sick with these platitudes. Ernst was not as stupid as he appeared.

"Faith and warfare would seem to have little in common, but of course, as a pastor, that's what you must say. But I say Hitler wants control of the Skagerrak. If he doesn't, he's a fool. The Skagerrak is important strategically, a waterway that connects the North Sea with the Baltic and gives access to Oslo Fjord. Of course he wants it, and the only way he is going to get it is to march right over us on his way there. And you tell me to have faith? I have faith. Mark my words. Faith indeed."

At that moment, Inge brought the rest of the food, gave Greta a nudge to put her plate on the table, called the men to sit, and asked the pastor to say the blessing.

"Of course, *Frue* Jensen. Let us pray." Karl bowed his head and offered thanks and they set to their meal. Conversation shifted to safer topics and when Ernst delivered Karl to the parsonage later that afternoon, the men shook hands. But it was at best a token gesture. A line had been drawn in the sand and each had taken the other's measure.

Ernst stopped back at the house after dropping off the pastor, and by this time Lars was home and was relaxing with a beer and the newspaper. Ernst helped himself to a beer as well and pulled up a chair.

"What did you learn about the passenger from the submarine?" Ernst asked. "I haven't talked to Volmer yet and it's been eating me up, wanting to know more."

"Nothing specifically. Yet," Lars added. "I did run the plate on the Mercedes. I only got a partial but it appears to be registered to a woman named Dagmar Strasser. I'm still working on that end of it. I followed the car to an apartment house in downtown Kolding, where they both got out.

"What did the man look like?" Ernst leaned in and faced

his brother directly.

Lars set the paper down on his lap and considered the question. "Tall and well-muscled. Not heavy, though. It was lean muscle. Maybe forty. Forty-five at the most. Closely trimmed blond hair. This question must be going somewhere, *Ja*?"

"I don't really know where it is going, but it's a fairly accurate description of the new minister, except for the age and the height. He looks to be closer to mid-fifties and is a bit stooped in his posture. I just have a feeling that something isn't right." Ernst studied the etched glass on his stein, a hart running through a forest of white trees. "I've just taken the new minister to the parsonage. He has a scar running from his eye to his chin. It's an old scar, but it's out of place, unusual in a minister."

"What are you saying? That a minister can't have an accident or cut himself?"

"No, of course not. But I've seen these scars before. It's a fencing scar."

Lars raised an eyebrow. "Our minister has belonged to a fencing club?"

"Of course that's just one possibility, but that would give him a rather elite background, wouldn't you think? Hardly part of ministerial studies."

"German name, German school, German scar. German spy?" Lars crossed his legs. "It would be most interesting if the man I am seeking is right here in town. It might be interesting to do some background checking on our new pastor in addition to the woman's. I'll see what I can find out."

Ernst nodded. "I might be wrong."

"These are dangerous times, brother." Lars shook his head. "You could be right."

Chapter Fifteen

London

Easy as one, two, three. Three was the magic number, Katrin always said, and John was beginning to believe it as the number kept running through his head. He had three days to assemble a team and report back to Whitehall. The pressure was beginning to build, even as the hourglass sand was running down. Today, Osterley Park. Tomorrow, Bletchley Hall, and the final day back to Whitehall to prepare for the airlift out. There was no cushion. The drop would happen and he must be ready with his team in place.

While the masses of population concentrated in the cities, the old estates offered two essential qualities the urban areas could not provide - space and privacy. Although many of these manors had been swallowed up as the cities grew, they remained oases surrounded by mature landscaping which sequestered them from public view. As he approached Osterley, John considered that wealth could be measured by proximity to the streets. The poor lived in tenements that fronted directly on the streets, the middle class had their lawns and sidewalks that gave some distance, and the wealthy had their curving drives that wound from the gated entrances to the dwellings that were hidden far from the commoners outside.

Osterley Park belonged to the last category. Originally in the country and now, due to the ever-expanding city population, in the western suburbs of London, it had been more a country retreat than a principal estate, built for a banker, Sir Thomas Gresham in the sixteenth century. When Queen Elizabeth I visited it and suggested that a hedge would be suitable in one part of the grounds, the gardeners were immediately set to work and the hedge was in place when she awoke the next morning.

The house itself was square, constructed of red brick with white stone details and it sported a turret in each corner of the building. The rooms inside were spacious, with Etruscan influences and rounded archways and semi-circular alcoves softening the exterior's geometric bluntness. These days the first members of the Local Defence Volunteers trained on the grounds. These volunteers, now known as the British Home Guard, were men who had served during the Great War and who were now considered too old to serve in the current conflict. Men too young to serve, but who still wanted to do their part to protect their homeland, drilled alongside their elders.

The creation of the Home Guard had come about as a direct result of Churchill's letter to the Chief of Staff. "What would happen if 20,000 enemy troops were to land on the east coast of England?" he asked. The result was the creation of the Local Defence Volunteers, charged with protecting the port of Dover, a port critical to Britain's survival. The Volunteers joined up in droves and began to train on the very artillery that might be required to save the whole of England. From the brown address book he carried, John had selected two names as his targets for today - two men he hoped to add to his own arsenal.

The first man he'd come to interview was Stanley Livingston and John wondered what the poor fellow had endured at school. It had no doubt toughened him, for he had distinguished himself during the Great War as a marksman of exceptional skill as well as a linguist with seven languages to his credit. John figured that if Livingston couldn't talk his way out of a fight, he had an alternative solution.

Livingston's build also enhanced his desirability, for he was average. Average height, average weight, nondescript appearance, eminently forgettable and therefore highly valuable. He could pass for an Italian with his dark hair or a German with his aquiline nose. His eyes were brown, his complexion was medium. He also had a mean right hook, and John touched his jaw at the recollection. They had had at it early on and that encounter had proved to be the beginning of a durable friendship. John hoped he would be willing for one more go round.

The second man was Chester Beedle. Unlike Stanley, Chet was remarkable in appearance. He was quite short, stocky with a tendency to portliness, bald, and sported a handlebar mustache that swooped gracefully from his upper lip to touch the tips of his mutton chop whiskers. He looked like a butcher, and indeed had been a meat cutter his entire working life. John had already found the slot he wanted him to fill in the heart of Berlin, a butcher shop that provided choice cuts for the elite dinner functions of the National Socialist Party.

Chet's language skills were limited but were exactly what John needed. Chet spoke Cockney English and working class German, the legacy of a grandmother who had emigrated to England in the 1860s in search of a suitable husband, having determined that she'd had her fill of thickheaded men. Why she had ever thought England would offer a thinner-skulled variety of the male gender was beyond both Chet and John's understanding, but she must have been satisfied, for she had met Walter Beedle and had set her cap for him. They had celebrated their golden wedding anniversary with a trip to London and were honored, along with several other couples, for their matrimonial accomplishment at a public audience at

Buckingham Palace.

Both men had answered his wire and were waiting for him when he arrived. They were quite a pair and John nodded to himself. They were precisely what he wanted. Yes, they would do quite nicely. Three hours and at least that many pints of lager later, John had secured their interest in the operation. After they'd all adjourned to the Cock and Whistle, the local pub, they'd done a bit of catching up, which took some time, as it had been nearly twenty years since they'd worked together.

"Blimey!" Chet took a hefty swig of his lager. "I thought I'd retired from the meat cutting. No more meat. That's what I said to myself. I said, 'Chester, old lad, you're done.' It just goes to show you, that you never know nothing for sure. If that isn't the God's honest truth." He looked thoughtfully at the bottom of his glass and signaled for another pint. "So, when do we start?"

"I can be ready tomorrow," said Stanley. There's nothing to hold me here. Nothing, now that my Bessie's gone." He smiled ruefully at his mates. "It was best. She'd lived her time. And when it's your time, well, there's nothing to do but answer the call. So here I am, wanting something to occupy myself and you show up. Just like that." He snapped his fingers. "It's fate. That's what it is." He clenched his jaw as if the idea needed further shaping in the mold before he let it go. "I'm ready." He unclenched and took a decisive swallow from his pint.

John was gathering his thoughts to find the best way to express his condolences at Stanley's loss, but Chet offered his own first. "Yessir. Bessie was a good old girl. She was a fine bitch." He paused and John's eyes widened. "There's not many bitches as have that many pups in a litter. Seventeen, wasn't it? And she raised 'em all. She won the pub pool with that last batch. Yes, she was a good hound."

There are times when there is really nothing left to say and John could only nod in sorrowful agreement. After a respectful moment or two of reflective silence in honor of the dear departed Bessie, it was decided that Stanley and Chet would leave for Whitehall in the morning. John left his mates to consider the possible benefits of another round and set off for his next stop, Bletchley Park.

As a recruiter, so far he was batting a hundred percent. Of course, the lure was powerful, the stakes were high, and he was dealing with an elite group who understood the odds.

Chapter Sixteen

London

John had been making good time since he'd left his lodgings. It was one of those most unusual English mornings – bright and sunny and even a tad warm. It was a grand morning for a motorcycle ride and the Harley-Davidson was performing beautifully. At his current rate of speed he estimated he'd arrive at Bletchley Park slightly ahead of schedule.

Last August, code-breaking operations for the British Navy had been physically moved to Bletchley, known familiarly as BP. Its official designation was *Station X*, which referred to its number in the chain of stations across England. It also was referred to as the Government Code and Cypher School, GC&CS, often irreverently referred to as the Golf, Cheese and Chess Society.

Physically, it was an estate 40 miles from London and situated approximately halfway between Oxford and Cambridge Universities, from which many of the team members had been recruited. A number of huts which were actually small frame dwellings had been built on the estate to house the chess masters, mathematicians, professors, and linguists who were all part of the team, referred to as Captain

Ridley's Shooting Party, and dedicated to deciphering the intercepted encrypted messages of the Third Reich.

This morning, John's first conversation would be with Mr. Eugene Abbingdon, chief of operations. Churchill had told John to be prepared for Abbingdon, but hadn't expanded on the warning. He'd given a throaty chuckle, which had caused John to raise an eyebrow and do some speculating. Nothing, however, could have prepared him for what happened next.

As John leaned into the last curve of the driveway, an apparition on a penny farthing crossed his path, causing him to swerve off to the side and plow into a boxwood hedge that then closed around the motorcycle, almost obscuring it from sight.

"What the hell?" John picked himself up from the ground where he'd been thrown and looked behind him, wondering if he'd been hallucinating. He removed his goggles and leather helmet and rubbed his forehead, which had hit the ground with a good deal of force. His nose was bleeding and his neck had taken a bit of a wrench. He blinked to clear away the cobwebs.

At that moment a craggy face peered into the hedges and a raspy voice inquired, "I say! Are you all right?" The craggy face's hand produced a clean handkerchief, which John accepted and pressed to his nostril to staunch the flow of blood.

"Awfully sorry, old chap. I didn't expect anyone quite so soon. I was exercising. Thought I'd have time for a few circuits." The craggy face was etched with lines of deep concern. "I've caused you a spot of bother. Oh dear."

The concerned face was wearing aviator goggles and hat with earflaps and the neck, which was the extent of John's range of vision at this point, was swaddled in an orange woolen muffler with fringe at least a foot in length. John wondered if perhaps he had also suffered a concussion, but the voice continued.

"I'm Abbingdon. You must be Chichester. Awfully glad to meet you. Are you able to navigate?" He looked concernedly at the position of the motorcycle. Concern seemed to be his hallmark expression and intensity his natural state.

John stood and brushed the dirt and leaves from his clothes. "Just give me a minute. I don't think I'm badly stuck, just wedged a bit. He gave his nose a final blot and stuffed the handkerchief in his pocket. Eugene withdrew to a respectful distance and waited with intense interest to see the results of the extrication.

The motorcycle hadn't suffered any damage and appeared to be merely resting on its side. John grabbed the handlebars and threw all his weight into righting the bike, which he then backed out onto the drive.

"Jolly good work, that. Excellent. Very good." Eugene's furrowed brow relaxed, reducing the crease in its center by a good quarter inch, although it was still a formidable cavern. "Just go on ahead and I'll follow." Eugene readjusted his cap and goggles and climbed back aboard his ancient bicycle with the huge front wheel and the miniscule back wheel, wobbling a bit before he got up enough speed to totter off behind John. They made an odd parade as they rounded the building and pulled up at the rear entrance of the mansion.

John set the kickstand on the motorcycle and turned to examine the penny farthing with interest. "Do the Jerries really understand what they're up against?" John asked.

"I beg your pardon?" Eugene asked, vaulting off the seat.

"I daresay there's nothing in their intelligence that will aid them in defending against this marvel of engineering. It defies the laws of gravity.

"Indeed." Eugene said. "Well, here we are and good enough for all that." He extended a bony hand to John in greeting. "We'll have a spot of tea and have a look see about your injuries. You do look better, though. Keep the handkerchief. I've a good supply. I tend to fall a bit." He looked with concern at his mode of transportation. "It does give one quite a good view, though. Even considering all the lumps and bumps one acquires. The wheels are a bit narrow, you know. Not much in the way of traction at times." He shrugged and led the way into the manor. "The locals think we're a bit off. Odd, actually. I've heard them say so. It's rather helpful, don't you know. Keeps the visitors and callers to a minimum. Actually," he added, turning his head slightly to the left and tossing the words over his shoulder, "we don't get visitors, come to think of it."

Removing his cap released a great quantity of red hair, mostly confined to the top of his head, and which now sprang to life as if released from hibernation. Even though cut short at the nape of his neck and neatly trimmed at the sideburns, the amount atop his pate would have provided enough nesting material for a covey of quail. His Adam's apple protruded to the point where it looked as if it might be painful. All in all he was a collection of bones and joints with an engaging personality and bountiful energy. John found him immensely likeable.

"I'm one of the fellows here, as you know. They found me at university – Cambridge," he added. "Mathematics department. It's all about numbers, actually," he confided, leaning forward to peer into John's eyes. "What I do now and what I did then, I mean. Everything is. Even the piano. I performed as a child, you know. Or perhaps you don't. No matter. One finds it interesting when a child can play Mozart." He led the way down the hall. "I still play the piano when I need to think. It helps sort the ideas, you know."

"I've heard that before. About mathematics," John said. "It does make sense. Music is almost pure mathematics, isn't it?"

"Indeed." They'd entered a small kitchen and Eugene was bustling about, setting the kettle on and rummaging for cups and saucers in the cupboard.

"How do you take yours?" he asked. "White? With or

without?" He was pawing through the cabinet like a squirrel in search of buried acorns, but he eventually produced a sugar bowl and pitcher, which he set on the table. He poured cream from a bottle into the pitcher, set a pair of tongs next to the sugar bowl, and hovered over the kettle.

"A watched pot, and all that," he said cheerfully, "but it's more about physics than wise old maxims, isn't it? And of course it's not a pot at all, so there you have it."

"Yes, indeed," said John, beginning to feel a bit dizzy with the abrupt changes in topic. "White with, please." English tea was nothing like its weak American cousin. Robust, hearty, and revivifying, it had fueled the Empire. John hoped it would do the trick for him.

"So." Eugene pulled up a chair and joined his guest. "I'm told that you are Dr. George Chichester. A very British name, if you don't mind my saying so."

"My own name is just as British," John laughed, "but it wouldn't do, would it?"

"Not at all. Not at all. We're used to that sort of thing here. Keeps everything tidy at both ends, if you understand my meaning. Would you care for a biscuit? I believe there's a tin somewhere." He looked around hopefully, but the counters were bare.

"I'm fine. This is just right," John said, raising his cup of tea.

"I've gathered a list for you. I think you'll find them up to snuff. All speak German as well as Danish. They'll be along individually after a while. I thought you would like a moment or so to review their dossiers before you meet them in person."

"That will be fine. Very good of you."

"Tut." Eugene said. "Not a problem at all. I've gone through your requirements carefully and I know you were specific, but…" he trailed off in an uncertain direction.

"Is something wrong?" His biggest fear was that he would be unable to fill the quota. There wouldn't be enough time to start over if the right people couldn't be found or weren't available. Timing was critical. Timing was everything.

"No, not wrong. Well, not necessarily wrong. Actually, it's all quite right, you see." Eugene set down the cup. "There are the three. There is an additional possibility I think you'll appreciate. I'll just let you decide for yourself." And with that he left to fetch the first candidate.

"One, two, three." John repeated to himself. "This will be easy as one, two, three. God in heaven, I hope that's true."

Within three minutes, Eugene brought John the first of the potential recruits. "Dr. Chichester, this is Mr. Basil Dunkling. When you have finished your discussion, Mr. Dunkling will alert the next person to come in. That will save time, I believe. I'll check in with you before you make your departure."

"That will be fine. Thank you very much," John said. "Have a seat, Mr. Dunkling," he indicated the chair Eugene had vacated. "You're a chef, I understand."

"Yes, a pastry chef, to be precise."

"And your other talents?"

"I'm a crossword fanatic, you might say. Have been most of my life. Started as a lad. My best time for the *Times*, if you'll pardon the play on words, is twenty-four minutes. That's for the Sunday edition, of course. The weekday selections I polish off in under ten. There are actually quite a few of us here. Even some elderly women you'd think were gaga by now. They're quite good at finding patterns, which is what it's all about.

"You're at liberty to travel," John said.

"Oh yes. No ties, if that's what you mean. Yes, I'm quite at liberty." Basil smiled. He was a short, stocky man of about thirty with a square face, a thick neck, and a pot belly.

"Thank you, Mr. Dunkling. You can send in the next person, if you would."

Basil Dunkling rose and was crossing the threshold when

John shot him a question. "What's the secret to a flaky pie crust?" John asked.

Dunkling didn't break stride, as he turned and replied, "Lard and ice water and a gentle hand."

"Thank you, Mr. Dunkling," John said. "Stay close. We'll all meet together after a while."

"Right. I'll send in your next victim," Dunkling said.

The next victim was Dena Cottle. She was thirty-two, about five feet two inches in height and slender, with auburn hair pulled back in a tight bun. She wore horn-rimmed glasses perched on the end of a pert nose. She had a pleasant face and a warm smile.

"I understand there's a test," Dr. Chichester. "May I have the question, please?"

John nodded. "*Jeg kunne tænke mig at besøge Danmark en dag.*"

"*Danmark er et fantastisk land,*" Dena replied.

"*Tak.*"

"You are most welcome. My mother is Danish. And I agree – you should visit Denmark one day, and I understand that prospect is coming sooner rather than later. Will I be coming along?"

"I believe so. You are a nurse. That will be helpful in more ways than one. "Do you have questions of me?"

"No questions, just one more piece of information you may need to know." Her expression grew serious. "My mother's maiden name is Cohen. I am a Jew."

"My mother's maiden name was Stafford," John replied, with a twinkle in his eye, "and I am unaffiliated."

Dena searched his eyes and nodded. "I see. I won't hold it against you," she smiled. "However, it could add a layer of complication."

"It's possible that any aspect of our lives could add a layer of complication. All the more reason to prepare carefully to ensure this doesn't happen. Would you please join Basil and send in the next person?"

"Gladly. A pleasure to be on board."

John rose from the table and stretched. Sunshine was streaming through the window and the room was heating up. He lowered the shade partway to block some of the light. When he turned around, he was convinced he had a concussion after all. Eugene had returned.

"I felt I had better do the introductions this time. This is what I meant. You see, it's quite all right, in fact, it's jolly good. You get two for the price of one. Well, you don't really, but it's nearly the same as." He stopped for breath, which gave his Adam's apple a respite from its violent bobbing up and down while he chattered on. "May I present Mr. Cecil Ackroyd," he looked to his right, "and Mr. Graham Ackroyd," he looked to his left.

Twins. John's mouth dropped open and he stared first at one and then at the other. The men were in their early fifties, about five foot ten and trim of build. Identical twins. Bald identical twins. Bald identical twins with Van Dyke beards.

John stood and walked to the doorway to shake hands.

"I'm the good-looking one," said Graham.

"And I'm the one who indulges him in his delusions of grandeur," said Cecil.

"I'll leave the three of you to chat," said Eugene, beating a quick retreat down the hall.

"Pull up a couple of chairs gentlemen," John said. "I'm all ears. Who's first?"

"Age before beauty," Graham said, nodding to his brother.

"Tedious, Graham, tedious. I'm all of six minutes older than he," Cecil said scowling at his brother. "But that's fine. On with the show. You want to know our usefulness to you and if we're up for the trek."

"That's correct," John said.

"Very well then. Both Graham and I have photographic memories. Before we get the Danish test, I must tell you that we've been studying the language intensively for the past two months and only need to perfect our accents. Isn't that right, Graham?"

"Yes, our ears will pick up the local dialect quickly enough, so that shouldn't be a concern," Graham said. "We're fluent in German, French, Norwegian, Italian, and Mandarin."

John stopped his note-taking and put his pen down. "Mandarin?"

"Righto," Cecil said. "We took that one up just for sport. Not only a completely different phonetic system but different tones for each sound. Incredibly interesting language."

"Well," said John. "One never knows when a talent will become useful. I'll definitely keep that in mind, although I don't believe this particular mission will involve the Chinese. But still, it's good to know. In addition to the languages?"

"Graham is a munitions expert. What he can't do with a stick of dynamite, doesn't need to be done. Of course he's also up to date on some of the more modern explosives, as well. When he's not researching novel ways of creating debris, he's a truck driver. I'm a heavy equipment operator," Cecil added. "If it's got an engine, I can handle it."

"We've talked about the risks," Graham said. "We're not married and nobody's waiting up for us. It will be a nice break from what we're doing now. Get a bit of fresh air and all that."

"Right," John said. "Let's join the others in the parlor."

The contrast between the opulent furnishings of the mansion and the stark furnishings of the huts, where the members of Captain Ridley's Shooting Party did their work, was dramatic. With its richly paneled walls, painted ceilings and wainscoting, Oriental carpets, tall windows with brocade draperies, and massive stone fireplace, the room was the very picture of a traditional country manor house.

Dena and Basil had taken up their stations in an alcove by the window and were comfortably ensconced in two of the overstuffed armchairs. When John and the Ackroyd brothers entered the room, Basil rose and helped them carry three more chairs to the alcove.

"It's time to get down to business," John began, placing his attaché case on the floor and taking a seat. "You've been chosen because of your various talents that may become useful to Britain at some point. I can tell you where your mission will begin and when it will begin, but no one can tell you the ending date. That remains to be determined. From the moment you parachute into Denmark, you will be on your own."

Expressions grew puzzled and Graham said, "Denmark is neutral."

"It is indeed," John said. "And very shortly it will under German occupation. Whether you will remain in Denmark or move on down to Germany, you will be behind enemy lines."

There were murmurs of understanding, and John continued. "You will be provided with new identities. You will go to work, socialize with friends you will make, and generally become productive members of your community. When your services are needed, you will be contacted. The procedures you will follow and the method by which you will identify your contact will be explained to you at your briefing when you arrive at Whitehall.

"If you have any reservations, this is the time to withdraw with honor. I will remind you that the Official Secrets Act is binding upon everything we have discussed today or will discuss in the future. If you wish to leave, now is the time." He sat back in his chair, crossed his long legs, stretched them out, and waited. No one rose to leave.

"Very good then. A car will be by tomorrow morning at 0800 hours to take you to Whitehall. You have the rest of the day to pack and put your affairs in order. I'll see you in

London." And with that, the four rose and left the room. He finished up his notes, bade Eugene and his penny farthing farewell, and set off to report the success of his assignment to the Admiralty and Winston Churchill.

Chapter Seventeen

Sankt Peder

"It's *piano*! *Piano*!" thundered the choir director. "You are not calling home the goats! And *sta-cat-to*!" He beat his baton on the music stand with each syllable. "Again! From the beginning and this time let's do it correctly. You must be one voice, one golden thread reaching out to lead the congregation to God."

The director, *Herre* Magnus Poulsen, lifted his arms and waved the baton above his head. "Listen to your neighbor and meld your voices together!" The choir members of the Evangelical Lutheran Church of the Redeemer of Sankt Peder were well into their weekly drill into the finer points of sacred music. *Herre* Poulson turned to acknowledge the entrance of the pastor. "Pastor, if you would please to have a seat in the front pew and be our audience, we will perform for you after our break."

Karl gritted his teeth and forced a smile. Choir practice. He'd forgotten about choir practice. It was one item he hadn't considered when he'd accepted this mission. Christ and good God Almighty. It was almost more than he could stand.

The choir was preparing for next week's competition in Copenhagen and had tacked on an additional hour and a half to its weekly practice time. Karl had a splitting headache, having endured for the better part of the evening, the screeching of Emma Steengarten as she conducted her own private competition to drown out the other eleven members of the group. The assault on his eardrums showed no signs of abating.

Now they filed into the church hall and arranged themselves around the long table with the red and white checkered tablecloth to sip tea or coffee and rest their overtaxed vocal chords. "No milk!" insisted *Herre* Poulsen. "It coats the vocal chords! And not too hot for the beverages!" Talking was permitted and the choir members wasted no time in catching up and sharing the latest gossip and news. Karl sat down with them and joined in the conversation.

"There's going to be some restrictions put on the fleet," grumbled one of the tenors, Hans Jorgensen. "It's hard enough to make a living without the Germans telling us where we can and can't fish."

"Where did you hear that, Hans" asked Karl, a concerned look fixed on his face.

"I heard it too, Pastor," Nils Rasmussen confirmed. "The talk is all over the docks."

"That's going to make things difficult," Karl said. "But how do you know it's true? It could be just a rumor. You know how stories spread."

"No, Pastor," Nils said. "I got it straight from the harbormaster himself."

"Really?" Karl said, shaking his head. "What's the harbormaster's name, again? I've forgotten."

"Aksel Spelman, Pastor," Hans said. "He knows."

"That could be," Karl said, making a mental note to add this name to his nightly transmission. "That could very well be."

"Intermission is over!" commanded *Herre* Poulsen. "Let us finish up!"

It was nine o'clock when the choirmaster dismissed his charges with the admonition to gargle with salt water three times a day and to remain out of the evening air, so as not to injure their vocal chords. Emma Steengarten nodded solemnly, as she wrapped her muffler three times around her throat, before setting out into the dreaded evening air.

Karl moved about the church checking windows and turning out lights, as the stragglers gathered up their belongings and spilled out the side door of the church in groups of twos and threes. He was returning the hymnals to the pews and stacking them at each end, while he mulled over the conversation he'd had in the church hall with the men. If they decided to create difficulties with the upcoming restrictions on their activities, measures would have to be taken.

The hymnals had been stacked haphazardly atop the upright piano that served as stand-in for the organ during the weekly drill, and as he reached for the next pile, one fell to the floor with a soft thud. As he stooped to pick it up, a shadow passed across the books, and he straightened and turned to see who had remained behind. There was a silhouette of a woman's figure, and as she entered the vestibule, the woman greeted him by name.

"Hello Karl, surprised to see me?" Dagmar's voice was as sultry as a Louisiana swamp. She'd made an impressive entrance. Her fur coat was unbuttoned, revealing a form-fitting red silk dress with deep décolletage. She made a show of pulling off first her right glove, then her left, examining them as if they were all that mattered at the moment. She rested a delicate hand across the back of the last pew and struck a pose. Cool and calm. She'd copied this from a poster featuring Marlene Dietrich and had practiced it until she was sure she had it down pat. Karl couldn't know she needed that pew for support, as her knees had gone weak and her heart was racing.

Surprised? Somehow he wasn't. It was just the sort of

theatrics Dagmar would think up. This was the perfect end to a thoroughly rotten day that he realized wasn't over yet. He had to get rid of her, and quickly. He turned back to the piano and finished straightening the books before responding, but she didn't wait for his answer and pressed her advantage.

"Don't you think you're just a tad out of your element?"

He now faced her and his eyes bored into hers. "What the bloody hell are you doing here and how the hell did you find me?"

She clucked at him in mock disapproval. "Such language from a minister and in church too. What would your congregation say?" She shook her head in disbelief. "And I thought I knew you. Just goes to show, you never can tell about people. They'll disappoint you every chance they get."

"You didn't answer my question."

"I didn't, did I? Hmmm. More's the pity." She looked around the church. "This is really charming. I love what you've done with the place. Stained glass windows, fresh paint. It's precious. Rather small though, isn't it? I should think you'd have wanted something more in keeping with your character. Larger than life. Perhaps the Vatican. Yes, I can see you in the Vatican, all those jeweled rings and fancy outfits. Vestments, I think they call them. Yes, that's more your speed. Pope. Of course you'd have to convert, but that shouldn't pose any problem for you." Dagmar's eyes narrowed. "You can convert from lover to bastard in the blink of an eye. Religion should be a piece of cake."

"Dagmar, answer me." Karl's voice had a dangerous undercurrent.

She gave a high, thin laugh. "You really shouldn't leave important papers in your jacket." She chided him. "Anyone could have found them. Found you," she added. She looked smug.

"Leave. Now."

"Oh no, darling. Come on. Admit it. You're glad to see

me. This," her arm swept around the church, dismissively, "has got to cramp your style." She now slipped off the coat and, draping it over her left arm, straightened her shoulders to show her breasts to full advantage. Sex had always worked before. "I've missed you."

"Are you alone?"

She made a show of looking around, behind her, even standing on tiptoe to see over his shoulder. "Looks like it. God, what a silly question. Of course I'm alone. I'm here to see you. Just little old me to see big, strong, and handsome you."

"Knock off the Southern belle impression. You're not Scarlett O'Hara, this isn't acting studio, and you're not all that convincing." He moved a step closer to her. "Did you tell anyone you were coming?"

She gave an exaggerated, exasperated sigh. "Of course not. What do you take me for? This is our little secret." She deposited the coat on the pew seat and moved closer to him, until they were close enough she could run her hands down the front of his shirt. "Of course, it's going to cost you if you want me to keep it. Our little secret, that is." She was playful. "Oh Karl, don't be like that. Let's go for a ride. I've brought the car." She encircled his waist with her arms and looked up into his eyes. "I'm sorry I blew up at you. I didn't mean it really. Well, maybe at the time, but that's over."

"You shouldn't have come here, Dagmar." He grabbed her arms to disentangle himself and she gave a sharp cry as he took her hands and pushed her away.

"Now what?" he asked, exasperated.

"I cut myself, and it hurts and it's your fault. You made me so angry." She showed her bandaged finger and tried her pout on him but that didn't have any more effect than her breasts had. She was running out of equipment to thrust at him.

"You are an idiot. You have no sense, no brains. You're putting us both in jeopardy. I really thought you were smarter than that."

"Oh fiddle. Who cares if I'm here? And no one will ever know I came if you just come with me now." She lowered her voice to a seductive whisper. "We can ride all night and find a hotel and get a room..." Her eyes were pleading. "Come on. You know you want to." She waited. Her eyes smoldered with carefully constructed desire and her lips trembled with rehearsed passion. She began to breathe slowly, allowing her chest to rise and fall before his scrutiny.

Karl looked around the darkened church. No one would want him until morning. Tomorrow was the housekeeper's day off. It could work. Why not? Nothing really mattered anyway. He let the tension go and relaxed his shoulders. It would be over soon enough and she'd not be a thorn in his side any longer. "Where's the car?" he asked.

She caught her breath and fluttered her lashes at him. "It's alongside the parsonage. I pulled in out of sight. I didn't want anybody to see me. I just wanted to see you. Needed you," she added. Her voice was soft and low.

"All right." He nodded. "Let's go out the side door. I'll drive."

She reached for her bag and propped it on her knee, rummaging until she found her keys, pulling out half the contents in the process. "Here they are," she said handing them over and stuffing things back in her purse. She brushed her fingers across the scar on his cheek and traced the outline of his jaw. "Whatever you want. I never could stay mad at you."

"I need to change." He looked towards the parsonage.

"Don't bother. I thought of that. There's a change of clothes in the car. I brought everything you'll need. You know, if you want, I could stay here. You could tell everyone that I'm your baby sister come to visit."

"Don't! Bad enough as it is."

"Oh? I thought it was rather good."

"You're a slut. How I ever got involved with you is

beyond me."

"You got involved because I wanted you to. Actually, it was Papa who ordered it at the beginning, don't you know?"

Karl's eyes widened.

"Oh yes. I was to see how you would work out. Test your loyalty and all. It worked out just fine." Her eyes traveled south. "Very Fine."

Karl was beyond speech. He stared at Dagmar, disbelief in his eyes. "You've got it wrong. Dead wrong. I'm nobody's patsy. Nobody uses me like that."

"Talk to Papa. I'm just the Party hack."

"You're the Party whore."

"But I'm a sensitive whore," she pouted.

He threw back his head and laughed. "Son of a bitch. You're really something, you know that?"

Dagmar just kept him fixed in her gaze. Her eyes were smoke and when she kissed him, he tasted fire. She had that effect on him, and she knew it.

"Not just yet." He pulled out his pocket watch and frowned. "It's almost nine o'clock. I have to check in first," he jerked his head in the direction of the parsonage. "You'd better come with me. We'll go out the side door." He shut off the rest of the lights and led the way from the church and around back to the rear door of the parsonage. He held the door open for her and she brushed past him on her way through. He caught the scent of her perfume.

"Don't these people ever lock anything?" She wrinkled her nose.

"Actually, no. They're very trusting."

"They're very stupid, if you ask me. I wouldn't trust them."

"And that's why you belong to the Master Race." He continued through the kitchen and down the hall to the stairs as he spoke, his words hanging in the air as she walked through them. "Trust is a highly overrated virtue. I only trust myself, but locking the door would raise suspicions, and so I don't. But I take precautions, nevertheless."

Dagmar shrugged. Karl's room was at the top of the stairs and the door was open. She tossed her coat and purse on the bed and walked to the window.

Karl unfastened his clerical collar and placed it on the dresser, then retrieved the radio from the shelf in the fireplace and set it on the desk, while Dagmar completed the tour of his room. She stopped at the dresser and picked up the collar, twirling it around her wrist.

"Put that back," the harshness of his voice startled her, but she blew a kiss at him and continued to twirl the collar.

"Touch. Touch. Touch." She jabbed at it with her index finger. Karl started to rise from his chair, and she decided this wasn't a good thing. "Sorry! I didn't realize you were still attached to this." She tossed the collar back on the dresser and returned to the window.

"Get away from the window. You're on display."

"Don't do this. Don't do that." Dagmar gave another theatrical sigh and sank into the leather chair. Her eyes continued to travel around the room and she listened to the clicks, short and long of the Morse code that Karl was transmitting to Berlin, trying to mimic the tapping with her toes.

Karl finished his transmission, removed his headphones, and was returning the radio to its nook, when Dagmar decided she could stand the quiet no longer. "Did I tell you Leni Riefenstahl had been a dancer?" Dagmar had kicked off her pumps. "Oh yes, I did. I remember now." She stretched out her legs and was rotating her ankles. "I have rather shapely ankles, don't I? What do you think?"

"I told you what I think. You are utterly shameless." Karl walked to the chair and held out his hands to pull her up.

"Will you help me?" Dagmar had perfected her little girl voice. "Please, Karl? Just this one little favor for me?"

Karl's face turned to stone. His eyes, his lips, everything became rigid before her eyes. "So that's what this is really all about?"

"If you care about me at all, you'll do this. Just introduce me to your friends. I can take it from there. It won't cost you anything. Promise me you'll do what I ask."

"You really had me going for a while. I'll give you that. But now I think it would be best if you just leave. For good."

"Don't forget what I know. And I will use it. If your stupid mission's such a big deal, then you'll want to do whatever it takes to protect it."

"You know, you're right," he said. There was a moment of deep regret in his eyes that puzzled her, as he reached up and cupped her face in his hands. She closed her eyes waiting for his kiss, but instead, with a savage twist he snapped her neck and let her fall, lifeless, to the floor. "Every actress should play a death scene once in her career, my dear. Yours came prematurely. Why couldn't you just have let it go?" He cursed her and God and his life and the hell it had become. He was no better than the vermin he worked for. Killing came easy now. He felt deep and utter despair and a gut wrenching pain.

Outside the church, evening shadows darkened and only the distant stars bore witness as Karl carried Dagmar's body to the car and deposited it in the trunk. He drove the car to the abandoned barn at the edge of the field bordering the parsonage and covered the car with a tarpaulin. He'd have to find some way to get rid of everything. "Dead or alive, you cause me nothing but trouble," he muttered as he closed the barn door and returned to his room.

Karl slept little that night, but good news greeted him the next morning. *Frue* Emma Jorgensen's heart had finally given out and she had died peacefully in her sleep. She had enjoyed poor health for years, and her standard greeting to callers never varied:

"I have no vitality today." She'd shake her head, incredulous at this new daily development in the state of her health. She'd been incredulous for ninety-seven years, from all accounts.

Karl received the news with an appropriate solemnity, but this was absolutely perfect. The answer to his prayers. He frowned. Not prayers, the answer to something else. Something primal. He dressed, breakfasted, and set out to call on the bereaved family, who'd decided after lengthy discussion that the funeral service would be held day after tomorrow. The death was not unexpected, and distant relatives had called to pay their last respects numerous times before Emma finally checked out. They had called regularly and frequently, no one really sure when Emma might actually do the deed. Also, Karl suspected, there was the matter of the will, as Emma was quite well off. So the doting relatives were all in attendance when Karl arrived.

"There'll be no viewing, Pastor and we'd just like a simple service. "Emma wouldn't have wanted a lot of fuss made," one of the daughters explained. The rest of the relatives all nodded sadly in unison. "Her soul is already with her Maker."

What they really meant, figured Karl, was that they wanted the old lady in the ground as soon as possible, so they could converge at the lawyer's office and get on with the reading of her Last Will and Testament. "Of course," he said. "Emma, I'm sure is already with the Lord and looking down on her beloved family." There was a bit of shifting in seats and throat clearing among the bereaved, but Karl continued. "Yes, simple and tasteful." Bloodsucking leeches, he thought. "The service will be followed, of course, by internment in the cemetery behind the church."

He broke free of the Jorgensens shortly before noon and moved to the next item on his agenda. He paid a call on Ole Sorenson, who dug the graves.

"Well, Pastor, that's sad news. Yes. Sad news indeed. Emma was the oldest woman in town, you know." Ole was leaning against a tree digging a small hole. "Even when I don't work, I work. I'm a planter, Pastor. Today I'm planting flowers. Tomorrow, who knows?" He gave a hearty laugh which allowed a river of tobacco juice to escape his lips and trickle down his gray beard. "I wonder who the oldest one is now." Ole considered this while he pulled a worn leather pouch from his pocket and pulled out a generous portion of chewing tobacco, which he stuffed in his mouth and worked it around to soften it up. "Abel Madsen, I think," he said. "*Ja.* It's Abel, all right."

"Very interesting, I'm sure, Ole," Karl said, cutting him off before he could relate Abel's life history. "However, right now we need to consider the wishes of Emma's family. The funeral service will be the day after tomorrow. I expect you'll want to get that taken care of right away. This afternoon, in fact, would be fine."

"If you think so, Pastor, but I think tomorrow would be time enough. *Ja.* Tomorrow."

"I really think today would be best, Ole. Once the job is done, it's done and you won't have to worry about it."

"Don't worry, pastor. I've never left one above ground yet." He chuckled and more juice escaped.

One more day then, Karl thought. One more day with Dagmar like an albatross around his neck. He turned to leave, but Ole called to him. "It's okay, Pastor. I'll do it. Seeing that you're trying to do the right thing for the family. I'll dig Emma's grave this afternoon."

That evening Karl whistled as he walked through the graveyard, checking on Ole's work. The Jorgensen family plot was in the far northwestern corner of the church graveyard, giving the deceased a commanding view of the ocean.

After midnight, he deepened the grave and brought the car around to the side of the parsonage. He opened the trunk, gathered up Dagmar's body and placed it on the ground floor. He returned the borrowed dirt to the grave, tamping it down uniformly with Ole's spade, which he then returned to the tool shed. Done and finished. Dagmar would cause him no more trouble. After *Frue* Jorgensen's interment, and after he disposed of her car, everything would be taken care of. Emma and Dagmar would share their quarters with a joint tenancy in perpetuity. He pressed his lips together in a thin smile. Dagmar was Emma's problem now.

Chapter Eighteen

Kolding

Schmidt and Ericksen's was hopping this morning. The joint was jumpin'. Every phone line was lit up and my arms were moving so fast, plugging in outgoing and incoming calls, that my brain was having trouble keeping up. If only this could count as exercise, I'd be svelte, but I knew from sad experience that tired arms did not make for slim hips and thighs.

With Helga just as busy, I'd have been able to risk listening in, but the heavy volume made it impossible, and keeping a key open for the entire call was necessary to avoid giving myself away with a telltale click when I connected or cut out. That kind of eavesdropping took time, a scarce commodity this morning. I would have to investigate the day's orders when the rush was past, and I was fairly sure today would give me good information. I needed Helga out of the office for this, and that might prove difficult. I'd need to come up with something soon.

Helga's adding machine tape had spilled over her desktop an hour ago and now was winding around one desk leg and curving around her chair and ankles like an albino boa constrictor. She had a pencil wedged behind her ear, another one clasped between her teeth, her hair had escaped its bobby pins, and deep lines of concentration furrowed her brow. She had the overall appearance of a woman on the edge.

Even the love of her life had rethought his entry after spying her grim face through the half-glassed partition that separated the office from the plant. He carefully backed away from the war zone, hands outstretched, palms facing outward as well, warding off the woman of his dreams. When Helga was in full battle mode it was best to just leave her be.

The one oasis of calm non-productivity was Dagmar's desk. Helga had supplied it with the first batch file folders early this morning and she had been adding to the pile at regular intervals since then, each increment accompanied by an increasingly dark scowl, but Dagmar was not in residence.

"That girl is the laziest, most self-centered......" Helga sputtered through her clenched teeth-with-pencil. "Not a telephone call. Nothing. In my day, we wouldn't have a job to come back to if we pulled a stunt like this. Just because her father is some big fool somewhere, that doesn't give her the right..." Helga was beginning to drool around the pencil. She made a slight slurping noise and shot a dark look at the offender's desk.

The work that had originated from the central office quickly spilled forth into the production plant, and by mid-afternoon, the pace there had also picked up noticeably. Wally had informed the crew they'd be pulling overtime for the next week and possibly after that as well. He had rolled up his own shirtsleeves, donned a white meat cutter's jacket, and was hard at work alongside his men.

When the lunch whistle blasted at twelve o'clock, it was a welcome relief from the hectic pace of the morning, and within a minute Wally rapped on the glass, holding his lunch box aloft, a silent signal that it was time to eat. Even Helga was ready to abandon her station for the duration, having had the entire morning to prepare her lecture to Dagmar. As we set to our lunches, she gave Wally the unabridged version.

"She'll be in this afternoon, and no doubt with a reasonable excuse or some song and dance." Wally was talking around his sandwich, a generous offering of meat, cheese, and bread. "If there's a problem, send her to me." He patted Helga's arm reassuringly.

But Dagmar wasn't at her desk at the end of the day. Irritation turned to concern, and Helga's attempts to reach Dagmar at home by telephone proved fruitless. For once she seemed at a loss for what to do.

"She probably had a family emergency or something like that," I offered. "You said her father was someone important. That means she's at least got him. Maybe she has other relatives as well."

"She seldom mentioned him. Her closest relationship is with herself." Helga bit her lip, an outward sign of a pang of guilt for being ungenerous. "She did refer to him as The Colonel, I think. But I don't think she ever used his name. Helga frowned. "It doesn't seem natural, not to talk about your family, but then she's…different. That's the most charitable term I can manage. Maybe we should tell the police?"

"What would we say?" Wally asked. "That Dagmar didn't come to work? They'll ask if she's done that before. We'll say yes. They'll snap their notebooks closed and tell us to call after she's been gone – I don't know – a week or something."

"I suppose that's true. But still," Helga shook her head.

"We'll cross that bridge when we come to it. If we come to it," I said. "I'm sure everything is just fine" With lunch now over, I returned to the switchboard. A nagging suspicion that all was not well stayed with me, however, and it was with a mixture of relief and apprehension that I shut down the switchboard for the day at 5:00, a half-hour later than usual. If Dagmar had met with foul play, the police would be investigating and they would begin with her friends and work associates. I did not need that added concern while I was snooping around on my own. It would be best if Dagmar came to work on Monday morning and put an end to everybody's concerns.

Chapter Nineteen

Sankt Peder

Dusk and dawn are Mother Nature's intermissions. It's the time when the stage crew changes sets and the actors change costumes. In Middle High German the word for this is *zwischerliecht*, "the time between light." In Danish, it's called *tusmorke*, "two darks." This simple difference of perspective is just one example of the differences that separate the Germans and the Danes. Regardless of the propaganda pouring out of Berlin that claimed the Danes were also part of the Master Race and should joyfully embrace their destiny, the Danes weren't buying into it. They knew that this twilight was the beginning of a long, dark night that would soon spread across the face of Europe.

It was twilight at the Volmer Jensen home and upstairs in her grandfather's study, Greta was sitting cross legged on the wool rug, making notes in her science journal. The fern fronds pressed between the pages made faint indentations on the blank paper and framed her writing with the look of embossed stationery. She wrote neatly, each entry beginning with a meticulously detailed and labeled sketch of her specimen fern, which she identified with both common and scientific names. Currently her interest was horsetail ferns and a Swede was causing her problems. Carl von Linne, known to the scientific world as Linnaeus, had developed the system of classification that was both occupying and vexing Greta at the moment.

Kingdom: Plant
Phylum: Pterophyta
Class: Equisetopsida
Order: Equisateles
Family: Equisatacea
Genus: Equisetum
Species:?
Scientific name: Equisetum something or other.

There were seven species of horsetail ferns in Denmark, and Greta was determined to find a sample of each to record in her notebook. The current specimen, however, had her stymied. *Palustre*? *Telemateia*? She picked up her magnifying glass and peered intently at the green frond that refused to give up its secret. She scowled and looked up at her grandfather. "*Tante* Katrin will know. She knows everything about plants. When is she coming, *Opa?* I can ask her then." Volmer was deep in concentration and didn't hear her. She sighed and put the glass and the fern down on the notebook.

Volmer was at his desk, transcribing his notes in preparation for his now nightly transmission to Dick. The smoke from his pipe circled his head and filtered across the room, hovering like a low-level stratus cloud in a heavy sky. At one point he frowned, set down his fountain pen and retrieved a heavy volume from his military history shelf. Consulting the index he traced an entry with his index finger, grunted in satisfaction, and set the book down on the edge of his desk, just as Greta looked up from her own writing.

"What do you read, *Opa*?" she asked.

He replied with a twinkle in his eye, "Words. I read words." It was a challenge, and a game they enjoyed. Now it was up to Greta to identify the source.

Her brow furrowed in concentration, Greta shook her head. “A hint, just one.”

“Elsinore.” Volmer arched an eyebrow and waited. He shifted his position slightly so she could see the darkening outline of Castel Grunespan in the distance.

Greta caught both clues. “Hamlet, Prince of Denmark!” She twisted to her left and regarded the shelves filled with books. “Have you read all of them, *Opa*?”

“Every one. Some more than once.”

She reflected on this. “The Bible too?’

“The Bible too.”

“Why, *Opa*?

“Why more than once? Well, some books, like your schoolbooks, must be read more than once to learn what they have to tell you. They are read for knowledge. Other books can be read at different times in your life and you understand them differently each time. There are layers of meaning and as you grow and mature, you discover something new with each reading. Sometimes, it’s as simple as revisiting an old friend. The story captures your mind.”

“The Bible is all of those, *Opa*.”

“Yes, little one, it certainly is.”

Greta squirmed to standing and walked over to the wooden stand that held the Jensen family Bible. Thin, faded ribbons marked important places in the Book, where the births, marriages, and deaths of generations were recorded. It held the history of her family. She rested a hand across the faint marks of centuries past. “There is order here, like my science journal.” Opening to the *Book of Isaiah*, she studied the ornate letter that began the chapter. “This is so beautiful.”

“It’s a story. A story in a letter,” said Volmer, as he explained the intricate details of the illuminated manuscript. “The monks labored all their lives in this endeavor. Each copy of the Bible was done by hand, and each chapter began with this," he pointed to the gold embossed letter.

"Illumination means light," said Greta, but her voice was a question.

"In this regard it means enlightenment," corrected Volmer. "The monks began each day's work with a prayer that their minds would be enlightened, and they drew their prayer here."

"They must have gotten really tired, doing this for their whole lives," she said. "Grandpa, why are some men good and some men bad?"

"Ah, now you speak of philosophy." Volmer pulled a thoughtful draw on his pipe. "Some will say it is the fault of life's troubles. Others that it is the work of Satan. All I know for sure is that we have choices. We may choose to do good or we may choose to do evil. We have the gift of free will."

"Hitler is doing evil," Greta said.

"He's using his free will to cause great harm, that is for sure." Volmer looked at Greta. "My father told me, when I was a boy and had asked that same question, that the same fire that melts wax, makes steel. It speaks to your character, little one. Trouble and difficulties are part of life. You cannot escape them. If your character is strong, then the troubles of life will make you even stronger. If your character is not strong, you will wilt like one of your ferns after it's plucked from the ground. He smiled at his granddaughter and touched her cheek with his rough hand. "There are difficult times ahead, little one. But don't fret. You will be steel." He chuckled softly and Greta blushed.

Chapter Twenty

Sankt Peder

Denmark is relatively small, as countries go, about half the size of South Carolina. It's made up of the peninsula, Jutland, which is attached by land, if not sentiment, to Germany. There are also over 400 islands, with the capital, Copenhagen, located on the largest, the island of Zealand. There is an extensive ferry system to link the islands with each other and the mainland, and the ferries roads, and trains, make Denmark an easy country to get around in. Mostly Denmark is flat. My mother used to joke that when the ants made a new ant hill it became a government-registered landform and its height was carefully entered in the national statistics as the new highest mountain in the country.

My nose was fogging up the window glass on the bus as I traveled across Jutland from Kolding to Esbjerg and then to Sankt Peder, and I cleared it with my sleeve so as not to miss a single sight along the way. It had been close to ten years since I had been back and the bus trip was reacquainting me with the scenery. While everything in Europe is on a smaller scale than in America, with so many borders to cross and customs stations to pass through, and currencies that changed with the borders as well, sometimes travel was at best, inconvenient. The language differences, though, were not such a problem. Most of us spoke at least two and sometimes three foreign tongues. French was the language of literature, German the language of science, but English was by far and away the most popular and the most useful.

Overall, people didn't travel extensively, and I wondered if the ones who did set off on their odysseys and never returned except, like me, to visit. And maybe the ones who wanted to travel were the ones who immigrated to America. Perhaps that was true. It was an interesting thought.

I did know that my family in Denmark did not understand just how vast a country America was. In fact, Inge spoke of New York and San Francisco as if they were within hailing distance of each other. She had begged me to bring her some souvenirs from the World's Fair, as if it were a grocery store down on the corner. I'd promised to try, and that was as good as a blood vow as far as she was concerned. So here I was, with my bag of presents for Lars, Inge, Greta, Anna, and Volmer, and a few extras in case another relative or two materialized during the course of the weekend. I wouldn't tell them I'd picked the souvenirs up at the airport instead of the Fair. I'd also found a rather ostentatious rhinestone ring as well and it now was doing substitution service for my wedding band.

We passed through wheat fields and oak forests, beech groves and along small rivers on our way to the opposite coast. I was relaxed, or as relaxed as I was going to get. The meat orders were coming in steadily from Berlin, and I'd gotten good shots of them with the small camera I kept in my pocketbook by the switchboard. Nothing of any great significance yet. The orders seemed to be fairly innocuous and spread out over large areas. If the big shipments were coming, they hadn't come yet.

Sometimes making the transfer of information on an assignment is difficult. This time, everything had fallen into place without a whole lot of extra effort on my part. The bus driver who had the Kolding-Esbjerg route was the brother in law of the harbormaster from Copenhagen who was the nephew of the wife of the English Ambassador in Copenhagen.

This chain was a bit complicated, but the result was that information from me could find its way back to England in the diplomatic pouch. And so, with everyone ready to do their part, the stressful part of this trip had been accomplished, the film transfer to the bus driver having gone off without a hitch. The actual conversation resembled something from a very bad Hollywood production. It was so bad, it worked. I'd purchased a bouquet of daffodils from a street vendor before boarding the bus, and the driver had provided me the expected greeting, "Daffodils are always nice, but yellow tulips are my wife's favorite flower."

Extending the flowers to him, and passing off the film as our hands touched around the stems, I allowed him a sniff, replying, "But tulips have no fragrance." Well the text lacked imagination, but these lines were not being penned by screenwriters. They worked and that was enough. Besides, the flowers really were for Inge, and she did prefer daffodils. Who was I arguing with, for heaven's sakes? Focus, Katrin, focus.

I had an entire weekend to visit with Inge and her family, and I intended to make the most of it. Even though Inge had faithfully sent photographs of Greta, the last time I had actually seen her she was only four years old. Hardly more than a toddler, and now nearly done with childhood. I knew I wasn't the first to note the fleeting nature of time, but the reality hit me hard. We moved through this life so quickly, with hardly enough time to accomplish what we must have been sent here to do. But these were deeper thoughts than I wanted to think today. For now I was doing the job I was trained for and one unexpected but welcome aspect of that was the chance to see my sister and her family and find out the meaning of Inge's urgent message. I'd pushed that thought to the back of my mind but it was still there, niggling at me. Now, I wanted an explanation.

We were nearly to Esbjerg now, and as the bus pulled into the station, I could see Inge waving heartily, standing on tiptoe as if that would give her a better look inside the bus. A broad smile on her face, tears running down her cheeks, and yes, a bouquet of daffodils in her hand. This was too good.

I yanked the old Gladstone bag from the luggage compartment and bumped off the bus, the suitcase jabbing me in the calves, as I swung down the stairs and onto the ground, where I was caught up in the onslaught of embraces and kisses. At some point we exchanged daffodils and Lars was finally able to separate us long enough to propel us to the truck, an arm around each of our shoulders for control and the Gladstone dangling from his right hand like an extra appendage. With Inge's daffodils in my right hand, and my daffodils in Inge's left, we looked as if we had stepped out of an oil painting entitled, *Homecoming.*

Lars, firmly in charge now, held the door as Inge and I climbed into the truck. He'd even managed to keep the Gladstone from whacking into my shoulder blade or collarbone, as he carried it along.

Inge was a non-stop news event.

"We had a submarine sighting!" she said. "And there was a man on the submarine who got off and rowed to shore. We all saw him."

"All?" I asked.

She nodded vigorously. "*Ja!* There was Lars and me and Volmer and Anna and Greta and Marta Jorgensen. We watched him. He didn't see us," she added.

"*Ja.* He was met by a woman. They drove together towards Kolding," Lars said.

"Lars followed them," Inge said. "He's still working on it."

Lars nodded, a grim expression on his face.

Conversation moved on to the new Pastor, Karl Mueller.

"He's nice enough," Inge said, although there seemed to be some uncertainty in her voice. She was tentative, searching for the right words to describe him. "He's a bookish type and he spends evenings reading quietly in the parsonage, alone."

"You seem worried, Inge," I said.

"I don't know. I mean he visits the elderly and the sick and there's nothing I can put my finger on, but, I don't know. Open. That's it. He's not as open as Pastor Lindstrom had been." She left it there.

Lars was frowning at the road ahead, as he merged into traffic. He didn't take his eyes off the road, but offered his own opinion. "He is a contradiction. There are secrets there, and I am not certain he is to be trusted. It's just a professional hunch. There is more, but it will keep until we're home."

I nodded. Professional hunches were usually built upon observation and experience. They were, for the most part, to be trusted. If Lars's hunches were true, what was the pastor's purpose here? Sankt Peder was hardly a hotbed of anything. It was a hardworking community that minded its own business for the most part. Friendly and welcoming, as well. A person would have to be a bit of an odd duck to ruffle feathers.

"We'll be having the Open House for Pastor after the Easter Sunday service," Inge continued. "It just didn't seem proper to have a celebration so close on the heels of *Frue* Jorgensen's funeral." Inge patted my knee. "You've come just in time to help bake."

What a devious mind my sister had. I no more baked than I crocheted with chain mail. "Bake?" I managed to put a world of meaning in that one word. "I don't bake. I have never baked. I won't bake." I sounded like a petulant three year old. If I had been able to stamp a foot, I would have. It would have emphasized my point. The most aggravating thing about my sister is that she ignores me when it suits her. In that regard she's a great deal like my husband. Now was no different. She changed the subject instead as a brief tactical retreat.

"Greta has a surprise for you. She's been working on it all week." Inge turned to see my face and she grinned, and I noticed for the first time that she and Lars had exactly the same smile. Maybe it was true that after so many years you started to look alike. Did I look like John? I wondered. I hope he didn't look like me. That would be unsettling.

The house had received a fresh coat of paint and looked ready for Easter itself. "We decided it was time to make a change, Lars explained. "So we went from that mustard yellow to a peach. At least that's what Inge says it is." He looked at her fondly. "She's got quite an eye for color."

She certainly did. The house reminded me of a fruit salad. With its peach clapboard siding and lemon yellow shutters, it was quite attractive in a healthy, edible way. The perfect house for a cook.

Velkommen Tante Katrin! proclaimed the festive banner that spanned the doorway off the front porch. Directly underneath it was my not so little niece, Greta, who was waving with both arms over her head, pointing to the sign as if somehow I would miss it unless directed to it. As most women do, with occasions both joyous and solemn, I was crying, Inge was crying, Greta was about to cry, and Lars was shaking his head at the strange ways of women.

Greta bounded off the front porch and raced to meet us, and I wrapped my arms around her and kissed her cheek, then held her back at arms' length to utter the words all women speak and all children dread. "Greta, you've grown! You're all grown up! You are so beautiful!" Greta accepted this with grace and Inge beamed. Lars had collected my bag and now proceeded up the stairs, calling over his shoulder that he'd put it in the guest room for me. He disappeared into the house, leaving us to our tears and laughter.

In my room, I spent a few moments freshening up and setting out the gifts I had brought for them. I hadn't had anything resembling a normal routine in the last two weeks, and I could feel it catching up to me. When I stood I could still feel the motion of the bus and the sensation that everything was moving very quickly extended beyond the physical. Time would soon bring my stay to a close and even though this was just one more stop on my whirlwind European tour, it was home, and for the weekend at least, nothing was going to come between me and total rest and relaxation. Of that I was absolutely and completely certain.

Inge had cooked and she had baked. No surprise there. We had an absolute feast. Nothing was burned, underdone, limp, or otherwise less than perfect, and after dinner we distributed our gifts for each other, and I felt something like a wise man, or woman, who had finally reached Bethlehem or Nazareth or wherever the Holy Family was living at the time. The specific geography escaped me. Whatever, I was home.

For Lars I had felt slippers made from the wool of the sheep my friend Ardis raised. She had soaked the wool and added Ivory soap flakes and worked it until it had become felt. The process was marvelous to watch and Lars slipped them on his feet and remarked he had never had a more comfortable pair. "And they will soften as you wear them and will last a long time," I said, as he stretched his long legs out to admire his slippers.

Inge's gift was a white bone china tea cup and saucer decorated with red roses and gold lettering that proclaimed "New York World's Fair, 1939-1940." I knew Inge loved roses, and there was an active group in New York trying to make the rose the official state flower. She enjoyed hearing that.

"You have official flowers in America?" she asked.

"Official flowers, animals, and some other things as well. Even the months are given official titles. I think May is Official Cheese Month, but I'm not too sure. Anyway, yes, everything is very official there."

"Such a country," she said.

Such a country indeed. For Greta I had brought a botany book about ferns of the world and her eyes lit up as if the very stars of heaven were held within her. "Your mama has told me all about your interests, and I thought this might be a good addition to your library."

"*Tante* Katrin, this is just perfect. I do love it. Truly." She reached across and hugged my knees, as she was in her favorite spot, sitting on the floor, Indian style. "This will answer my question! I told *Opa* you would know!"

I hugged her back and opened my own gifts. Inge's had a suspicious shape, and I just knew what it was. "Oh. Inge," I said. "You really shouldn't have." But she had. This tome was *The Complete Muffin Cookbook*, and I knew I would spend many pleasant hours, perusing the art contained therein. It was good to know that in this changing world, there still remained some constants. Inge was one of the constants in my life and never tired of her mission to turn me into a cook worthy of the Nissen name. That I collected her books and proudly displayed them solely for their art was beside the point.

There was a sweater Greta had knit for me, a robin's egg blue with hand painted buttons of miniature bluebells with delicate green leaves. I was embraced by family and especially I was surrounded by Art.

Chapter Twenty-One

Sankt Peder

"Are you ready for a talk?" I was drying the breakfast dishes, while Inge washed. Washing dishes is the perfect time and place for a heart to heart. One of the advantages of being a woman is that you have the camaraderie of the kitchen, a place that rightfully has been called the heart of the home. And I had been patient as long as I could.

Inge paused with a soapy plate in her hand. "Just wait a little longer. There's something I want you to see first. Wait until tonight?" Her face was as serious as I had ever seen it, and I could only nod my assent.

"All right, but remember I'm on the bus tomorrow and won't be back until the weekend."

"You'll know everything tonight. I promise."

And we left it at that.

The parsonage was a white clapboard home that had housed Sankt Peder's clergy for well over a hundred years. The congregation kept it in good repair, and as a result of their efforts, it had a comfortable, lived-in, welcoming kind of feeling about it.

The minister's study was located on the second floor. Dark wood paneling and rows of bookshelves lined the wall cater-corner to the large casement window that opened onto a handsome view of the ocean. While the beauty of the view was lost on Karl, the utility of it was not. He sat before it by the hour, his high-powered spotting scope secured on its tripod and open at his side, a small journal, with six neatly ruled columns. Each column had a title: *Name of Vessel, Type of Vessel, Country of Origin, Date Spotted, Heading*, and the last column was simply labeled *Kill*, a testimony to the effectiveness of his personal assault on the Allied naval forces. Red Xs in this column followed the entries for the *SS Athenia, HMS Ark Royal, HMS Courageous, SS Clement, Stonegate, HMS Royal Oak, Rawalpindi.* Merchant ships and passenger liners all with a final destination of Davy Jones Locker, courtesy of the man known as Ronin.

Each night at 2000 hours, Karl sent on the day's sightings to Berlin via wireless transmitter. Following his nightly contact, he replaced the transmitter and his journal on a shelf he had constructed inside the fireplace in his room.

Everything was neat and orderly, although one loose end from the Dagmar incident pestered him. He still needed to move her car from the barn and return it to her apartment. Wednesday. This Wednesday, his free day, he would drive it away and return by bus and the job would be complete. He actually regretted having killed her, and that regret surprised him. There might have been another way, but there was no time to waste, and even though she had been useful, he shook his head. Useful. Well, she had provided some diversion. She'd also followed orders, most of the time. She'd shoved the old man into traffic, where the autobus had finished him off. That had saved him some work and gotten him here more quickly than if he'd had to kill the pastor himself. But he couldn't trust her, and that had cost her.

Outside the window, looking up from the shadows, Inge whispered to her sister. "This is what I wanted you to see. He is always watching the sea. Marta Johanssen saw him first and she told Anna, who told me."

I processed this chain of command. Sankt Peder had elevated gossip to an art form.

"We are the Daughters of Gefion and we watch to protect our homeland," Inge drew herself up proudly. "We are going to help the Allies. Somehow." Then she continued, "And always with the telescope. I think there is something going on." She gave a firm nod of her head. I wanted you to see for yourself. What do you make of it?"

I reminded myself that nothing, nothing, was going to spoil my quiet enjoyment of family this weekend. Absolutely nothing. This was just a stroll, a sisterly stroll through the neighborhood before bed. "Perhaps he just loves the ocean?" I was reaching here. There was something fishy going on. I groaned at my own pun. Inge might be inclined to exaggerate a bit, but these were dangerous times, and the minister's reclusive behavior seemed at odds with his calling. "No," I reassured her. "Something doesn't feel right."

Above our heads the window shade was lowered, and shortly thereafter the lamp was extinguished.

"I have a feeling there is more to this man than meets the eyes," Inge still stared at the now darkened window.

"Or less," I added.

"And there's one more thing that's strange. I'll have to show you."

We walked down the path past the parsonage and followed the dirt driveway that led to the barn in the field at the rear.

"I'm not wearing the right footwear for tromping across the pastures, Inge," I said, pausing to kick a stone out of my right shoe. I looked like an ostrich with an itch. Or maybe it was a flamingo. I paused. It wasn't important and Inge had moved on ahead.

"In here," she whispered, and motioned for me to hurry up. I abandoned my efforts at rock removal and caught up with her.

"It's right here," she said, as she lifted a tarpaulin from a vehicle parked by the far wall.

It was a black Mercedes and a brand new one to boot. I looked at Inge and shrugged. "Whose car is that?"

"I don't know. I don't know how long it's been here, but I don't think it's been here very long. There's no dust on the tarpaulin. Greta told me about it just before we left. She'd been off on one of her plant hunts and she got curious when she saw the barn door closed. It's never closed," Inge added.

I stole a quick look behind me and then opened the driver side door. I reached over to the glove box and rummaged through the papers inside. "Good God Almighty," I said. "This is Dagmar's car." I backed out quickly and motioned for Inge to lower the tarpaulin.

"Did you say Dagmar?" she asked.

"I did, why?"

"Dagmar Strasser was the name of the woman who was driving the car that picked up the man dropped off by the submarine. Lars found that out when he followed her back to Kolding and traced the license plate. He's still waiting on more information."

"Dagmar is a Nazi spy?" Suddenly several pieces fell into place. It explained her erratic work schedule and possibly her extended absence from work. Was her assignment over? But why was her car here? Strange. "Dagmar is the file clerk at the meat plant in Kolding, where I've been working," I said.

Inge's eyes grew wide. We heard a rustle outside and froze. "We'd better get back to the house before someone comes asking questions," I said and Inge nodded. We turned quietly and made our way back home, disturbing a raccoon foraging alongside the barn.

Lars was sitting on the front porch reading the paper when we arrived back at the house. "I was ready to go looking for you, he said. I was starting to worry." He set down the paper. "She's my second in command, Katrin. She can do what I cannot. Men in Sankt Peder do not routinely stroll along the streets arm in arm," he smiled. "What is the report tonight?"

"Watching out to sea with the telescope, again," she said, "and some more news on that woman. Exciting news, Lars. Her car is in the parsonage barn! Katrin found the registration papers in the glove box."

"She works at the meat plant, Lars", I said, "but she's not been seen for several days now. It's possible she's moved on."

Lars nodded. "If her only job was to be available to escort the passenger, she may have. Strange she'd leave her car behind, though. I'm still working on the connection between the passenger and the pastor. Mueller will have his free day on Wednesday. If he goes into Esbjerg, I will have time to search the parsonage," Lars said. "I'm doing a background check on him right now. I've got a man watching the woman's apartment. If she surfaces, we'll know."

"He's watched everywhere he goes," Inge added.

"Exciting evening. Anyone who thinks the country is a peaceful, quiet place, has never been here. Oh, I almost forgot, Inge," Lars said. "Anna called. She needs the punch bowl for the reception. I told her I'd tell you when you got back."

Inge nodded and she and I went into the house to fetch the bowl. "The English are rationing gasoline." Inge, still the champion of the *non sequitur.* I figured this was heading somewhere, though. "And food. So are the French. And now the Germans have been told to turn in their radios." She pressed her lips together and nodded her head. She'd located the punch bowl on the pantry floor, behind the canning supplies.

"It will come here too, you know." She wiped a tendril of golden hair out of her eyes.

"I think that's pretty much a certainty."

"I've never asked you to tell me what you do." She

looked at me, her eyes steady, as she hauled the bowl out onto the kitchen counter.

"Inge."

"No, I don't need to know. That's not what I'm trying to say. Very soon, life is going to change and there is nothing I can do to stop that. Perhaps it will never be the same again." She took a deep breath and smoothed the front of her dress with her hand. "I'm not a clairvoyant, but I can see this future clearly, at least the immediate future. We will lose our independence to that monster from Austria. While there is still time, I want to cash in our inheritance, den hundrede tusinde. I have a plan for it. I need your blessing. Our money will be gone after the Nazis are in control. Then it will be too late."

So, there it was. Her reason for the note with the check.

"Inge," I began, "that is your money as much as it is mine. Mama and Papa wanted us to use it as we saw fit. You have that right. Of course you can cash out. I'll write the permission letter tonight for you to take to the banker on Monday." So that was all she needed from me. That was simple, but no, there was a devious gleam in her eye that told me there was more. I decided to sit down and hear it all.

"We will need supplies. Guns and ammunition, I suppose." Her lips were pursed as she accessed the contents of a mental inventory she had created. "And petrol. We will need to lay in supplies of petrol." Then came her little bombshell, a word that turned out to be quite apt, given the circumstances. "With your share added to mine, we will make a good start." The prosecution rested her case, having presented it to the jury for consideration.

What I have always admired about my sister is her ability to frame her requests in such a way that a person would come across as a complete heel if she were to deny them. She is a gifted negotiator. The Daughters of Gefion were shaping up to be formidable adversaries.

I asked, "Inge, when did you take up firearms?"

"Next Monday." Her voice was prim, and her hands were folded in front of her.

I winced at the thought of Inge with a Gatling gun or a Thompson. "Have you talked to Lars about this?"

"*Ja*, I told him."

"You *told* him. And?"

"And that is that. I am already looking for a suitable place to hide our equipment. A barn will be good, and I am investigating the parsonage barn tomorrow. It is convenient, yet out of the way. There is the problem of the minister, though." She looked concerned. "But we will deal with that, somehow."

So far she had secured funding, generated a supply list, had checked into somc promising real estate, and was probably already recruiting volunteers for the Danish Resistance. The thought that there might be other Inges throughout Denmark and France and the rest of Europe scared the hell out of me. It also made me fiercely proud of my sister, the Amazon housewife.

"So you will help. *Ja*?" It really wasn't a question but rather a statement of purpose. Recruitment wasn't going to be a problem for her either, I could see.

I tried one more tack. "Inge, this is noble and wonderful and very brave. But you have no idea what war is really like. There is death and pain and suffering and big bombs that blow things up. Really big bombs." I wasn't getting anywhere. "Boom!" I tried a feeble sound effect to no avail. No one was going to blow up Inge's munitions dump.

"Inge, war is…hell!" Thank you, General Tecumseh Sherman, for the assist here.

Inge was fired up now and all hell was literally breaking loose right here in the kitchen. "And you think living under *Der Führer's* Third Reich is going to be heaven? That, Katrin, will be hell on earth. The Germans will take our sons and husbands and make them fight for them. And if they refuse, the Nazis will kill us. Who will be left to fight then,

Katrin? Old men and children and women. We didn't ask for this. We have no choice. We must finish what they have started."

I knew there would be no winning this argument. Her closer was air tight.

"You can only die once. It should count for something." Her face flushed, she trembled with the force of her words. And now, having chalked up her first victory in the European Allied Campaign, Inge produced pen and paper and secured her first military contract. I wrote the letter and signed it right there in the kitchen.

"Come, Katrin. Come look at the night sky with me." She held out her hand and with her arm across my shoulders, we walked to the window. "Remember what Mama used to tell us when we were children?" Inge pointed up at the stars. "Those are God's candles. He put them in the heavens so the darkest night would shine." She turned to look in my eyes. "The darkest night is coming but we are God's candles on earth. We will shine until the night is past."

That night as I sank into the soft depths of the featherbed, I realized just what I had been sent here to protect. It wasn't the commerce of nations, although that was important. It wasn't the rightful rule of law, although that was important as well. It was more than either of those things. It was the fundamental security of home and hearth. I wanted my family to be safe from harm, and even more, I wanted everyone's family to be safe. It was really just that simple.

Chapter Twenty-Two

Kolding

I'd returned to Kolding after a restful weekend and had walked straight into a hornet's nest, with Dagmar the absent queen bee or hornet or wasp around which all the buzz was happening. She had not shown up to work again today, and Helga, Wally, and I decided that I should visit her apartment after work. I wasn't keen on getting involved in this little drama. John had warned me about just this sort of thing. Involvement. It was my middle name. But what was I to do? They needed my help. And for all I knew, so did Dagmar.

By this time my old bicycle legs had returned and I cruised across town without strain to Dagmar's digs, which were in a well to do section of the city. It was obvious she wasn't hurting for money, and I wondered if the Nazis paid their spies this well or if some inheritance was the source of her income. Perhaps she was moonlighting somewhere after hours at the plant. Whatever she did paid well.

A quick scan of the street didn't reveal anything unusual. Some pedestrian traffic, bicycles moving along at a good clip, and a few automobiles parked by the curb. Inside one, a man was reading a newspaper. Probably waiting for his wife, I guessed.

There was no answer at Dagmar's door so I rang up the landlady, a peroxide blonde, whose hair was pinned so tightly into a bun that the skin was stretched at the corners of her eyes. The heightened color of her cheeks was due in part to the spiderlike network of red and blue veins that crosshatched their way across her face. This woman's favorite libation was not coffee, not tea. This woman got about the day's business in a serious fashion. She stared at me through bleary eyes and heaved a ninety proof sigh. Her breath could kill a camel at three kilometers, and I backed up a respectful distance to give the vapors a little room to dissipate. With her feet planted far enough apart to ensure some balance, she tightened the sash of her bathrobe. I expected she'd be thus casually attired the rest of the day.

Dagmar's landlady, *Frue* Nilsson, was a suspicious sort and it took a few minutes to convince her I was on the up and up. No, she hadn't seen Dagmar. She didn't keep track of her tenants, as long as they paid their rent on time and didn't have noisy parties. I had an idea that she did keep very good track of her tenants and suggested that maybe Dagmar had asked her to keep an eye on the place while she was gone. Of course that would mean she'd need to be able to keep them open, something that I doubted she could manage far along into the course of the day. But you never knew. Some alcoholics seemed to function on a marginal level for quite a while until their bodies gave out.

"We're just so worried about her. It's not like her to miss work. She's always so punctual and responsible," I lied through my teeth. I figured a caring concern might break through the roadblock. "Could we just check to be sure she is not ill? I knocked and knocked on the door but there was no answer. Not a sound. Everyone is so worried," I repeated. "Maybe we should call the police?" I found myself matching her slight sway, as I tried to maintain eye contact. That did it. No way did she want the cops beating down her doors.

"Wait there." She wobbled a bit as she turned, and in a

few minutes, she returned with a ring of keys and clanked upstairs to Dagmar's apartment like the drunken porter in *Macbeth*. She scrutinized the assortment like a bridge player determining trump, finally settling on the desired key. She rapped on the door, while she kept one eye semi-focused on me. I could tell she figured I hadn't knocked hard enough or long enough or maybe even had the wrong apartment, but I just smiled expectantly and waited.

Her result was the same as mine. No result at all. She closed one eye to narrow the playing field which probably consisted of several doors and a multitude of keyholes, and inserted the key. In spite of avowed disinterest, I could tell she was burning to see what was inside. What was inside was nothing. Well, nothing in the shape of Dagmar, at least.

The apartment was your basic three room flat, four if you considered the bathroom. The rooms were spacious. There was a parlor, kitchen with dining area, and bedroom. The front door led directly into the parlor, which led into the kitchen. The bedroom door was to the left of the parlor, and the bathroom was off that. But it was the furnishings that stopped us in our tracks. The landlady halted first, causing me to nearly walk up her back. I gave a whistle and the tipsy landlady's eyes bugged out of her head. I checked my watch. Yep, still 1940, but you couldn't prove it here. We had walked into the Palace of Versailles, the Louvre, and the hideout of Genghis Khan all rolled into one. Louis XIV furniture, Persian rugs, and Rembrandts on the wall gave a decidedly rich flavor to the flat. The theme was money. The unifying color was black. The effect was Opulent. Ornate. Ostentatious. Overdone. Overwhelming. Holy shit. Seeing is believing, but this defied comprehension.

Whenever I'm faced with a problem of gargantuan proportions, I find it helps to break it down into manageable chunks. I decided to approach the lair of Dagmar in the same way. Once my eyes had adjusted to the gloom that permeated the place, in part caused by the drawn damask draperies and heavy shades, I took stock. The Persian carpet in the parlor was a deep maroon with black and cream sculpted designs. The one in the bedroom was of similar design in the same colors. We were talking major capital outlay.

"Boulle." I breathed the name as I examined first the armoire, then the console table by the front door.

"What?" *Frue* Nilsson was following on my elbow, her keys still dangling from her hand. All she needed was a chatelaine and she'd fit right in at court.

"Boulle," I repeated. "Andre Charles Boulle. The cabinet maker to Louis XIV." I looked at *Frue* Nilsson. "These are priceless antiques." I examined the ebony wood inlaid with tortoiseshell and brass, the gilt and bronze mounts. The marble and granite table tops. Against the far wall there was a cabinet shaped like a sarcophagus, set on scroll legs, like a table, with drawers beneath. And dividing the parlor from the kitchen was a cabinet with a serpentine front and carved feet and panels. Entwined serpents with golden fangs framed an oversized mirror that would have reflected the view outside the window, had the drapes and shades been opened. As it was, the glass was dark. In this kingdom, for the room seemed more suited to a man than a woman, there was no fairest of them all. It was all strange and marvelous.

Two Rembrandts hung from the wall on golden ropes. *The Night Watch*. Surely this was a copy, but I wasn't really so sure. I studied the subject matter, the group of city guardsmen waiting the command to fall in line. Two men in the front, one in yellow, the other in black, and a little girl, also dressed in yellow. Directly opposite, watching the men was *Portrait of a Lady with an Ostrich Feather Fan*. She seemed unimpressed with the guardsmen.

The bedroom door was ajar and I opened it the rest of the way. A massive bed, intricately carved, occupied center stage. A circular canopy hung suspended from the ceiling, and rich damask bed draperies in black and cream and deepest red were tied by each bedpost with silken golden ropes. Above the bed, still one more Rembrandt, *Bathsheba at her Bath."* I was struck by the quasi-pornographic effect of it all. Indulgence. Satiety. I wouldn't have been surprised had a satyr shown itself. In fact I actually was hoping one would. It would have been a nice touch, but it didn't happen.

The closet was full, as I had expected it would be. One section of hangers held work outfits, business dresses, skirts, blouses, and sweaters. Then there was another grouping of designer gowns, furs, lingerie and dressing gowns. There were at least a dozen pairs of Italian pumps in coordinating colors lined up beneath the gowns. The other side of the closet housed a man's wardrobe, also decidedly upscale. Where Dagmar's tastes ran to Italian, the man's were French. Who was the mystery man? Was he paying the rent? I looked at the landlady, but she just shrugged, shook her head, and hiccupped softly.

Very interesting, and that, with certainty, was the queen of understatements. So there was more to little Dagmar than met the eye. A great deal more, it seemed. I wondered what her story actually was, but there were no answers here, just questions layered upon themselves like a wedding cake. I thanked the landlady, who remained standing agape in the middle of the room. Speechless, she raised a hand in farewell, stunned into sobriety, and I let myself out of the apartment. I paused at the bottom of the steps and looked back up the stairs. I'd give a week's salary to find out what her secrets were. Not that I was nosy, just professionally curious. I grinned. It was an advantage to be inquisitive in our line of work. No, I corrected myself, it was an absolute necessity.

Our AWOL employee had been transformed into a mysterious femme fatale. Which one of Dagmar's personalities, I wondered, was actually missing? Regardless, I believed that when, or if, Dagmar returned, she would find her rent had been substantially increased. It appeared she could afford it. I had a bad feeling about this. No woman worth her womanhood walks away leaving that much Italian shoe leather behind. I wondered just how much I should share with Helga and couldn't find any good reason to withhold what I had found out. It didn't impact my assignment in any way, and she and Wally might be better off knowing more about their little file clerk. No, tomorrow I would report my findings to Helga, and if Dagmar had not rematerialized by then, it was definitely time to call in the authorities.

As I pedaled back towards my room, I set the problem of Dagmar aside and switched into professional espionage mode. I needed a strategy that would permit me to photograph those orders that had been placed today. One caller had identified himself as Quartermaster something or other. That would mean he was in charge of supplies. It was a good lead. I just needed to find the paperwork that matched. It would work out, I told myself. It had to.

I maneuvered through the streets, and pulled up at my lodgings. My thoughts had so thoroughly absorbed me, I couldn't recall having negotiated the last several blocks. I had gone on autopilot. That lapse had me chastising myself. I couldn't afford not to be aware. Ever.

Once upstairs in my room, I retrieved my camera from its hiding place, which was a cereal box in plain sight on the center shelf above the little hotplate that sat on the counter. *Frue* Pedersson supplied breakfast and dinner, but provided the necessary equipment for those wishing to make a light meal in their rooms.

My fingers closed around the small rectangular box I'd stuffed two-thirds of the way down the box of Kellogg's Corn Flakes. I crunched a few flakes as I withdrew the camera from its hiding place, took it out of the protective box, and stowed it in my pocketbook. I was replacing the cereal box on the shelf, when the colorful illustration on the front spoke to me. It wanted me to eat some. I was a bit hungry and if corn was now suitable for breakfast, why not for a bedtime snack? Leave it to the Americans, I thought, to figure out how to turn an ear of corn into flakes. It tasted fine and even better than corn, and didn't get stuck in your teeth.

I padded downstairs with the box of cereal, took the bottle of milk from the ice box, a banana from the fruit bowl on the table, the sugar bowl from the counter, a clean teaspoon from the dish rack on the sink, and seated myself at the table to create a gourmet delight. No bowl and no knife to slice the banana. This simple, convenient meal was becoming more complicated than I'd anticipated. Why are the simple things the most difficult? I sighed and pushed myself back from the table to correct the oversight, glancing out the kitchen window on my way back to the sink.

Darkness had fallen quickly. The night was clear and stars sparkled against a backdrop of black infinity. The streetlamp cast a golden circle of light on the cobbled street and spotlighted two lovers walking hand in hand in the cool night air. My own lover was absent from me and I missed him. Cold cereal is cold comfort on a lonely night. The room seemed suddenly too small and too big at the same time and the sounds of my eating echoed in the stillness.

I cleaned up after myself and trudged up the stairs to my room, where I laid out my clothes for morning. It promised to be a busy day and photographing those orders was the most important thing on my list. Bless her. Dagmar wasn't much help when she was at work, but she was turning out to be extremely useful *in absentia*. As a distraction, she worked really well. No one was the least bit interested in what I was doing at the switchboard console and now I was fervently hoping she'd be gone at least another day. That would be enough. Just one more day. I gave my pocketbook a pat for luck and climbed into bed.

Chapter Twenty-Three

Kolding

Bicycling Danes bound for the central business district and the outlying industrial sector resembled a flock of well-behaved migratory birds, legs pumping industriously in the human equivalent of wings. A newcomer to the flock, I merged politely into the stream and found my slot in formation. Danes are organized, efficient, and healthy. I am healthy too, I muttered, giving my all to keep up. Ten minutes later I arrived, skidded into my spot alongside the plant, set the kickstand and stood on quivering underpinnings. Achieving an effortless appearance was going to require effort.

I had beat Helga this morning, but that was by design. When she arrived fifteen minutes later, it was still ten minutes before the official start of work, and I was busily alphabetizing the file folders on Dagmar's desk. I looked up as she entered and greeted her with a helpful smile.

"I'll get these cleaned up today when there's a lull at the switchboard," I said. "Just stack today's to the left of the short pile," I pointed to the ones I had already sorted for the filing cabinet, "and I'll do them as I can."

Helga scanned her own desk which was heaped with

work and nodded. "How did you make out yesterday? Was she home?"

"Not home and no sign of where she might be." I set the files down. I asked, "Did she ever mention a boyfriend?" Maybe she and *Herre* what's his name were having a romantic rendezvous in Copenhagen. Maybe she had eloped? I discarded the thought. She had left her sexy lingerie at home, along with her Parisian perfume and expensive jewelry. No, it just didn't add up. Wherever Dagmar was, she hadn't planned on being gone this long.

"No, no one that I recall. All she talks about is becoming an actress, the next Sarah Bernhardt." Helga struck a pose with the back of her right hand covering her forehead, chin uplifted to an imaginary spotlight. Her head bobbed downward. "She's really not a bad sort, just young."

Helga was feeling generous this morning. Wally had that effect on her and since Wally had decided that it had been too late to walk home after their supper together at Helga's house, they had spent the night in unbridled passion. So Helga had roses in her cheeks that matched the roses in her dress, and there was a sparkle in her eyes. She was utterly adorable. A woman in love.

Dagmar. Dagmar, on the other hand, might be young, but the woman whose life I had glimpsed in that apartment yesterday was no innocent. I straightened up the first batch of filing and carried a new stack over to the switchboard, setting it to the side of the console where I could work on it between calls. So far, I had not run across the military orders. There was a full day's work ahead of me here and if fate worked the way it usually does, the orders would be at the bottom of the pile.

Helga stood in the center of the office, hands on hips, biting her lower lip. "I'll talk to Waldemar. He'll know what to do next." She set her handbag on her desk and pawed around inside until she produced her compact. She freshened her lipstick, blotted her lips, and left in search of Wally.

Even in times of duress, a woman understands the importance of looking one's best. Helga never missed an opportunity to look good for Wally.

With Helga off on her mission, I turned my attention to my own. Two small orders headed to Berlin, and one larger one being shipped all the way to Dusseldorf. Not the big one, though. Not the one I was looking for.

When Helga had brought Wally back to the office, they were deep in animated conversation, and now they stood alongside Dagmar's desk, which had become sort of a silent partner in their discussion. If it harbored any secrets, this was its opportune moment to reveal what it knew. However, the only sign of human occupation was in the form of Clark Gable, framed in gold filigree, and holding court center stage front. "To Dagmar with love, Clark Gable." Clark had a rather distant expression on his face, but it might have just been the dust covering the glass.

"Have you gone through her drawers?" Wally asked, looking first at Helga and then at me.

I bent my head over my work, trying to repress an evil thought. It was the idea of Helga going through Wally's drawers. I speculated if he wore floral boxers to coordinate with the ties. I shook my head to clear the idea. It was a bit more than I could handle.

"Of course not!" Helga said archly. She was incensed.

Wally's face was a mask of blank innocence. He really was a dear. "Well, then it's time we did," he said. He looked expectantly at Helga who looked at me, desperation in her eyes at the prospect of violating Dagmar's privacy, even if it was for her own good. I was all twisted around – my head was facing them, my left elbow was holding my place in the folders and I was transferring a call with my right hand. It was a fairly awkward procedure and I felt like a circus contortionist.

"Well..." Helga was still unconvinced. She looked at the desk as if it were a living creature, then at Wally, then back at me. "Of course, we must. I will look." She still didn't like the idea, but Helga was a woman who did her duty. She rubbed her hands together and straightened to her full height, before moving in for the assault. She pulled out the chair and seated herself, looking for all the world like a concert pianist about to attempt the *Goldberg Variations* on a barroom upright.

Beginning hesitantly, Helga picked up steam and confidence as she worked her way down the left side of the desk. The first drawer was stuffed with cosmetics. There were bottles of nail polish, lipstick tubes, barrettes, rouge boxes, face powder, nail files, and the other accoutrements of feminine pulchritude. The second drawer was where Dagmar stashed the back issues of her movie magazines. Helga was now plowing ahead with enthusiasm. She rummaged through the lot, shaking her head the while. The wide center drawer held the standard office supplies, none of which appeared to have seen much use. The remaining two right hand drawers proved just as fruitless, until Helga pounced on a photograph. She let out a long low whistle, which brought Wally's head leaning over her shoulder.

The photo in question was of Dagmar with a German officer. They appeared to be attending some type of society function, as Dagmar was dressed in a blue silk gown with silver pumps and matching purse. She was also wearing diamond hair clips and a diamond choker that looked to be worth a queen's ransom. All this was nothing, however. It was the figure on Dagmar's left that drew Helga's attention. The soldier's array of medals and ribbons indicated he was a career man. The single oak leaf displayed on both collars caught her eye and she swallowed hard and fell back in her chair. The roses had left her cheeks, which had turned an unbecoming shade of pale.

The man in question was *Standartenfuhrer*, the highest field officer rank in the *Schutzstaffel,* known as the *SS*. A cold chill ran down my spine and I'm sure Helga's spine as well. In the *Waffen-SS* the rank was considered the equivalent of an *Oberst*, a Colonel.

"Who's that?" Wally was riveted on Dagmar's curves. Even his deep and abiding love for Helga had not dulled his masculine appreciation of the feminine form.

Helga didn't reply. She tilted the photo to catch the best light from the window, and her eyes swept from Dagmar to the face of her companion. She let out another whistle, this one quite a bit longer than the first. "That's her father," she finally pronounced. "The age is right, the rank is right, the resemblance is there." She lifted her eyes to Wally and me. "That's the colonel, and we have a problem."

Helga dropped the photograph on the desk as if it had suddenly become too hot to hold. Wally had lost interest in the voluptuous Dagmar. My stomach turned over, and the room seemed to have become cold as death.

"I will telephone the police and report her missing." Wally spoke with a total lack of enthusiasm. He looked around the room. "Let's clean up and make sure everything is in order." He frowned at the tottering stacks on Dagmar's desk. This wouldn't do.

I jumped in. "I'll take them all now. There's room next to the console on the floor." Without waiting for a response, I abandoned the board and swooped down on the desk, gathering the lot in my arms and anchoring it with my chin. Somehow Clark had gotten caught up in the harvest, and his jaunty chin preceded me back to my station. It was a rather nice picture, and I set it down next to me for company. I could almost hear him say, "Frankly my dear, I don't give a damn where you put me." Clark and I had work to do.

Wally gave an absentminded nod and strode off down the hall to place the dreaded call. With police came questions. I for one was going to be short on answers.

Chapter Twenty-Four

Kolding

The police officer who showed up at the office later that afternoon to complete the report was a clean cut, pleasant-looking, earnest young man of about twenty-four. His blond hair was regulation cut, his uniform was neatly pressed, and his creased brow suggested he was not making any inroads in dispelling a tension headache. The clipboard he carried was filled to the straining point with forms. He was thoroughly prepared to document the disappearance of the lost battalion.

Helga showed him to a chair next to her desk, and then she sat, hands folded on her blotter, waiting nervously for the officer, Sergeant N. Andersen, to begin.

Producing a pen from his jacket pocket, Sergeant N. Andersen flipped a page over the top of his clipboard, cleared his throat, and began to work his way down the Missing Persons form.

"Name?"

"Helga Bruegger."

He entered this information in neat block letters on line one. I craned my neck to see how long the form was. It was a substantial document.

"When did you last see Fraulein Bruegger?"

Helga was now flustered. "No, I am Helga Bruegger."

"You are obviously here, then. Who are we talking about? Who is the missing person?" He drew a line through the first entry. I suspected his tension headache was worsening by the minute.

"Dagmar. Dagmar Strasser."

And so it went, with bumps and starts for the next ten minutes or so. There was not much to tell him, and even though he asked the same few questions in a variety of ways, our responses didn't vary. Our inability to fill the paper with pertinent information and his strained expression told us we were not doing our part to fill in the blank spaces. We were not Observant Citizens. In short, we were a disappointment.

What we told him was that Dagmar hadn't come to work Friday or Monday. We knew nothing of her associates or her habits outside the office, and we had gone to her apartment to check on her welfare. She wasn't there and her landlady did not know where she'd gone. We had come up short. Yes, we did have a photograph of her, which Helga handed over with a cautious gesture. And that is when Sergeant N. Andersen turned a most unattractive shade of green.

Wally entered the office and the sudden burst of noise from the plant caused the Sergeant to startle, but it relieved the painful silence that had settled over the room. Wally looked at the officer and then around the room, assuring himself that we had made it neat and tidy. Helga had even fetched the goose feather duster from the cleaning closet and had flicked it over every surface, to the point of standing on a chair to catch the transom. For my part, I had stacked the files under the switchboard, in two neat piles that were camouflaged by my chair. The office would have passed muster from the most meticulous mother-in-law. The Sergeant didn't seem to notice or care. He had bigger worries than a cluttered office.

Helga continued to be her most helpful self, introducing

Sergeant N. Andersen to the subjects in the photo. "I believe that is Dagmar with her father," she said, pointing to the Colonel. "I mean, of course it is Dagmar, and I don't know for sure about her father, but you can see the resemblance? They are obviously related. And she did call her father The Colonel." Helga paused for breath. She had pretty much exhausted her store of information. "You are welcome to take the photograph." She held it out to him. Good riddance, I thought.

At that moment, our young officer was no doubt fervently wishing he had taken the barking dog complaint that had come across his desk that morning and left this time bomb to someone else. Anyone else. He stared at the photo like a condemned prisoner contemplating the gallows, groaned audibly, and I could feel he hoped he wasn't looking at the end of his career. He gathered together the remaining shreds of his professional ambitions, attached the photograph to his clipboard, and left his card.

"Do not hesitate to call if you think of anything you might have forgotten or if *Froken*, I mean *Fraulein* Strasser should return. *Especiall*y if *Fraulein* Strasser should return," he emphasized. His tone was more pleading than official, and I felt sorry for him. He was heading into deep and murky waters. I could only hope we were not going to be caught up in them as well.

There wasn't much to say after he had left. Now that the police had become involved, we had to come to grips with the fact that something was truly amiss. Helga did not appear to be gripping all that well. In fact she was wringing her hands like an understudy to Lady MacBeth, in the depths of a deep inner turmoil. She looked at me and said, "I should have explained what I really meant."

I didn't understand and waited for more information which wasn't long in coming.

"It's just that the way she looked at Wally made my blood boil," she forged ahead. "I told her that if she tried anything with him, I'd kill her. I didn't really mean it. Well, not entirely. I think one of the meat cutters may have overheard me." She raised her eyes to me, embarrassment and defiance struggling for dominance. My money was on defiance to win with embarrassment a long shot to place.

This was a new wrinkle, but I spoke gently. "Helga, whatever you said doesn't mean beans. You're overwrought just now and you're not thinking clearly. No one thinks you had anything at all to do with Dagmar's disappearance. Confession may be good for the soul, but in this case, don't go borrowing trouble." I hated when I mixed up my aphorisms like that. Still, I think the point was made. "If you give the police that sort of information, you may bite off more than you can chew. They'll be obligated to look at you as the prime suspect in this mess. We don't know anything more than we told the police, do we?" I was still a little unsure of what Helga might spit out, but she just shook her head, forlorn. Her conscience was troubled, but it was only troubled because she was innocent. Protecting your territory is right up there with the maternal instinct and self preservation. And Wally was Helga's personal territory.

"What do beans mean?" Helga at least had listened to me, and I hoped she would take my advice to heart.

"Beans mean it's not important," I smiled, and continued my slow progress with the paperwork, while I offered occasional uplifting platitudes as they occurred to me. "Hope. That's the ticket. We need to keep up our hopes. Hope springs eternal, and all that sort of thing." I was trying to jolly her along. What else to say? My mother always had a saying for everything. Her favorite had been "Where there's life, there's *Generalquartiermeister des Herres*!!!!" Eureka. I had hit the mother lode. Good lord in heaven!!

"What did you just say?"

"Nothing." I managed a weak smile. "Just trying to remember what my mother used to tell me when I was feeling at loose ends. I've lost it right now." Fortunately

Helga was sunk somewhere between hopelessness and despair and not caring much about anything. So as she turned away I slipped the long searched for file inside the March issue of *Screen Romances* under Clark's approving gaze. I winked at him. The Quartermaster General of the German Army was about to mingle temporarily with the likes of Garbo, Bergman, and Lake and become a film star in his own right. Such an honor.

Helga gave a weak smile in response and was still pushing paper around her desk in a desultory fashion when the five o'clock whistle blew. By then she was more than ready to call it a day. Reaching for her coat and hat, she heaved a sigh of relief to be done with the place until morning.

"I'll be right behind you. Just want to finish up this little bit." I spoke over my left shoulder while I made a show of straightening up. "Don't wait for me." Please don't wait for me, I prayed under my breath. Just go. This won't take long. I just need a few minutes alone.

She didn't need me to tell her twice, and I closed the door after her, waiting until I heard her heels clicking down the hall, as she went to meet Wally for their walk home. No doubt she would unburden herself to him and he would be flattered by her confession. Any man who has a woman willing to kill for him has got to feel studly. Waldemar would be cock of the walk tomorrow.

I locked the door, opened the movie magazine, and scanned the paperwork. This was the biggest shipment Schmidt and Ericksen had ever made. The order was so huge it would need to be shipped by rail and it wasn't headed south but was to be sent north and that was all I needed to know. It was the proof Churchill needed that German troops would soon be on the move, headed north through Denmark and on to Norway. I took the camera from my jacket pocket and snapped two pictures of the army's order.

Paperwork back in file folder, camera returned to pocket,

and heartbeat noticeably racing, I took a calming breath, straightened my shoulders, and set out for home. Four days until I could dispatch the goods via the bus driver. Four days to guard the film with my life. Four days that would seem like four years.

Chapter Twenty-Five

Berlin, Germany

"Today we rule Germany, tomorrow the world!" The exhortation still rang in Eric Strasser's ears. Like the phoenix rising from the ashes, Germany was resurrected and for better or worse had married itself to the cause of Adolph Hitler, now *Der Führer*, who had been in exceptionally good form this morning. The dying echoes of the *Führer's* voice were supplanted by the chanting of the enraptured crowd, "*Sieg Heil! Sieg Heil!*" Tears streamed down the cheeks of men and women alike. The Master had done his work again. The Savior. The Messiah. Of course, the music helped. Selected for its emotional appeal, it soared and electrified the air.

As Strasser muscled his way through the phalanx of officers guarding the offices of the *Wehrmacht*, there was a determined set to his jaw that conveyed the look of a man on a mission, as indeed he was. This mission, however, had nothing to do with military operations. It was strictly personal and concerned his daughter, Dagmar, who was vexing him no end, as usual. Also, as usual, her timing could not have been worse.

The din on the clerical front was deafening. There was

noise everywhere. Voices raised in volume as telephone conversations became arguments, secretaries transcribing line after line of text from dictaphones, typewriter keys clacking and bells dinging to signal the end of the line, the slap as the carriage was flung back into position. There was a palpable energy to the room with its row upon row of desks, and everyone engaged in some type of activity. Paper was everywhere.

Strasser's aide, Martin Koebler, had a telephone receiver pinned between his left ear and shoulder as he continued to pound away on the keyboard. A cigarette clenched between his lips and a pencil jammed between his right ear and temple added to the image of a pincer crab with all claws engaged.

With the honed instincts of the well schooled, Martin's right arm picked itself off the keyboard and flung itself out in a *Heil Hitler* salute. He continued to type, with never a break in his rhythm, and before Strasser could acknowledge the salute, Martin was back at work and Strasser was holding a file stuffed with papers. Strasser did a quick head shake, his eyes traveling from the file in his hand to Martin's desk. Martin was a magician; nothing short of sleight of hand could have achieved this transfer.

Strasser furrowed his brow and regarded Martin more carefully. This might be a talent they could use down the road. He filed this thought away for later consideration and entered his inner office, locking the door behind him. He sat down at his desk and proceeded to examine the files, dossiers on the staff of Schmidt and Ericksen.

The General Manager was a Waldemar Hedegaard, a native of Kolding, fifty-five, single, five foot six, portly, brown eyes and balding. No visible scars, no visible taste either, as Strasser squinted at the photo accompanying the description. Hedegaard was sporting a bow tie splotched with some kind of big red flowers. He wondered about Hedegaard and whether his single status and floral outfit indicated some sort of moral perversion. Strasser raised the corner of his lip in disgust. This type would be weeded out shortly and the day couldn't come soon enough.

Helga Bruegger was the Office Manager, born in Copenhagen, had moved to Kolding fifteen years ago. Also single, fifty-three, blonde and blue eyed and tall. Five foot eleven and with a weight to match. This was a depraved lot. Strasser tapped his finger on the photograph. She was a big, buxom woman and didn't seem at all self-conscious about her attributes, as she regarded the camera with an even gaze.

The switchboard operator was a frumpish sow by the name of Hilda Sorensen.

Hilda and Helga. It sounded like a women's *kaffeklatsch*. Sixty-two, five foot five, average build, grey hair, brown eyes, large mouth, wide nose. She gave ugly a bad name.

There were twelve meat cutters, whose descriptions were all similar. Similarly vague, and Strasser frowned at the incompleteness. Incompetence was rampant. He rang for Martin. "Where is the information on the meat cutters? Who are the supervisors?" Strasser waved the file in the air.

"I will check on it immediately, *Herr Oberst,*" Martin said, frowning and beating a fast retreat back to his desk where he placed a phone call upstairs.

Strasser could hear Martin screaming at the person on the other end of the phone. Within two minutes he knocked once on the door and entered. "Intelligence has nothing more, *Herr Oberst.* They did not consider them important."

Strasser grunted. "That will be all, Martin."

"Ja wohl. Heil Hitler." He shot his right arm into the air at the same time he opened the door with his left hand and escaped back to his desk.

Strasser set the file aside and steepled his fingers over it. He did not like going into a situation half-prepared. After a few moments he leaned back in his chair and folded his hands behind his neck. There was a hairline crack in the plaster near the light switch and he stared at it, but his thoughts were miles away.

Dagmar had gone missing from work, and that is where he would begin to search for her. There was nothing on the surface that would indicate her co-workers were responsible, but appearances were often deceiving. He would find out what they knew. He rang Martin with instructions to have his car made ready, and that he would not need his driver for the time being. He checked his pistol and returned it to his holster.

There was one more file to take along and study. This one was stamped *Top Secret* and had come straight from the *Führer* himself. Inhaling sharply he rose from his desk. By the time he returned, Denmark and Norway would belong to the Third Reich. He grabbed his attaché case, stuffed the files inside, and left the office via his private exit. The weather had changed and now fat raindrops pelted him and he tucked his head down against the shock of the cold, wet wind.

His car was waiting for him with the motor running and an officer on guard by the driver's door. The officer, a lieutenant, snapped to attention and saluted as Strasser approached. Strasser gave a perfunctory salute, the lieutenant closed the door and returned to attention, and Strasser pulled away from the curb.

First stop would be Dagmar's apartment, then her workplace. His jaw clenched. She had always been a headstrong girl and her insistence on making her own way, within limitations, of course, was infuriating. She lived in a dream world, where his reasoned arguments fell on deaf ears. She wanted a career in film. He could arrange that. The Ministry of Culture was gearing up for full production and she would have her pick of roles. But all his pleading had not changed her mind. Hollywood was all she talked about.

He frowned. Her disparagement of Leni Riefenstahl might work against him at some point. She must be made to see these comments must stop. He suspected that jealousy was at the heart of her comments, and for that he had to accept the blame. He had doted on her, given her everything she had ever wanted. And now this. Anger and concern distracted him. He saw the curve almost too late, overcorrected, and nearly went off the road. The tires of the staff car, a 1937 Mercedes Benz 290L Cabriolet, squealed in protest. The twin flags on the fenders snapped and fluttered, twins of the turmoil raging within him. The Swastikas emblazoned on the fabric were carried along on the wind, and Strasser pushed on as well.

The first portion of his search met with failure. Dagmar's car was not parked anywhere near her apartment and Strasser didn't quite know how to read this. If she wasn't here and wasn't at work, where could she be? Even for all her foolishness, this was not like her. He let himself into her apartment with his own key. If he were paying for this place, he damn sure had a right to be inside.

But nothing. No trace of a struggle, nothing out of place, as far as he could tell. He stood in the middle of the parlor and looked up one end and down the other. Her purse was gone, as was her fur coat. So she had left and apparently under her own power.

Strasser chewed on his lip. If he found out nothing more at the meat plant, he'd return and take the place apart. He let himself out and sped away, to the undisguised relief of Dagmar's landlady who had seen the staff car arrive and had wondered what the Nazis were doing this far north. She didn't like it one bit, but prudence indicated she stay inside and out of sight and she'd watched the Colonel come and go from behind the safety of her curtained window.

The man reading the newspaper in the automobile parked across the street also watched Strasser's arrival and departure with interest. He set the paper down on the passenger seat and he returned to police headquarters to report.

Chapter Twenty-Six

Kolding

I had bundled up against the morning rain, but to little use. My stockings were soaked and my shoes were sponges, dribbling water each time I came to the down stroke on the bicycle pedals. My rain bonnet had slid back in a nefarious cooperation with the mild headwind I was encountering, and water seemed to be defying the laws of physics, flowing upstream from my wrists towards my elbows, through my coat sleeve that was acting as a wind tunnel. Still, I pedaled resolutely onward, wet hair plastered against my forehead, each strand dripping and sending a steady stream of water flowing down my nose, forming a lake out of the folds in my neck scarf. To finish off a wonderful start to the day, I was coming down with a cold. My throat felt scratchy and I had begun sneezing, my own mild contribution to the wetness of the morning air.

"I snoze a sneeze into the air." How did the rest of that go? My mind was fogging in along with the atmosphere. I shook my head and a scattering of drops flew from my bonnet. Grimly, I hunkered down for the last push. My first order of business was going to be a cup of hot, strong coffee. But just then, just when I had decided that I couldn't possibly get any wetter, a two-toned cream and grey Mercedes convertible, violating every regulation in the traffic code, passed me on the left and cut across in front of me as it negotiated an illegal right hand turn. The effect was the equivalent of a one-two punch. Whatever didn't splash me from the side, managed to connect in the front. I raised my hand in a farewell salute, while I contemplated the exotic, glamorous image of international intrigue I had become. I was an embarrassment to spydom and was also probably incubating pneumonia, and double pneumonia at that. In my misery I hadn't processed a full description of the car, but that was soon to change.

It was only five minutes later when I arrived at work, but it felt like a lifetime. I parked my bicycle alongside the building and slopped around to the front door. It was in this condition that Helga found me and bundled me off through the vestibule, down the front hall, through the meat plant, and past the wide-eyed staring of the cutters to the dressing room. With an efficiency that was comforting and a manner that was encouraging, she boomed reassurances at me, while she searched for clean towels and something suitable for me to wear.

I rubbed myself dry and the rough friction of the industrial grade towel restored my circulation and warmed me. Perhaps I would survive after all. On the other hand, my wardrobe options were slim and the best Helga could produce was a knee length white meat cutter's jacket. She did find a men's leather belt and that at least cut down on the updraft as I moved back along the corridor to my work station. My own clothes were sharing line space with aprons and towels in the back part of the building. The clothesline looked overdressed from my perspective, but my outfit did add a splash of color that alleviated the whitescape.

With my blonde hair released from its turban, my tresses hung limply around my face and straggled halfway down my back. My nose, now cherry red from sneezing and dripping, was in conspiracy with my throat, also now probably cherry red and moving from scratchy to sharply sore. In short, I felt lousy.

Helga studied my appearance for a moment and then brightened. Removing her floral hair ribbon and bow from its accustomed nest above her left ear, she gathered my locks in a fat ponytail, which she tied securely with the ribbon. She anchored the bow atop my head and stood back to regard the effect.

"Not too bad! You'll be just fine. Of course you will!"

And so indeed I was, bolstered by her concern, and with white coat, black belt, floral ribbon and bow, and oh yes, the extra pair of felt slippers that Wally kept in the locker room for when his ankles began to swell and his feet ache, I returned to the office.

I was a vision splendid. It is important in the profession to blend. And at least as far as the floral aspect of my attire went, I did just that. Helga had her floral skirt, Wally his tie, and me the ribbon and bow. We looked as if we were partners in a florist shop, but we pressed on to the front office where I settled in at the switchboard.

I figured the morning could only get better. It certainly couldn't get any worse. But it is not a good idea to think this way; it tempts fate. I had been surveying my little kingdom, my soggy, dripping kingdom. I was queen of my own nutshell, to paraphrase Hamlet, and the realm was in need of some extensive renovations. My pocketbook was sitting in its own puddle, and I knew the contents must be just as wet. I needed to get them out of there.

I dumped my pocketbook onto the desk and was sorting out the wet from the not so wet when I was interrupted by a burst of cold air as the front door opened and an unpleasant looking fellow in a German officer's uniform walked in. He was frowning at me, why I couldn't fathom. What I could, and did fathom, was that this was the much dreaded, but expected visit from Dagmar's father. Crap. He looked just like his picture. I was face to face with a really nasty looking individual. Why today?"

"*Guten morgen Fraulein.*"

"*Guten morgen, Herr Oberst,*" I replied. I smiled politely and waited. I found it interesting he was speaking in German. He probably figured that sooner or later we would all have to speak it anyway, and was cutting some corners.

"You are not *Fraulein* Hilda ..." Strasser looked at me, reproach on his face. That was the trouble with Nazis. You couldn't do anything right, even if you hadn't done anything wrong.

"That's correct. I am not." I continued to smile. I knew what his game was and was itching to see just how far I could push him. He took another tack. Good tactical maneuver.

"I am here to make inquiries concerning *Fraulein* Dagmar Strasser.

"You will want to speak with *Froken* Bruegger," I beamed at him and placed a call on the intercom. "She will be here directly. She is in the plant, distributing work orders." I returned to my sorting, leaving the Colonel to entertain himself while he waited.

When Helga did return, Wally was right by her side and had transformed his short frame into the physique of a warrior. Arms crossed against his chest and feet planted on the concrete floor, he couldn't have set down roots any more firmly had he been an oak in the forest primeval beset by murmuring pines and hemlocks. His jaw was set, his gaze was firm, and he was not the least awed by the presence of one of Hitler's right hand men. Or if he was, he wasn't letting it show.

Strasser's eyes traveled from Wally to Helga to me and back to Wally, taking in our sartorial splendor, no doubt. His spit and polish uniform was the only drab piece of clothing in sight, and his only splotch of color, his array of medals and decorations, was outranked by the sheer magnitude of

Helga's cabbage roses.

The comic veneer of the situation didn't conceal the serious underlying nature of the colonel's visit, and I had no doubt but that we would each be favored with a private audience. I didn't like it. With one more military order to photograph, and the Quartermaster scheduled to place a follow-up to the big beef order today, along with detailed instructions for shipment, I needed to be at my post and not tied up with the Colonel when that call came through.

With my back to Strasser, I transferred the camera and my pistol from my handbag to my jacket pockets. While he spoke with Helga, I finished drying off what could be dried, and lined up the rest of my items in a neat row across the console to evaporate. My handkerchief, which I tented over an empty flower vase, gave the effect of a makeshift shrine and judging from the proximity to Mr. Gable's picture, it looked as if I belonged to a star cult that worshiped the film god with sodden trinkets.

Strasser, with Wally on his heels, left to grill the cutters in the meat room. He was going to start at the bottom and work up. Helga had returned to her desk, where she sat rigidly, alternately mopping her damp forehead with her handkerchief and wringing the handkerchief as if she were doing laundry. She was pale as a cube of Swiss in a mousetrap. In the silence, the grandfather clock in the corner ticked off the minutes. I'd never remembered it being so loud and each tick brought Helga closer to the edge.

When the Quartermaster rang through at nine-thirty, Helga was more than glad to have something to do, and she typed up the order with brutal force, her fingers assaulting the keyboard, each stroke a punch directed at the office intruder. Ripping the sheet out of the roller, she tore a corner and left a jagged edge at the bottom. Her hands were trembling.

"Chin up, honey. He'll be gone soon and you'll both be fine." I tried to sound more confident than I felt.

Her eyes brimmed with tears. "It's just the beginning. The beginning of the end."

"Hey, come on. Don't sound so morose. It's not a funeral. What could the Gestapo possibly find that would harm either of you? There's nothing you need be afraid of."

"I wish that were true." She gave a wan smile and took a deep breath. Something had changed and had led her to a decision. Her eyes were now bright and clear, the tears were gone. Her hands no longer trembled.

That was the moment I realized what courage really is. So many times we are seduced by grand, heroic displays of daring do, but really, that's not it. Courage is so much more than that. It's the cumulative effect of a myriad of individual acts of bravery that lead ultimately to the victory of good over evil. In this case the act was the simple unknotting of a neck scarf. For in so doing, Helga revealed the Star of David that hung suspended from a simple silver chain around her neck. She folded the scarf and set it aside, giving it a dismissive pat with her hand. She looked at me with deliberate eyes and I felt tears well up in my own.

"And Wally?" I asked.

"No. Wally wishes only I should be safe. The scarf was his idea. It is too late for scarves now."

"Go wash your face and fix your lipstick. Some day you must meet my sister. She's got your kind of spunk. I think you'd get along famously."

Helga pursed her lips and exhaled, a mighty sigh. "I wasn't sure…" Her voice trailed off.

"King Christian has said it best, I think." I tried to recall the exact words. "We are Danes. We are only Danes here."

Helga located her lipstick tube, then left to attend to her face repair in the bathroom. While she was occupied, I managed to capture the last of the orders on microfilm and snap the roll of exposed film to a small clip attached to my hosiery garter. The film was cool against my thigh, a vivid contrast to the heat flushing my face. When Helga returned from her mini-toilette, she enfolded me in her ample arms and kissed me on the cheek.

"Hilda will be returning Monday morning," I remarked by way of changing the subject. "I'll miss you and Wally, but I'll be glad to get home."

Before Helga could mist up again on me, the door from the cutting room opened and a granite-faced Wally and a beet-faced Colonel entered the office. Strasser's visage was a mix of exasperation, frustration, and indignation. He was pissed, to phrase it coarsely.

"Your workers are idiots!" barked Strasser. His words went literally over Wally's head, as the Colonel had a good nine inches on Wally. "They are dumb. But they also seem to be deaf and blind as well!" Strasser's volume was increasing, but Wally just stood by impassively. It was a brilliant strategy. Strasser might command a legion, but Wally was Napoleon on the best day of his life.

Strasser, unused to being ignored, turned to confront Helga, who rose from her chair to meet his gaze head on. She was close enough to his height that he could not use his to intimidate, and with her shoulders straightened, back erect, and chest thrust out, she was majestic. Helga was a 42 DD, and at the moment her cups were running over.

It wasn't Helga's ample charms that caught Strasser's eye, however, but the symbol she wore. His eyes narrowed, and I slipped my hand inside the jacket pocket where my pistol waited. My fingers tightened around the grip, but the moment passed. An icy calm had replaced the heat of anger, and I feared this even more. Whatever he did next would be deliberate and methodical. What he did next was dismiss her. "Your time is almost over," he said. And then he addressed me.

"*Fraulein*, your name please." You are not *Frau*…"

I resumed restocking my purse, and I answered without raising my head. "I am Frokken Katrin Nissen, the temporary replacement. And this is my last week," I added as an afterthought. "I'm afraid I don't know anything."

Strasser snorted and fixed Wally in a glare. "That is most unusual. Someone here who doesn't know anything."

I shrugged, and when I did look up, it was straight into the two most reptilian eyes I had ever seen. The little hairs on the back of my neck bristled. Snatching my handkerchief from its drying rack, I faced him directly on and gave my nose a good blow. He only recoiled slightly, when the handkerchief slipped a bit and he got the full blast.

"I'm coming down with a cold," I explained. "Got thoroughly drenched on the way to work this morning. And then some idiot in a Mercedes sprayed me with enough water to float an ark." I added a mild sneeze for good measure and stuffed the now once again wet cloth into my pocket. I rose from the console. "I need to use the powder room," I said, pushing past him. I had only gotten as far as the cutting room when a rough hand grabbed my shoulder, spun me around, and the other hand slapped me across the face.

"Insolent bitch!"

Strasser had a hand like the hind end of a pig and the effect of the slap sent me reeling into the cutting table. Grabbing the edge of the board for support, I barely kept myself from falling to the floor. That would not have put me in a good position. And I think instinct or reflex surfaced, for as I straightened up, I grabbed the nearest boning knife and made a neat incision between the Colonel's fifth and sixth ribs and, thrusting upwards, stuck him in the heart. Assuming, that is, he had one. Coming in from the side, I had the satisfaction of seeing the sheer surprise in his eyes before they closed forever.

Strasser's curse plus the loud slap had alerted Christian, Martin, and Jurgen, the cutters, who had vaulted the center table to rush to my aid. They were joined almost immediately by Wally and Helga, who had raced from the office. Helga had a hefty ceramic paperweight the size of a bowling ball in her hand, and Wally was wielding a meat cleaver. The sight was impressive as battalions went.

Jurgen prodded the inert form with the steel toe of his work shoe. Fists still clenched, he was taking no chances. “Snakes are still dangerous, even when they appear dead,” he remarked, giving a final jab.

“At least you can eat a rattlesnake,” I said. “They’re really good grilled with a little garlic and butter. Taste like chicken.” I looked up to see a confused array of faces. “Really!” They remained unconvinced, but Wally had gotten a strange expression on his face and then burst out laughing, a deep roar that shook his belly like Saint Nicholas.

“Katrin, my dear,” he said, “not to worry. Sometimes they taste like beef.” He motioned to the men to collect Strasser. “You and Helga go back to the office. I’ll be there shortly.” He turned to Christian and said something that I couldn’t make out and Christian burst out laughing as well. This little private joke seemed to be making the rounds of the men and Christian shared it with Jurgen and Martin with the same result.

Helga and I looked at each other with the dawning of realization. It was preposterous. Brilliant, but preposterous all the same. I loved it.

Back in the main office, I finished packing up and was ready to turn the switchboard over to Helga for the remainder of the day. Wally was true to his word, and it was only five minutes later when he returned with Strasser’s neatly folded uniform in hand, which he held out for me to take. “We’ve cleaned it up as best we could. You may have a use for this,” he said. “I think you are quite a bit more than a switchboard operator.” He winked at me and turned to Helga. “Telephone the Quartermaster and inform him the shipment will be ready on time. We must keep the German troops fed.” He roared as he returned to the plant.

“The car!” Helga’s face paled. “Oh God in heaven. This doesn’t end.” She gave a moan.

“I’ll deal with the car. It’ll be gone in a jiffy, and so must

I. Be right back." I gave her a reassuring smile and retraced my earlier steps down the hall. This time I completed my journey and retrieved my drying clothes. Back in the office I finished packing up. Helga would take care of the switchboard until Hilda returned on Monday. I fished through Strasser's pants pockets until I found the car keys, then wrapped my sweater around his uniform, slung the strap of my pocketbook over my right shoulder, and gave Helga a farewell embrace. "Tell Wally goodbye for me," I said, "and take care of each other."

Helga nodded, "And you too. We will not see you again, will we?"

"You never can tell, Helga. You never know what the future has in store."

I let myself out and my jaw dropped as I beheld the car awaiting its driver, outside the plant. It was the same Mercedes that had soaked me on the way to work. "Damn," I said, for lack of something more original. "There is justice in the universe after all." I eased myself into the driver's seat and turned on the ignition. The engine roared to life and I wasted no time putting distance between me and the meat plant.

The sensation that someone else besides me was in the car dogged me. I couldn't shake it. It was a sense of negative energy or maybe some electrical disturbance in the air caused by the storm. More likely it was the residue of Strasser's malevolence. I'm not superstitious generally, but I did crack the window a bit, just in case whatever part of the Colonel might be lingering behind needed a way out. It's best not to take chances with the forces of evil.

I wondered if it were possible for cars to take on the personalities of their owners. This car was designed to intimidate, just like the Colonel. Cold, austere, and powerful, it was well suited to an aggressive type. I didn't think it could ever be purged clean.

It wouldn't take long to reach the coast. I had no idea

what to do next, but I figured something would come to me when I got there. So I hadn't any plans to stop until I spied the briefcase out of the corner of my right eye, right smack dab on the passenger seat. I'd been so intent on getting away that I hadn't even noticed it until now.

Pulling off at the next wide spot in the road, I parked the car in a grove of beech, sheltered from the elements and from the view of passersby.

Of course the case was locked, but a quick study of the keys on Strasser's ring produced the one I needed. The clasps sprang back against the leather and I had a vision of Pandora's Box and the havoc it had unleashed upon an unsuspecting world. Sure enough, there was havoc to spare among the contents. Strasser's briefcase was a traveling file cabinet and the documents were arranged chronologically with the most recent on top. A cursory glance told me that this information needed to get to headquarters and I loaded the camera and began filming as fast as my fingers could move through the pile of papers. It was only as I was replacing them in the case that I stopped to read the one on top and my blood ran cold in my veins.

The Fuehrer and Supreme Commander of the Armed Forces

Berlin, 1 March 1940

TOP SECRET by Officer Only

DIRECTIVE FOR "FALL WESERUEBUNG"

The development of the Situation in Scandinavia required the making of all preparations for the occupation of Denmark and Norway by a part of the German Armed Forces ("Fall Weseruebung"). This operation should prevent British encroachment on Scandinavia and Baltic; further it should guarantee our ore base in Sweden and give our navy and Air Force a wider start line against Britain......The crossing of the Danish border and the landings in Norway must take place simultaneously…it is most important that the Scandinavian States as well as the Western opponents should be taken by surprise by our measures.

Occupation of Denmark ("Weserueung Sued") Added to this, having secured the most important places, the Group will break through as quickly as possible from Guenen to Skagen and to the east coast. In Seeland bases will be captured early on. These will serve as starting points for later occupation.

(Signed) A. Hitler.

As I read, I had forgotten to breathe, and now I was hyperventilating. I concentrated on breathing and, slamming the briefcase shut, hiked up my lab coat and added one more roll of film to the garter. I tossed the case into the back seat and pulled back onto the main road, throwing gravel. Just one more woman with a pink rose hair ribbon, clad in a white lab coat, hiding two rolls of top secret microfilm on her thigh, driving a German staff car across the midsection of Denmark and bound for the coast with the hounds of hell snapping at her heels.

Chapter Twenty-Seven

Sankt Peder

"Drop down dew, o ye heavens. Thou art my sword and my shield." I was blending a couple of Psalms or some half-remembered Bible verses, but I think God still caught my intention, as the rain continued to drench the countryside in torrents. The plan I had promised myself would evolve as I drove on towards the coast was still a bit hazy, but so far it involved Inge, the bus driver, a hot bath, and some luck. I was only doing about 40 kilometers an hour, in order to keep from hydroplaning off the road, but with each landmark I passed, Sankt Peder was inching closer.

I blew into town pushed along by an east wind, arriving at Inge's house just as the rain slacked off and the skies brightened. As the sun broke through the clouds, the mist began to rise from the fields, and along with the mist, my spirits rose as well.

I drove the car into the barn nearly running over Inge's chickens which had sheltered there and which were now lined up in a row that spanned the doorway, considering with their miniscule chicken brains whether or not to venture back out into the puddled yard. I could almost hear the worms surfacing and figured that any chicken worth her stuffing would make haste to head towards the buffet. With a great deal of clucking and fussing, they parted and made their move, the lust for the hunt having triumphed.

I was leaning against the driver's door for support, eyes closed and burning, my burst of adrenaline having been depleted by the wild ride, and feeling none too steady on my feet, when I heard the unmistakable dulcet tones of my sister.

"Good Lord! What happened to your face?"

I opened my eyes, or rather my right eye, for the left one wasn't responding all that well. Considering what I was wearing, how I had arrived, and the fact that I had a neatly folded SS uniform under my left arm and an attaché case dangling from my right hand, it was as good a greeting as any. And my face did hurt. It was probably a deep shade of magenta by now and by tomorrow would be turning green and yellow as well. I could be my own Easter egg. I pointed to the uniform by way of answer and managed a weak smile. "I killed the Colonel in the meat locker with a boning knife." A fleeting idea passed through my head, but I couldn't quite grasp hold of it before it escaped. But Inge was talking, and her voice chased the thought away.

"What did you do with the rest of him?"

I didn't want to cover that ground again, and I suspected it was more of a rhetorical question, so I worked around it. "I need some help."

"No doubt." Inge eyed me with an appraising look. "But first, let's get this car covered over and then get you inside for an ice bag, a hot bath, and a stiff drink.

I love my sister. Nothing ever fazes her, and even if she had her priorities out of whack, she would wait until I was ready to talk. So I did. "First the car, then the hot drink, then the ice pack, then the bath. Then another hot drink." My teeth had begun to chatter and I was shaking uncontrollably.

"Hypothermia," I stuttered.

"Shock," Inge surmised.

It is a fact of nature that our bodies betray us. They stiffen, they break, they fall victim to disease and age, and there comes a time when sheer will power has to carry us through. And this was that time for me. I felt like a marathon runner whose wind is spent but must go five more miles or fail. And the stakes were much too high to stop and rest for very long, and failure could not be, must not be, an option.

So five minutes later, the car secured with a canvas overcoat, I was sitting at the kitchen table, wrapped in a warm woolen blanket, sipping hot coffee laced with whiskey with one hand, and holding an ice bag to my face with the other. My throat hurt, my nose was running, and I punctuated the conversation with occasional sneezes, while I navigated through the surreal floating effect that a low-grade fever can produce. At times, I felt I was observing myself from a distance, and connecting the handkerchief with my nose was becoming a hit and miss affair. It is difficult work, being a glamorous woman of intrigue and international espionage. Extraneous thoughts and nonsensical ideas wandered in and out of my consciousness. I wondered if Mata Hari had had a sister. It became obvious she never had a brother-in-law.

"Good Lord! What happened to your face?" Lars was home. Damn and double damn. No point in even trying to smile. He was peering at me with the practiced eye of law enforcement and the jig was up. "Time to come clean, I think. *Ja*?"

"I need to find the bus driver," I croaked. No point in wasting time here.

"She's delirious," Inge explained to her other half. "She wants to get on the bus."

"What bus?"

"I don't know. Just a bus." Inge waved a helpless hand. "Any bus." Inge was at her most helpful self. The maternal instinct can really affect a woman's rational thinking. She insisted on treating me as if I were a slightly demented, daffy old aunt who needed humoring and maybe a hefty shot of laudanum and now they had begun discussing me in the third person.

"Help me get her up to bed. She's as stubborn as a post and she won't cooperate. I've been trying to put her in bed for the past hour. She needs a good night's sleep."

Inge's cure for everything was a good night's sleep. Often, to her credit, it worked. Not this time, however. "Dough!" was the way my refusal came out. It's hard to hold court when you're all stuffed up. "I need to find the bus driver." Lars, bless his soul, sat down and waited. He motioned for Inge to take a seat as well. Now I really felt like a decrepit monarch. My loyal subjects were waiting for my addled brain to make some sense. The safety of the realm was at stake. One more lubricating snort of coffee and I launched Phase Two of The Plan.

"The Germans plan to invade Denmark on the 9th of April," I began. "That is less than two weeks from today." Lars stiffened in his straight back chair and Inge nodded, her worst fears confirmed.

I continued, "They expect to make short work of Denmark on their way to Norway. We are not their primary objective, just a piece of ground they need to pass through, and they don't anticipate any resistance." Inge snorted, and I held up my hand to ward off her patriotic rebuttal.

I turned towards the briefcase on the table and pulled it onto my lap. "The documents are here," I tapped the case. "And also here," I reached under my blanket, parted the lab coat and unsnapped the microfilm from my garter, setting the two rolls on top of the case.

Lars leaned in and studied my face. "So where does the bus driver fit in?"

"I need to get this film to him when the bus pulls in today. He takes them to the next stop." I looked at the clock on the wall above the icebox. "In an hour," I added. "I have to go."

"No." Lars left no room for argument. "You are absolutely in no condition to go out. You've got a fever and you'll drop in your shoes half a kilometer from the house."

I stuck out my tongue at him, but it was a half-hearted gesture, as I hated to admit he was right. I wasn't even sure I could stand without support, let alone venture downtown and wait at the bus station.

"We just have to hand these off? That's it?" Inge was plotting.

"That's pretty much it. Except that we need to be sure he's the right driver. There's a pass code, of course, and two baskets of rolls," I added.

Inge squinted at me, trying to determine whether this last part was the fever talking. She looked doubtful.

"I go up to him and tell him that these are for his wife," I said, holding up an imaginary basket of rolls. "Then he asks what kind of rolls they are and I answer sweet French rolls. He says he really prefers pumpernickel with his beef roast. Then I give him the basket of pumpernickel rolls with the film hidden on the bottom under the napkin."

"What if he doesn't say the right thing?" Inge asked.

"Then I just give him the basket of sweet French rolls and get the hell out of there as fast as I can with the basket of pumpernickel rolls." I was fading quickly, and it was just at that moment the back screen door slammed shut. Greta was home. Inge caught Lars's eye and he nodded.

Greta swung the strap of the book bag from her shoulder and let her school texts drop to the floor with a thud. She scrunched her face and tilted her head, studying me with an expression that bore a remarkable similarity to that of her mother. "Good Lord. What happened to your face, *Tante* Katrin?"

If only I had had the presence of mind to have had a sign made up before I came home, I could have hung it around my neck like a leper and avoided all the questions.

"Your aunt Katrin was in a fight." Inge was deriving a significant amount of vicarious pleasure from this situation. "She won."

Lars groaned but Greta was seeing me in a new light. She

approved wholeheartedly, and pulling out a chair, sat herself down and gazed at me as if I were Joan of Arc. I think the fever reminded me of poor St. Joan, burning at the stake and all that.

Lars looked at Greta, then at Inge, back at me, and finally fixed on his daughter. "Greta, we need you to do something very important while you are delivering your eggs today," he said.

She looked at her father and then at her mother and then back at me, serious expressions all around. As I explained what she was to do, her expression became serious as well and her brow furrowed, but I could see the light dancing in her eyes and felt a bittersweet moment pass between us. Greta was about to leave her childhood behind, and there would be no turning back for her.

Outside the window, I watched Inge's chickens hunt and peck on the lawn and up and down the drive, a squadron of ambulatory feathered typists. The sun, now shining with the freshly scrubbed brilliance that only comes after the rain, caught the prism dangling from the window shade and cast a rainbow on the far wall of the kitchen. Everything seemed so ordinary and peaceful.

"And what do I do after I give away the basket, *Tante* Katrin?"

"You finish delivering your eggs and then come home. This is just one additional stop on your route. And that is the way you must think of it," I emphasized. "Nothing unusual, nothing out of the ordinary."

Greta took a deep breath and straightened her shoulders.

Chapter Twenty-Eight

Sankt Peder, mostly

From the Reichstag balcony above the parade grounds, Adolph Hitler watched his troops pass in review. The waiting was almost over and he was euphoric, almost giddy. Soon, very soon the world would feel the unleashed might of his fury and would tremble and quake at the approach of his forces. Right arm extended, he blessed the troops as the martial music swelled and filled the air, underscored by the orchestrated beat of thousands of jackbooted feet slamming in perfect synchrony against the stone floor. And under the pavement, the earth trembled.

From his bedchamber in the Admiralty, Winston Churchill fumed and sputtered as he read the morning's briefings and barked at his orderly, whose function these days was to serve as listening post and verbal sparring dummy. He had absorbed quite a beating these past few weeks and knew that the Admiral's patience was nearly exhausted. Clad in his dressing gown and slippers, Churchill paced the length and then the breadth of his room, each step a soft, silent accompaniment to the ticking of his bedside clock. Just one hard piece of intelligence was all he needed to move and end this agonizing wait. It must come soon before it was too late. And throughout the realm, the people watched the skies and prayed for a miracle.

From the unlikeliest places and in the most unlikely of guises, deliverance comes. In this case, deliverance was a fourteen-year-old girl with flaxen braids and cornflower blue eyes, and she pedaled a red bicycle with white wicker baskets that straddled the frame housing the rear wheel. Greta Jensen had set out on her weekly egg route, a task that had been hers since she had turned eleven. Twelve dozen eggs were securely in place in the wicker baskets secured to the back fender, and the two baskets of rolls were nestled inside the wire basket secured to the handlebars. Greta had lined the baskets with padded muslin and painted the wicker white, adding a sprig of daisies and a border of ferns around the basket lids. She and her mother had been partners in the egg business ever since Greta had asked to help.

Greta kept careful records and had plans to increase the number of customers this year and perhaps add other products to the route. Milk and butter would help fill out her product line. She was almost ready to approach her mother with her ideas.

Inge kept Greta's share of the profits in a special fund that would pay her way at university. She was proud that Greta would go to university, the first person in the family to do so, and both Lars and Inge were firm on this. Lars was convinced Greta would become a teacher; Inge was just as certain she would choose nursing. Greta announced, however, that she would study science, specifically, paleobotany. This disclosure sent her father to the dictionary and her mother to wondering if her child was in reality a changeling, left on the doorstep.

Greta smiled inwardly remembering her father's only question, "Who will pay you to be this paleobotanist?" He wanted his daughter to be secure. When she had replied her intention was to become a professor and teach others, his chest had swelled with pride and he told everyone he met about his daughter who would be a professor one day.

She carried her science journal with her on her weekly rounds, and in it she recorded her sightings of flora, especially of ferns, which she loved. She sketched and measured and labeled them with their scientific names and each week shared her research with her grandfather, who encouraged her interest in botany. He always had something new to share with her and she looked forward to their discussions. Today there was no time for ferns. Today everything was different, and Greta realized with a flash of insight that her time of waiting was over. And while she focused her thoughts on what she must do, at home her family waited and prayed for her safe return.

Greta had practiced her simple line until she was satisfied that nothing in her voice or her tone would betray her racing heart. "These are for your wife," she informed the air ahead of her. "These are for your wife."

The bus station was not overly busy on a weekday afternoon, and she parked her bicycle close to the street and set the kickstand. Lifting the rolls from her basket, she placed one handle over each arm and stood waiting for the passengers to alight.

"Greta, isn't it? You are far from home." It sounded like an accusation. Pastor had approached unseen from the grocery store on the corner and was now blocking her view of the driver. "Have you come to help me with my groceries?"

Greta shook her head violently. "I am here for the driver. Excuse me, please." She tried to see around him and he laughed as he held his ground, forcing her to stop. Only yesterday Greta would have blushed and the teasing would have continued. But yesterday belonged to another life, and to her amazement, her color held as did her composure. She lifted her eyes to the pastor and repeated. "Excuse me, please," and he let her by. Greta felt a power coursing through her, the power of her sex. She had passed through the portal of childhood and emerged on the other side, a woman.

Turning her head slightly, she nodded, the gesture both an acknowledgement and a dismissal. She addressed the driver. "These are for your wife," Greta smiled, extending the basket of French rolls.

The driver was a young man, thin to the point of boniness, with a uniform that held hopes he might eat his way into it. It appeared the cloth might wear out before he achieved that distant goal. Even the hat floated over his skull, resting precariously atop his head, wobbling with each movement. His expression was kind but blank. "I'm not married." He said this with a sort of wonderment, as if this were something he had never considered before, but now it might prove interesting to pursue.

Greta's mind was racing. Behind her the minister waited, before her the driver was the wrong man. She was to leave. Aunt Katrin had said if this happened she should leave. But then one straggler, an ancient man with a carved wooden cane, appeared in the aisle and limped towards the exit door. Greta stepped aside to let him pass and he winked at her. "Don't worry. Ole will be back tomorrow. His wife is having a baby! That makes six. Six Gustafsons. If it's a boy, they're naming him after me." His wrinkled face beamed. "August Gustafson. That's quite a mouthful, *ja*?" The old man chuckled as he made his way down the steps and hobbled around the corner.

"Oh." Greta tightened her grip on the baskets and moved off the bus, both baskets still dangling from her forearms, her hands clasped together in front of her. Ole Gustafson. She knew the name, but not where they lived. She could find this out and still deliver the film. How to do this was the problem. She was chewing absently on her lower lip, as she took the rolls back to the bicycle.

The pastor was shaking hands with someone across the street, but as she looked, his eyes locked onto hers and she felt a sudden chill. He was still keeping an eye on her. Why? She didn't like it and suddenly she felt vulnerable and in danger.

She reached under the napkin and touched the film, reassuring herself, but as she looked up again, saw the pastor heading back her way. She fingered the streamers on her handlebar grips as her mind sought a way out.

"Greta! Wait just a moment. I can help you." Karl had a broad smile on his face, but there was no reflection of it in his eyes, which were cold and hard.

"*Ja*, Pastor," Greta said. "Slow and calm," she told herself. "Careful, measured breaths."

Karl plucked a basket from its nest on the handlebars. "I am off to visit the new mother now. I shall tell her this is a gift from the parish." He patted her on the cheek and she did her best not to flinch, as he quickly moved down the street, with his stolen offering of pumpernickel rolls. "I hope you choke on them. You are an evil man," she muttered and felt not a shred of guilt at her words. And with that, she mounted her bicycle and pedaled for all her might in the opposite direction. The closest safe haven was her grandfather and grandmother's home.

"I need your help, *Opa*. *Tante* Katrin is sick and Papa and Mama and *Tante* Katrin gave me a job to do but I couldn't because it was the wrong driver and the minister stole the rolls and I think he is very bad and I hope he does not know what I was doing but I am not sure." Greta had run out of breath, but Volmer had managed to follow the gist of her words.

"Greta, it is all right. You did the right thing. Now start over and tell me exactly what happened. Start at the beginning or as close to the beginning as you need to and try not to leave anything out." Volmer's voice was gentle, but his strength carried a reassurance and Greta knew that she could tell him everything. And so she did.

As she wound down her story, a mix of emotions coursed through Volmer. Fear, anger, and finally, sheer unmitigated relief and admiration for his granddaughter. He stood and embraced her, holding her tight against his chest and kissing the top of her head. He laughed out loud and she grinned from ear to ear. "And so," Greta concluded, "I figured I had better put the film somewhere where he didn't have a chance of getting it. That's when I thought about the handlebars. I pulled off the grip, jammed the film inside the hollow metal, and quick as a jiffy replaced the grip. Smooth as silk!"

When Anna entered the room, both Volmer and Greta looked at her and burst out laughing again. "I think you two have swallowed a canary," Anna remarked. "Perhaps you will tell me about it?"

"Sit, Anna," Volmer said, motioning to the chair next to him. "It is quite a story, and our Greta is the heroine."

So once again Greta recounted her story and when she had finished, the next step had become obvious. Anna would collect a few friends from the Ladies Guild at the church and they would call on Frau Gustafson, with a hot meal for the family and a receiving blanket for the infant. While the ladies oohed and aahed over the newest Gustafson, Anna would hand the film to Ole and that leg of the mission would be accomplished.

Anna rose from the table, her mind already working through the details. Volmer bent his head to Greta and whispered, "She will be ready and out the door in less than thirty minutes, and she and the women will be at the Gustafsons' home in under an hour. Mark my words." Volmer nodded his head solemnly, a veteran observer with many years of experience in these matters. When Anna did bid them farewell, Volmer produced his pocket watch, and tapping on the glass, said "Just like clockwork."

For the first time that day, Greta laughed.

While Anna was at the Gustafsons', Karl Mueller sat by his study window observing shipping activity off the coast of Sankt Peder. It appeared the British ships had increased their visibility, but there did not seem to be an orchestrated effort to interfere with Norwegian shipping activities. Still, it bore keeping a close watch.

He could sense a shortening of the time line and decided it was nearing time to pull out. Karl was no fool, and he knew that while he was useful to the Reich, he was also expendable and they would not worry unnecessarily about his welfare, should they decide to move ahead of schedule. He frowned, thinking of the car still hidden in the barn. He had planned to return it to Dagmar's apartment today, but a pastoral emergency with the Knudsen family had spoiled that plan.

Herre Knudsen had decided to take comfort in the arms of the village tart but he had left a trail a blind German Shepherd could have followed. Frue Gertrude had entered the little love nest and while the whore escaped unscathed, Herre Knudsen had not been so fortunate. He still sported a large lump where the wooden rolling pin had made contact with his thick skull. Karl's services as mediator and counselor had been called into play and by the time the once again happy couple departed his office, it was too late to make the necessary connection home.

Setting the binoculars down on the window sill, he continued to stare out the window until a faint smile crossed his face. He would leave after all the Easter festivities had been concluded this weekend. He would leave under cover of darkness, and he could leave in Dagmar's car.

Chapter Twenty-Nine

Sankt Peder

Feverish dreams peopled with grotesque distortions of human forms passed through my mind, while the room pitched and swayed like a ship tossed about on angry seas. I had entered a world that only the minds of Dali and Picasso could have conjured up. Abstractions solidified into a cubist nightmare. I floated through forests of skeletal trees and swirling mists of black and lowering clouds, beset upon by ravening creatures of darkest mythology. *Mareridt.* The spirits that sat on sleepers' chests and filled their dreams with terror.

All night the fever raged and when I awoke after dawn, the bedclothes were drenched in sweat. The storm having spent its fury, my fever had broken. My body once again belonged to me, weak and helpless as a newborn, but victorious over the demons that had beset me through a long and desperate night.

It must be morning, I thought, watching as the first rays of sunlight filtering through the lace curtains created doilies on the wall. I lifted my right hand to catch the golden drops on my fingers and watch them spill into pools of honey onto the coverlet. Nature had emerged from its bath, freshly scrubbed and shining. It was a glorious day. I listened to the sounds of birdsong, voices wafting up the stairs from the kitchen, and the sound of footsteps treading on the staircase.

Inge opened the door and set down a tray of tea and toast on the nightstand by the bed. She felt my forehead with the back of her left hand and nodded approval. I had passed the fever detection test. She fluffed my pillows, helped me sit up, and then helped me into my bed jacket. The tea was hot and sweet and fragrant, Inge's secret of adding a spoonful of apple juice to each pot and a spoonful of honey to each cup. It also reawakened my appetite, and I attacked the toast with enthusiasm. My thoughts clearing, I remembered what had transpired yesterday, and I set the toast back on the plate and asked Inge how Greta had fared.

"It was a most interesting afternoon," she began, and I settled back on the pillows and listened to the story. And it was quite a story.

Before Inge had finished her tale, Greta had joined us and was sitting on the edge of the bed, supplying an additional detail here and there.

"Mama said I should stay home from school today and rest." She laughed. "I don't need rest. Mama is the one who needs rest. And when Mama is tired, we all must sleep." The sun on her hair created a halo effect, and her eyes sparkled like blue diamonds. We were back on track.

I finished my breakfast and after a short nap, at the insistence of my sister, I awoke refreshed and ready for a bit of activity. I dressed in a pair of borrowed slacks and matching sweater and went downstairs, where Inge was folding laundry and singing softly to herself.

"I'm feeling better and would like a bit of fresh air. How would you like to walk with me out to the barn and take a good look at that car?" I asked. "There may be other surprises for us."

Inge gave a final pat to the bath towel she had set on top of the stack and untied her apron, tossing it onto the back of the wooden chair.

"Let's," she said, "I'm ready for a break. The laundry is never ending."

The resident barn owl which had settled in for her day's sleep on a rafter above the hay loft, signaled her displeasure at the disturbance, and with a soft rustle of feathers, floated deeper into the barn to resume her nap.

We removed the canvas cover from the car and let it settle to the dirt floor in a crumpled heap. "Where do we start?" asked Inge, studying the vehicle with a critical eye.

That was a very good question. We checked the glove compartment, which interestingly enough, actually held a pair of men's leather driving gloves. Nothing in them, nothing else in the compartment, not even a registration. I guess the Nazis didn't bother with the more mundane details of car ownership. And what police officer would actually pull one of them over and ask to see the documents? Not anyone who was contemplating retirement on a regular schedule, that was a given.

The rest of the front seat proved just as barren, but when we attacked the rear seats, we made our first discovery. Each of the armrests opened to reveal a deep compartment. The left hand side was empty, except for a pack of cigarettes, but the right hand side housed a Luger. It would be an impressive addition to Inge's arsenal. She lifted it out and balanced it in her hand. "It's heavy," she remarked, weighing it in her open palm. "Bullets. Do you suppose there's any bullets?" She was off on the hunt, peering deeper into the cavity and then checking under the floor mat.

"You'll have to add them to your shopping list," I said, absorbed in my own search of the convertible top. It seemed thicker than normal, and I ran my hands across the top and underneath it, making it into a sort of sandwich. I shook my head and set about taking the top down.

"Holy Mother of God!" I yelped, as the top and bottom layers of the cover parted to reveal a radio antenna. "Where there's smoke," I muttered. A short while later I discovered fire, which was housed in the trunk in the form of two short-wave radios. Inge's eyes bugged out as she recognized what we had uncovered.

"One more time through," I said and shifted my attention back to the front seat. The leather upholstery was luxurious, a soft beige, as were the side panels of the doors. It was only after I had examined them for the third time that I saw the slight depression in the panel of the driver's door, and pried it open with my fingers. Inside was a sheaf of papers filled with names, odd number combinations, and some handwritten notes.

I sat down on the dirt floor and rifled through them, but couldn't make out the significance of the numbers. One name, however, did ring a very loud bell, and I called Inge over to me in a whisper, even though there was no one else around.

"What'cha got?" Inge struggled out from beneath the car. She had a smudge of grease on her forehead and cheek. She had been checking out the undercarriage.

When I had said "One more time through," she had decided to be thorough. She was wiping her grease-covered hands on her housedress, but didn't seem to notice.

The list of names was alphabetical. What a surprise coming from the Germans, I thought, but as I reached the fourth name on the third page, the surprise was on me. There was Sankt Peder's not so beloved pastor, Karl Mueller, although the name was a parenthetical addition to one Hans Schwarz. Karl Mueller was Hans Schwarz?

"I knew it!" Inge said. "We all did. Now we've got proof! He has to be the man who came from the submarine. Lars will be overjoyed to get this. He's still waiting on more details about the woman who picked him up. All he has is a name, so far, and an address," she added.

I nodded absently, as I continued my search.

Finally, satisfied that there were no obvious secrets left,

we replaced the canvas. We had amassed quite a collection of artifacts. Inge loaded the radios and the antenna into a wheelbarrow and with me toting the Luger and the sheaf of papers, we were farmers returning from the field with a strange harvest indeed.

Chapter Thirty

London

"History will be kind to me," Churchill said, "for I intend to write it."

"Only the victors write history," John reminded him.

The Lord High Admiral grunted. "Do you play chess, Breckenridge?" Churchill was presiding over the morning's staff meeting from his bedchamber. "Fine game, fine game. It's an intellectual exercise in warfare, you know." With the morning's second cigar at hand and a magnum of champagne opened and at the ready, Churchill had breakfast under control.

John was balancing a cup of coffee on his lap, a minor heresy in the realm, while he rifled through the morning's briefings. "I play a little," he said.

"You try not to sacrifice any of your players, of course. But certain players are more valuable than others at different stages of the game." He looked up. "As long as you understand that, you can prevail."

"Checkmate is the end of the game, sir," John said.

"The German system does not reward initiative. I don't believe I would have fared well, had I had the misfortune to have been born across the Channel." Churchill was scrutinizing the mashed cigar that had fallen victim to his latest teeth grinding episode. "That fact, however, and I am referring to the former," Churchill made a looping gesture with his hand, "will stand us in good stead."

Churchill reached across the bed and set the cigar on his ashtray, an odd-looking item shaped like a pagoda with a small trough on top to hold the cigar. A gift from a friend, he was never far from it and never traveled without it.

"So where do we stand, Sir?" John was standing by at the ready.

"Two items of interest today." Churchill handed the file for Operation Wilfred to John. "The help we've received from your wife has finally broken the impasse. The microfilm she sent indicated German plans to move north towards the coast. The War Cabinet was disinclined to believe the reports coming out of Denmark, but now they have no choice but to move on them. They'vc verified that the document is Hitler's directive for *Operation Weserubung,* and we've finally gotten the green light for our plans."

Churchill's plans to mine the waters off Norway had actually changed several times since he had designed the operation last year, shortly after the German invasion of Poland. Originally, the plan would have had the troops landing after the mine laying operations, but it was ultimately decided that no troop landings would take place unless the Germans landed first or demonstrated an intent of violating Norwegian neutrality. Plan R4 would accompany Operation Wilfred. In this plan the Allies would proceed to occupy Trondheim and Bergen and destroy the Soia airfield. The R4 expedition would be transported in troop ships with an accompanying light cruiser force.

"But why did the Cabinet doubt the intelligence coming out of Denmark? Isn't that why they put people there in the first place?"

Churchill snorted. "It's the same old, same old story. Shortsightedness and a strange mixture of condescension and arrogance. Because *we* would never land a military force on a hostile shore without first securing control of the seas there, *we* assumed the Germans pursued a similar policy. A near fatal error. Now they agree that we need our chaps in Denmark and in several other key places as well."

"It seems to have played out the way you wanted, sir," John said.

"We're on track, at any rate. That brings us to the second item of business today. You will be in place before the operation commences. The fighting will begin in earnest within the next two weeks, and you will be in harm's way. There's no telling how long that situation will hold. We will not be able to extract you. Are your men aware of the conditions?"

"Yes, Sir. They are ready to move on your orders. Six men and one woman. The Dane will be given the necessary information in time to prepare for our arrival." John ran down the list of names, destinations, and assignments. "When your man in Berlin gave us the heads up that Hitler fancies an elite SS populated with Germanic men from the 'proper countries,' Norway, Holland, Denmark, and Sweden, we decided it was time to salt the ranks.

"Three of our men will move to the police forces in various cities across Denmark, where their distinguished service records will mark them as prime candidates for the honor of serving the *Reich*. Basil Dunkling and the twin brothers Cecil and Graham Ackroyd – all three are linguists and marksmen and all thoroughly vetted." John looked up at Churchill, who nodded.

He continued, "Stanley Livingston will establish himself as a dealer in fine art, with an ability to 'locate' rare and valuable items for a price. The high mucky-mucks in the Nazi Party are not above a bit of individual 'shopping' when they have the opportunity. We've fixed him up with credentials and a passport that reveals extensive travel to the Orient. This will give him plenty of legroom to operate.

"One late addition to the troupe is Dr. Alistair Fleming. He will head for Berlin, where he will be researching the occult and items of especial interest to *Der Führer*. We have a shopping list for him and suspect it won't be long before our academician is appreciated for his contributions to Hitler's stockpile of antiquities.

"Dena Cottle will be taking up residence at her family's estate on the German-Danish border, where she will lavishly entertain. Our friend Himmler has his little Himmler-Havn in Schleswig-Holstein, and I fancy he will soon find himself on her A-list.

"Chester Beedle will begin work in a butcher shop in Berlin, a prime location, as it supplies meat for the Party's functions, and I am bound for Copenhagen as the Reverend Martin Schoneborger, to spread the Gospel and organize my little Bible study groups. We've covered considerable ground in the past two weeks. Wish we'd had a bit more time."

"You've had the time there is. And now you've only to be patient a trifle longer."

"What's our transportation?"

"The best we've got, an Armstrong Whitworth Whitley V. It's got a cruising speed of 210 mph at 15,000 feet and a fuel capacity of 837 Imperial gallons. Should be enough to get the job done," Churchill said.

"I have more news for you," Churchill continued. "A colonel in the *Wehrmacht -Standartenfuhrer* Erich Strasser has been a thorn in our side for quite some time. I am pleased to report that the thorn has been removed." Churchill looked to John. "Katrin has done yeoman – excuse me – *woman* service here." He chuckled. "The news over the wire from The Dane is excellent. Katrin has dispatched Strasser for us. Nicely done, that. However, he has or had, I should say, a daughter. She is herself an agent of sorts. Not a very good one," he added. "Used her mainly for small jobs, mostly providing transport for mobile operatives. She's been involved with one of these men off and on for the past two years. He's good. Very good. Code name is Ronin."

"How do you know how good he is?" John asked.

"Because we've used him ourselves at times. But that's immaterial at the moment. The girl is of interest to us. With her connections, she may be someone you will find helpful to know, if you can arrange a meeting – and I have every confidence you can do so. Just an idea."

"A Lutheran minister and a Nazi," John said. "I guess there have been stranger combinations."

"Have been and will be," Churchill continued. "There is a problem, however. She has gone missing. Failed to show for a rendezvous, but she has also not been to work in a week or at her apartment either. The girl's name is Dagmar. She works at the plant with your wife." Churchill watched John, waiting for his reaction.

"Really."

"You are mastering the art of understatement," Churchill said and chuckled. "Just like a true Englishman. Strasser's aide is one of our chaps. Been there since the Beer Hall incident. Nice fellow, name of Martin. Mother is German. He knows Dagmar's habits, but we need him where he is. This job requires someone outside." He stabbed the paper with a pencil and flicked it back onto the bed where it settled in among its mates. "We don't want to risk him being exposed. We have plans for him," Churchill added. We want Katrin to find her."

"That's *all* Katrin has to do? Find someone who's gone missing somewhere? No further information available? I'm surprised you don't send a Girl Guide to do the job."

"Actually, we have some encouraging prospects in the Girl Guides," Churchill replied.

There was an edge to John's voice. "With all respect, Sir, this is nuts. It's time for her to come out."

"Details," the Lord High Admiral said. "She'll work them out."

Chapter Thirty-One

Sankt Peder

Raising my glass high, I proclaimed, "To Home and Hearth! It's the little touches that make a house a home. Lace curtains, the aroma of freshly-baked bread, the portraits of loved ones, the German staff car in the barn, top secret documents in the buffet along with the best tablecloths, a short wave radio transmitter in the upstairs study, and undercover agents, spies, and patriots in every nook and cranny!" I was inspirational. I loved my family. I was tipsy.

We had settled ourselves around the dining room table after supper. Lars had brought out the aquavit, and we had been toasting everyone and everything. I had run out of people and so had decided to honor the venerable farmhouse. We had an unspoken agreement to be festive.

Volmer's toast, "To the family business!" and Anna's "To the Ladies Guild and the Daughters of Gefion!" put the next round's responsibility on Inge, who did herself proud. "To the motor pool and the munitions dump!" Greta had been allowed one small glass and was nursing her drink to be able to participate in each round, while the rest of us, including, Lord help me, Anna and Volmer, set a mighty pace. Anna's cheeks were getting pinker with each round, and I noticed a devilish twinkle in Volmer's eye. Gussie the cat had stopped by to visit and was staring at us with her usual cross-eyed look of boredom. I had plans to toast her on my next turn.

Lars had just called for the next round when a loud rap came at the front door. For a moment all was silence, then Anna's hand went to her mouth, Volmer's eyes narrowed, Inge hiccupped, and Greta looked around expectantly, waiting to see where this interesting development would go. Inge and I snatched up our glasses, propelled Anna into the kitchen, and left the men to deal with our evening visitor. It was an excellent tactical move. Besides, this is where the knives were kept.

It took some effort to propel Anna, but by the time we got her through the door, Lars had returned his hand and glass to the table. Volmer thrust his jaw in the direction of the door, and Lars nodded. He rose, straightened, and gave a modest belch as he negotiated the short distance to the door, which he peered at intently before locating the doorknob. He flung the door open with a mighty swing, and watched as the two individuals standing on the doorstep merged into one figure, which unfortunately turned out to be Pastor Mueller, who had stopped by to collect the hymn selections from Anna for tomorrow's Easter service.

Lars carefully repeated the request, as if it had been uttered in a foreign language, and cementing it in place in his mind, slammed the door closed in the pastor's face. He stared at the door, processing the surprise departure of the pastor, shrugged, and set off to the kitchen where he relayed the information to Anna, who handed him the requested slip of paper and motioned him back to the door with a wave of her hand. Opening it more slowly this time, Lars was satisfied that the pastor was where he had left him. He gave him the paper, wished him good night, and firmly shut the door once again. He waited a moment or two before checking the doorstep, but the minister had departed.

Giggles from the kitchen and a dignified chortle from Volmer in the dining room greeted Lars upon his return from messenger duty. He bowed with a flourish and yawned. It was time to put the party to bed and I was ready. Lars and Inge collected Greta and they called out their "good nights" as they let themselves out the door for the short journey home. I trudged upstairs to bed and Volmer waited for Anna while she put out the cat and turned off the lights. Finally, they climbed the stairs together, Volmer's hand in hers.

Outside the house, a figure turned away from the parlor window and disappeared into the darkness.

"I'll be back shortly," Volmer said to Anna, as he tied the belt of his bathrobe and slipped his feet into leather slippers. Anna was seated at her vanity, the long ivory-handled hairbrush in her hand. Her hair had always been unruly and she'd been trying to tame it for the past sixty years. It showed no signs of giving up the fight, but still each night she coaxed it with a hundred strokes. Tight curls stretched under the caress of the bristles, only to spring back into undisciplined coils each time she set them free. Anna sighed.

Volmer's tread was soft as he crossed the hall to his study. Each night since Volmer had first sent on the news of the submarine, Dick had told him to be standing by at eleven o'clock every evening. It was five minutes till the hour, and as he waited, Volmer stood by his north window, bathed in the light of the moon. The countryside was as bright as day, and he could see the cat stalking a mouse in the yard below.

When Dick's message came through, it was short, a mix of letters and numbers. Volmer deciphered the message, using the simple cipher code they had devised many years ago. When he had finished, he sat back in his wooden chair and read the message: *Company coming. RSVP for eight at seven* was all it said. He took a deep breath before replying. His own message was just simple, "The company is welcome." He then took the paper with the transcribed message and struck a match to it, watching as the flame spread up from the corner to cover the contents, turning it to white ash that fell from his fingers to the ash tray on his desk. He stirred the residue with a pencil, shut down the radio, turned off the lamp, and went to his bedroom.

"Anna, are you sleeping yet?" he asked softly. "I need to talk with you."

"No, Volmer," she said, "I was waiting for you." She sat up and patted the down comforter, inviting him to come and sit down beside her.

"They are coming tomorrow night, Anna," he said.

"It had to come," she answered. "Come to bed, Volmer. We'll go early in the morning to tell Lars and Inge and make our preparations."

"*Ja,*" he said. "That is best," and he climbed into bed beside her.

Anna rolled over and wrapped her arm around him. Ten minutes later, Volmer sat up. "We should get started now, Anna," he said. "I can't sleep."

"I'll make coffee, Volmer. You gather the family."

Chapter Thirty-Two

Sankt Peder

"We're sleeping so little that morning only comes every other day around here, it seems." Lars was grumbling into his coffee cup.

"Drink your coffee, Lars, and wake up," Inge chided.

"I'll be right down," I called. John always called my trusty blue chenille robe my traveling bedspread, and as I snugged the belt around my waist, the warmth that enveloped me made me feel just a bit lonesome. In the few weeks I had been away from home, so much had happened. So much would still happen. One of my slippers had pulled a vanishing act, so I settled for it and supplemented it with a sock that was hanging out of my dresser drawer for the right foot. Thus attired I went downstairs to join the family.

"I will make more coffee," Inge said.

I had to smile at the rituals we observed. Dear Inge. No matter what the occasion, there was food and drink. She unwrapped a plate of currant muffins she had brought and set them alongside a pitcher of cream. Cups and saucers waited for the coffee. Volmer stood at the head of the table, a sheaf of papers nestled in the crook of his arm and the almanac by his plate. He looked for all the world like a lord chamberlain waiting on the queen to arrive.

"Sit Katrin. Sit Inge. Sit Greta. Sit Anna," Volmer began.

We complied, four obedient Schipperkes.

"The wire has arrived and English come on the evening," he said, "between sunset and moonrise. The sun will set at 6:29 tonight. The moon will rise at 7:51. We have a window of approximately an hour."

I nodded. We had been waiting each day for news of the drop date. At our last meeting of the Daughters of Gefion we had planned for this event. I remembered the women, brightly clad in their red and white, assembled in Inge's parlor.

Over coffee and muffins, they had received their first military briefing. It was a small core group, consisting of Inge, Anna, Marta, Barbara, and Ilse, and they had already made one difficult decision – not to include Gunda. There was too much uncertainty with her, and although she had a good heart, she couldn't be trusted not to say the wrong thing at the wrong time to the wrong people. This was best. They'd have meetings where they just gossiped, and Gunda would be welcome at these. It was the way it had to be.

"How will this work?" asked Marta. "What do we do?"

I had told Inge how the drop would work and she explained this to the women. "They will come at tusmorke, before the moon has risen," she began. "The plane will come from England and the agents will parachute from the plane as it passes over our north pasture. We will have lanterns to light their way in and we will make a circle with the lanterns to bring the people safely in. We will need homes for them for a short time until they can safely leave and begin their missions."

The women's eyes were bright and clear with understanding. "There will be eight of them. One, I understand, is a woman," Inge continued.

Marta was counting on her fingers. "I can take three. It will be a bit crowded but it will work." She nodded decisively.

"I can take one," Barbara offered. "Arne says this is a fine thing we are doing. He is proud of me." Inge smiled at Barbara, still on her honeymoon and offering her home for strangers. She was proud of all of them.

"Nils and I can take two as well," said Ilse.

"And Lars and I will also take two. It is settled."

Anna said, "We may not have much notice, but check the hymn board every day. The first hymn that has a number will tell you it is the day to assemble."

"So. We know they are coming and we know what we are to do. It is beginning, then, isn't it?" asked Ilse, and everyone knew what she meant. The women finished their coffee and left to tell their husbands what they had learned and to fill the lanterns with oil and to trim the wicks. Just as it was done in the Parable told by Jesus, so would it be done in this small town in Denmark.

That had been yesterday. The English invasion, or at least a miniature version of it, would parachute into Denmark in advance of the German invasion and disperse throughout the country, coordinating the Resistance and sabotaging the *Wehrmacht*. The intelligence I had gathered had revealed the timetable of Hitler's Operation *Weserubung* and with this knowledge Churchill had decided it was time to move the agents into place and gather his forces for *Operation Wilfred*.

John would be coming and I would be leaving, but for a brief moment, before I left for England via Sweden, I would see him. I wanted to shout and to laugh and to cry all at once. To touch him. To hold him and kiss him and tell him how much I loved him. How much I would always love him. Always and forever. I took a deep, ragged breath. Volmer and Anna were watching me, and their eyes were warm. I smiled.

"John will be coming. He will deal with Karl Mueller," I

said. "That will be one problem solved.

"*Ja*. And the women are ready. Marta every hour asks me when they will come." Anna shook her head. "I think she fancies herself a Madame DeFarge. She has even forsaken crocheting to learn to knit. Her heart is good. And who knows? Maybe she will strangle a Nazi with that scarf she is making. It is already long enough to throttle a battalion. It's red and white," she added, "she wanted it to be in the colors of the Danish flag."

The War Council of the Nissen-Jensen Family, now fully staffed, proceeded with the next item on the agenda, passing on the information to the townspeople.

"We have selected certain hymns," explained Anna, as she consulted the Lutheran hymnal she had brought downstairs with her. "We settled on two for sure, but didn't know about the time. We need to find one for that."

"We get the congregation's attention with "A Mighty Fortress is Our God." Anna bit her lip as she continued to scan down the index. "Then we sing "Bless this Day."

"I picked that one," Greta said.

"It was a good choice, little one," Volmer said.

"Don't forget this is Easter Sunday," I said. The minister is going to wonder why you're changing the hymns at the last minute."

"We'll worry about that later. The less he knows, the better. Here!" She found the hymn she was looking for and opened to that page. "My Blessed Savior Seven Times Spoke." She sat back and poured herself a cup of coffee, pleased.

"It's a little obscure," Volmer said. "I don't think the congregation knows it."

"Doesn't matter. As long as it tells them it's the time to gather in our field, we'll stumble through it. Julianne will play loud enough to drown us out anyway. That woman has the hand of a road mender when she plays the organ."

"She's almost deaf," said Greta. "Too bad the organ

doesn't have a volume control switch."

We ran through the logistics of the coming night. Everyone knew what to bring and where to gather. After we dispersed, I spent the waning hours of the night copying information from Strasser's papers to pass on to John. I would take the originals back to Whitehall with me, but John would have what he needed to get his own work done.

Unanswered questions haunted me, mostly what had happened to Dagmar and how that might affect Wally and Helga. Her father was out of the picture, but what was her connection to Karl Mueller, alias Hans Schwarz? What did the list of names and numbers mean? I didn't like leaving loose ends behind. There was nothing I could do now to get answers. They would come in their own time, if indeed they came at all.

I sat for a moment at the vanity, examining my face that looked so much like my sister's and like Greta's. What a strange thing family is. Mine wasn't all that out of the ordinary - that wasn't what I meant. It was the oddness of looking around at other people in the room and finding they looked a great deal like you. It was unsettling and yet comforting at the same time. "Strong genes," Mama had said. "The Nissen women had strong genes." Restless, I paced the room and then decided to take my strong genes outside for a breath of fresh air.

It was still and cold. I could see my breath and I made little puffs of it, tiny clouds that hung for a moment on the chilled air before they disappeared. Footsteps on the cobblestones caused me to turn and I saw Inge, coming down the path to join me. I smiled and raised a hand in welcome.

"I couldn't sleep either. So much will happen today I can hardly stand it."

"It will get started soon enough," I said. "This is the last bit of quiet, I think, for quite a while. Where is Lars?"

"Snoring like a woodcutter. He is shaking the bed he snores so loud." Inge made an exasperated face. "That's another reason I couldn't sleep."

I chuckled. "Inge, I have something I want you to give to Greta, when it's time." I reached into my coat pocket and extracted a worn silver thimble. I took Inge's hand and deposited the thimble in her palm, closing her fingers around it. I patted her hand and repeated, "When it's time."

"No! Oh, no! This is not right. This is yours to give her yourself when she has a child. You are the eldest daughter." Inge's eyes were wide. "No! You take it back. You will do it. That's what Mama told us and what her Mama told her. Don't break the chain." She pushed the thimble back at me, but I shook my head.

"Inge, take the thimble, please do it. Besides, the chain is already broken. I have no daughter, and you do. It is right you give it to her."

"You are stubborn, and I can be just as stubborn. I will not do it. I will keep it for you until you come back. Then you will give it to her yourself." Inge bobbed her head furiously and I knew better than to continue. I sighed and agreed.

"When the war is over, I will come back and we will give it to her together."

"That is better. Enough foolish talk. You speak as if we will never see each other again. I know better."

I hoped the Fates were listening, because if my sister had decided we would meet again in this life, it would be so. I had no doubts. And I also had no doubts but that we would both be exhausted if we didn't get some rest. I looked at Inge and smiled. "And now we must salvage an hour or two of sleep this night."

She returned the smile and we walked back inside the house together.

Chapter Thirty-Three

Sankt Peder

I should have been tired. Hell, I should have been exhausted. Adrenaline. It must have been pure adrenaline that had me pumped up. That and the knowledge I would be with John tonight. With so much happening, I hadn't slept even an hour. And now the sun was streaming through the window, a clear, bright Easter Sunday morning. Although the weather outside was still crisp, the weatherman had promised a high of 12 degrees Celsius today, so by the time we headed home from church, it would be almost shirtsleeve weather, well maybe long-sleeved flannel shirt weather. I would need my warm woolen coat this morning, that much was sure.

Inge had loaned me her best dress, a silk shantung in a glorious shade of emerald green. She'd added her matching cloche hat. "You wear it. It's Easter Sunday. That's that." And she draped it over my arms, set the hat on top, and shut the door firmly behind her, leaving me to yell "Thank you!" at the doorknob.

I ran my hands over the shimmering fabric, in a hue deep as pools of glacial waters. I would have to do something about my face, however, if I were going to do justice to the dress. Over the course of the last forty-eight hours my bruises had yellowed, and apart from looking like a woman in the end stages of some exotic liver disease, I was feeling pretty good. I applied a thick coating of face powder and analyzed the effect in the mirror. I resembled a porcelain Geisha doll, white as snow. If I didn't move my mouth too much, or blink too hard, or sneeze, it might last until church was out.

Losing interest in my mirrored reflection, I spied the Easter basket I'd set on the bed. Sometime during the night, Greta had placed the basket outside my door. Nestled in a bed of straw there was a chocolate bunny, colored eggs, and a spun sugar hollow egg in delicate shades of pink and blue and yellow, with a country scene inside of little chickens and daffodils. There was a note attached, "For your trip. Love, Greta."

I contemplated the nature of chocolate, which I consider to be an essential building block of life. Appropriate and suitable for all occasions. Hot chocolate with fresh marshmallows on a blustery winter day, rich chocolates with cream centers after an evening on the town, chocolate bars with almonds and walnuts by a campfire in the wilderness, chocolate cake with rich chocolate frosting on birthdays, chocolate sprinkles on vanilla ice cream and chocolate fudge-double decadence anytime. Death by Chocolate. My eyes were glazing over. I bit the ears off the rabbit and crunched my way downstairs to breakfast.

We were all a little fuzzy this morning, and breakfast was as quiet as last night had been raucous. Good strong coffee, stollen, and kippers helped some. I picked at my food. Picked at my first helping, picked at my second helping, and decided not to pick at a third. Most of the fare was disappearing without any extra help on my part anyways, and besides, Easter dinner would be an elaborate affair. I could tell from all the bowls covered with waxed paper and the ham that was waiting on the sideboard. It would do my appetite good to get a little exercise before the next meal.

Upstairs again, I climbed into the dress and wiggled until it fell over my hips, smoothed my hair and attached the cap with my hatpin. I slipped into my black pumps and gathered up my black gloves in my left hand. The rabbit in the basket looked rather lopsided, so I decided to even him out. I bit off the nose. You can never have too much chocolate. It provides energy and after all, we would need it. We had a full day ahead of us, and it revolved around church, the center of the woman's universe.

Kirke, køkken, børn had defined the role of women in Scandinavia and Germany for centuries. Now the modern world was tugging at the fabric of tradition, loosening the threads and causing established patterns to unravel. In the countryside, change came more slowly, and the old ways held sway. "Church, cooking, children" was still a fair description of the events unfolding this Sunday in the parish hall of the Evangelical Lutheran Church of the Redeemer of Sankt Peder, as the Ladies Society set up before church service for the Open House to welcome the new minister.

Each woman had staked out her own section of the long wooden tables that had been spread with red and white checked gingham cloths, and each dish was positioned to showcase its eye appeal. The whole setting up process hummed with efficiency, the result of perfected practice. It was a rite of passage for a young woman to create and present her signature dish, a tradition that had both its good and bad points. For those possessing talents in the culinary arts, the laurels were piled high. Unfortunately, for those whose offerings fell short, custom still deemed that the parish would endure many years of their efforts as well. And so, Bobbie Jensen's strudel disappeared quickly and the stalwart congregation gamely chewed away at Christina Ingalls's undercooked potato salad, year after year after year.

Everything was as I had remembered. The mop and the bucket were still in the corner closet. The kitchen sink still held the dish rack perpetually filled with cups and saucers. The huge pots that served up vast quantities of noodles and soups were stacked atop the cupboards, and just looking at them I recalled the slightly scorched hot chocolate that had seared its memory into my childhood. Other childhood memories surfaced. Chipping off pieces of ice on a hot summer's day. Picnics on the church lawn in the summer time, all of us with berry-stained faces from the pie-eating contests. The memories flooded back in a warm current of comfort. With hands on hips I surveyed this gentle kingdom.

I had been spared the cooking and had been assigned to set up and clean up, which suited me just fine. Any meal I didn't have to cook was a good one, as far as I was concerned, never having aspired to membership in the sorority of cooks, and Inge's efforts notwithstanding. With full length aprons covering our dresses, we received the bowls and platters of food that arrived in a steady procession. Our assembly line moved the food from the kitchen across the pass through space in the wall and onto the linoleum covered counter, from which other helping hands completed the transfer to the long tables in the hall, where my job was to ensure that each dish had the proper serving implement and all bowls were covered with waxed paper.

A short hallway connected the Parish Hall with the church proper. With windows lining both walls, the corridor was awash in light. It had been many years since I had attended a church service at home, but the familiar cadences of my native tongue reclaimed me quickly to the fold. Little had changed. The church was a sturdy boxlike structure with a crooked steeple that listed slightly to starboard, bent but not bowed by the fierce winter storms that had buffeted it over the years. Its weatherworn exterior had recently received a fresh coat of white paint and, thus decked out in its own Easter finery, it sported its steeple like a jaunty Easter bonnet. The church had spunk. Set back from the busy street, it was a hub of neighborhood activity. The women's group met here Mondays, the men's on Tuesday. Bible study on Thursdays and Choir Practice on Fridays, left Saturdays for weddings and funerals, Sundays for church school and worship. Wednesday was its traditional day of rest, and the pastor shared in that. Even a building deserves respite.

Some buildings intimidate. They are cold, unwelcoming structures, while others are warm and inviting. It's the basic difference between a house and a home. I had seen pictures of the majestic cathedrals of Europe - Notre Dame of Paris, Chartres, even the Vatican seemed to be more proclamations of man's achievements than tributes to the glory of God. Architectural wonders, they left me cold. God was closer to me here, and I to Him. A church is much more than a building. It is a community. And here the community was my family.

Coming here was coming home. I think it was the personal, homely touches that the important churches in all their grandeur could never achieve. For example, the cross-eyed Jesus oil painting that beamed upon the congregation and that had been the effort of *Frue* Schlenkmeyer, an aspiring artist who had more piety than talent. She had donated it to the church, which displayed it prominently and proudly in the hall. It wasn't a Rembrandt but still, it was a reasonable likeness, and a myopic Savior seemed infinitely more compassionate than one with perfect vision.

The well-worn plank floors glowed with the patina of age and the rows of white pews bore the scuffs and scars of generations of worshipers. My grandmother, Julianne, had prayed here, and her mother, Ingeborg, before her.

The flowers were fit for a cathedral. Snowdrops, the first flower of spring, daffodils, Easter lilies, hyacinths, and tulips had transformed the interior of the church into a spring garden. With the food taken care of, we were carrying the finishing touches with us, fern fronds that Greta had brought from her last foray into the small wooded lot that bordered the town. Many were still curled, soon to unfurl into a lacy filigree of green background to contrast with the pastel hues of the flowers. I had my own little secret burden. The rabbit was hitching a ride inside my pocketbook, although he had lost his front paws between the front door and the neighbors' home. I munched in contented silence.

Greta busied herself arranging the fronds, while I held the rest of her supply and followed her from vase to vase. Needing another fortifying nip from the bunny, I lifted him out of his den to consider which part to eat next. Greta stopped with her labors and held two small sprigs behind his head. "Replacement ears," she said and laughed. "Really, *Tante* Katrin, you should save some for later. You will be hungry."

I nodded in agreement at the wisdom of this and snapped off the head, offering her half. She accepted and we savored the treat in conspiratorial silence. All that was left now was the hollow body and a couple of rabbits' feet. Not especially lucky for this fellow. "After all," I said, "what possible use could there be for him now except to finish the job?"

"There are some choices, *Tante* Katrin. You could make him an ashtray, if you smoked, that is." She tilted her head, considering the possibilities. "Or a key holder!" She laughed and reached into her bag and deposited a set of car keys into the bunny.

"Greta! Not funny! You're getting germs in my food," I said but my eye settled on the keys. "Where did you get these? Don't tell me you've been driving?" I looked at her sternly.

"I wish. Nope. That sure would be fun, though. But I found these right outside in the cemetery when I was digging ferns. Right in the middle of the *equisetum silvatica*. Thought I'd add it to the announcements today," she said. "They have to belong to somebody."

We continued to peer down into the rabbit waiting for it to divulge more information, but all was silence. The bunny wasn't talking. Well, I had eaten the head quite a while ago. I fished out the keys and it was then I saw the Mercedes logo. Our possible pool of owners had now shrunk considerably. The only Mercedes automobiles that had graced the neighborhood of Sankt Peder comprised a field of two, the staff car that was hiding out in Inge's barn, and the car that we had seen in the parsonage barn. Both were out of their element, as I was sure not very many of these classy cars spent much time in barns of any type. An elegant garage seemed more their style.

"Let me take these, honey, if you don't mind. I think it would be best if we don't advertise that we have them just now."

Greta's eyes widened, but she nodded. "Do you think they have something to do with you know what?" She moved her eyes towards the minister who had emerged from his office where he had donned his vestments.

"It's possible," I said, tucking them into my pocketbook. "I'm going to check on something. I'll be back in a few minutes." I left Greta to finish up the fronds and slipped out the side door of the church hall.

The parsonage barn was mostly used for storage by members of the congregation, so it wasn't unusual to see someone from the town carrying boxes or tools in and out. It was unusual to see vehicles stored there, though, as these were precious few and those were used regularly. In the time since Inge and I had happened upon Dagmar's car there, no one had seen nor heard from her, and her trail had grown cold.

The car was still there under its tarpaulin. I hated questions without answers. It left everything so unsettled. I decided to search out Inge and run a theory or two past her.

"Do you recognize these?" I pulled the car keys out of my purse and dangled them in front of her face.

Inge shook her head slowly. "They've got the Mercedes logo. But I know for a fact that they don't belong to *our* car." She reached into her own purse and pulled out a matching set. "I figured to be ready if I needed to drive it somewhere."

So there we stood, dangling two sets of keys in each other's face and looking like a couple of amateur hypnotists. "These are Dagmar's," I said. "They have to be. But she's nowhere around and her car is still in the barn. So?"

"So?"

At that unfortunate moment, the pastor passed by on his way to the sacristy. He paused ever so slightly at the mention of Dagmar's name, but didn't stop. I wondered what the connection was. Find the answer and we might just find Dagmar. Regardless, Karl Mueller bore careful watching. He was a dangerous man.

The first notes of the organ prelude interrupted this line of thought and we took our seats. I slid into the pew and settled myself, smoothing my skirt and straightening my Easter bonnet, Inge's emerald cloche that hugged my head. If the food waiting in the hall was a study in textures, the church itself was a study in color - a riot of color. The spectrum of hues on the millinery that crowned the females of the parish echoed the flowers in the vases. Ribbons and bows, feathers and lace moved like waves in the ocean and wind in the meadow grass. Interspersed in this pastel landscape, the dark browns and grays and navy blue men's suits provided contrast and balance.

While the women took pleasurable note of each other's dress, the men had resigned themselves to the discomforts of stiff collars and ties. They endured this ordeal once a week as well as for weddings and funerals. It was the price they paid for domestic tranquility, although they would have been just as devout in their work clothes.

All heads were now bowed in prayer, and I realized I had been wool gathering, and the cold gaze of the minister bored through my distraction. Dropping my gaze to avoid being a giraffe in a heard of emus, I assumed a posture of prayerful reverence. That was another thing I remembered about church, my mind tended to wander at inopportune moments.

I was always being chastised for drifting away from the program. I sighed.

Certain hymns are traditionally associated with the celebration of Easter, and according to the song board, this morning would be no exception. But just as the pastor began the call to worship, Anna rose from her seat in the Amen pew and replaced the selections with new ones, to the undisguised displeasure of the minister. He stopped in midsentence to fix her with a disapproving glare while a soft murmur swept through the congregation.

"A Mighty Fortress is Our God," authored by Martin Luther himself, had transformed the call to worship into a call to arms, and while Karl could only puzzle at the change, the congregation joined in unison to raise their voices to God. Reverent, prayerful faces had taken on a firm resolve and their strong voices filled the church.

The sermon didn't sit well with the congregation, as the pastor spoke at some length on the virtues of obedience to earthly authority, citing the "Render to Caesar" advice that Jesus had used to answer His questioners. I caught Volmer's eye during this and he pursed his lips as if he had tasted something sour. I had to hide a smile behind my bulletin. People were beginning to fidget, and when the Andersen baby began to wail, his mother smiled at her neighbors, who smiled back.

Whether the pastor felt he had made his point, or had tired of competing with the tiniest parishioner, the sermon drew to a close, and with this, little Jacob Andersen drifted off to sleep. The silence was deafening.

We belted out "My Blessed Savior Seven Times Spoke" with several mistakes but a great deal of spirit nonetheless and then swung into the Recessional Hymn, "Bless this Day." Anna had done her job well. The congregation had understood the message and everyone would be in place tonight. Gathering our belongings, we awaited our turn to file out and shake hands with the pastor, greet neighbors, and make our way to the hall. My back had stiffened and I twisted left and right to loosen the kinks, and it was then that a shaft of light streaming through the stained glass window reflected off something on the floor underneath the pew in front of me. It took a little twisting, slumping, and sliding down in the bench, but stretching out my leg as far as I could, I was able to nudge the object with the toe of my shoe and coax it within reach. It was at once familiar and foreign. I knew immediately what it was and to whom it belonged, and it didn't belong here. It was Dagmar's diamond-encrusted barrette.

For a missing person, Dagmar was ever-present. Why here? When here? Inge and I needed to hash this out, but in private. The first opportunity might come at the meal that awaited us in the hall.

The men heaped their plates and the women fretted about their waistlines but still managed to take most of everything so as not to hurt anyone's feelings, and children tried to skip straight to the desserts. As I looked around, my heart was full. Everything was perfect. Of course it was perfect, Karl was gone. Odd, perhaps he had gone to his office. It just didn't feel right, one of those intuitive moments when you realize that something is out of whack. I excused myself from the table to check out my hunch.

The church hall is a spacious room with a hallway at either side. The effect is rather like ears on a box. The ear on the west side leads to the Church proper; the one on the east to the minister's office, the storage closet that is crammed as full as Fibber McGee's, the bathrooms, and the side entrance. The ladies' room is closest to the office, and I never could understand why. It made for some delicate situations when bodies collided, but today I was grateful for the proximity of office to bathroom, as I could try the handle and if I were interrupted, could slip into the bathroom and hide. The door was shut and locked. That probably meant that Karl had left and didn't want anyone snooping around while he was gone. Gone where? Everyone was in the hall; there was no one to visit. Even *Frue* Gundersson had been wheeled into the church for Easter.

Considering our plans for the evening, I wanted a minute by minute accounting of Karl's whereabouts. We would need to find a way to encumber him so he didn't come upon us at H-hour. This would be difficult to arrange if we couldn't find him.

"Any idea where Pastor Gestapo has gone?" I asked Inge when I rejoined the family.

She looked surprised and then looked around the room. "He was over there," she said, pointing at the head table which now had an empty chair. "I don't know where he's gone. Do you think he's up to something?" Inge sounded hopeful. "We could track him, like they do in the movies. I saw a western film with John Wayne and he had an Indian scout who did the tracking." Inge looked around the room again, as if she expected an Indian scout to materialize from among the good folk of Immanuel Lutheran.

"No scouts, no John Wayne, and no United States Cavalry," I pointed out. "We're on our own." Why when everything needs to fall into place does something always go wrong? Karl was a slippery devil, I gave him that. But I didn't like it and I had a bad feeling. The pastor did not return to the hall before we left.

The feeling only got worse when we returned home. The front door was wide open. "Greta, did you forget to close the front door?" Inge asked her daughter.

"Why is it always Greta? Greta this and Greta that. I know for a fact that I couldn't have shut the door because my hands were full of ferns and I was the first one out." She was filled with righteous indignation.

"Hold on." I said. "Just a minute. Before you ask me the same question, I wasn't the last one out." I was a tad defensive because I just might have been the last one out.

"No," said Lars, "I was the last one out, and I shut the

door." We regarded him with mild suspicion. "Just go in. It doesn't matter."

But it did matter. The buffet drawer was gaping open, the tablecloths and napkins had been emptied out of it and lay in a heap on the floor, and the top secret documents were gone. If you've ever been the victim of a crime, you can understand the sense of violation that we felt. Your home and your person should be sacrosanct, but all too often, aren't. The odd thought occurred to me that this was not a simple burglary, but rather an act of war. We were on the front lines. Somehow that seemed to change the situation significantly, at least on a psychological level.

It didn't take any great mental acuity to figure out who the thief was. I cursed myself under my breath for being stupid. Last night when we were toasting, Karl must have been prowling about, listening. The copies I had made for John were still in my bag, so we hadn't lost the information. However, with Karl in possession of the originals, he also had access to that same information. I wondered what his plans were. Whatever he intended, it didn't bode us well, I was sure.

"I've got an idea. If I'm not back in twenty minutes…" I left the rest unspoken, wheeled around, grabbed the pistol out of my pocketbook, and raced out the front door, where I spied Greta's bicycle. I rammed the kickstand up, tossed the gun into the wicker basket, hiked the dress up as high as I dared, mounted the bike, and headed back to church.

Chapter Thirty-Four

Sankt Peder

Pedaling a three-speed bicycle in a silk shantung dress is like riding sidesaddle in a bathrobe and just about as elegant. Balancing the need for speed with a modicum of modesty, I'd hiked up my skirts to give me some leg room and was pumping for all I was worth, a Danish Margaret Hamilton minus Toto in the basket. Where would he be? Karl not Toto. Church office? Possibly. Parsonage? More likely. Time was not on my side and I had to choose correctly the first time.

The situation reminded me of the climax of every Grade B suspense film I'd ever seen. The ones where the hero has to defuse the bomb that conveniently has two wires laid bare for his inspection. He looms over them with his snippers. "Cut the red one," urges the perspiring police captain. "No! Cut the blue one," screams the telephone repairman. Finally our hero positions his cutters around the red wire, then pauses for severe dramatic effect before severing the blue one, just as the countdown on the timer reaches one second. How did he know? Luck. That's what I needed right now. Blind, dumb luck. A perspiring police captain and telephone repairman also would have been welcome.

"Oh, what the hell," I muttered. "Eenie, meenie, minie,

parsonage. Less public and more privacy. If Karl needed privacy, he would make straight for his living quarters. He had perhaps a fifteen minute lead on me, and I only hoped that I could reach him before he did what I expected he would do. I swept into the drive, churning up gravel in my wake, and bailed off the bicycle. I leaned it against the house, out of sight, and made for the front door.

The front door was oak, with a hand carved mahogany cross affixed to the panel above the brass door knocker. The door was massive and sturdy. It was also locked, probably for the first time in its history. No one locked doors in Sankt Peder, least of all a minister. That in itself showed me I had chosen wisely, and in this case, it wasn't to keep out the devil, the devil was already within. What Karl didn't know, that everyone else did, was that the rusting key resided atop the narrow lip of the wood trim above the door. It had been set there when the door was installed, for lack of a better place to store it. This made a forced entry unnecessary. Even rusted, the key slipped easily into the lock and I said a silent prayer of thanks. I let myself in and shut the door quietly behind me.

I stood in the hallway, listening, and then the creaking of floorboards above my head indicated Karl's whereabouts. He was moving about the study. Gun gripped in my hand, I climbed the stairs. It occurred to me that once we were rid of Karl, the parsonage would need a thorough cleaning and disinfecting. Probably a rededication was called for, as well.

The study door was open, and Karl was standing by the desk. He sensed my presence, and for a brief second he froze, then straightened and turned to face me. Judging from the equipment on the desk, he had been assembling a wireless radio and had nearly completed the job. He was about to transmit and his text lay before him, the documents I had lifted from Strasser's automobile. I took a steadying breath.

"Step away from the desk," I reinforced the command

with a slight jerk of my head.

Karl's response was a cold half smile and his lips remained pressed together.

"Now," I said. "And keep your hands where I can see them." I was not going to play games. He either moved or I had plans to drop him where he stood, but I didn't want to risk smashing a perfectly good radio. Parts were going to get extremely difficult to come by as time went on.

Obviously not a fan of American movies, Karl kept his hands in front of him, but didn't raise them in surrender. He moved towards the dresser and stopped alongside, his eyes studying mine, appraising me. When he spoke his tone was condescending. His voice was derisive. "Are you prepared to use that gun?" He managed to combine a sneer with a laugh. Very irritating.

"I am and I will. Count on it."

He turned his hands palms up, indicating the ball was in my court. I reached into my pocket and pulled out the car keys Greta had found. Slipping the ring through my index finger, I dangled them before his eyes. "Lose these?" I asked.

"Wh…" He stopped himself. Gone was the air of superiority. In its place, I detected something cold and calculated.

"Dagmar had to have had them when she drove her car into the barn," I said, tossing them on the desk. "Oh yes, we found Dagmar's car in the barn. Why she was here at all is a mystery, and why she hid her car in the barn is an even bigger one." I waited for some kind of reaction. When none was forthcoming, I added, "People have been looking for her, you know. Especially her father. The Colonel," I added.

"He won't find her," Karl spat.

"I know that."

Karl's eyes narrowed at my quick response. "I don't see how."

"You don't have to. Just believe it."

He drew back into himself and his color faded. "What do

you want?"

"Mostly I want what is on the desk there," I said, motioning to the papers. "But I'd also like an answer."

"Why not? Ask away."

"Where's Dagmar?"

"Why do you care? What's she to you?"

"I don't care, especially. And she's nothing to me. Let's just say I'm the curious type." This seemed to amuse him.

"Your guess is as good as mine. Maybe heaven, maybe hell, maybe some place in between. You could ask her yourself, but she won't answer. She's right over there." He turned his head and looked out the window towards the graveyard and a cold chill went through me. "I answered your question, now I want something from you."

This game of cat and mouse was wearing thin, but I had to find a way to keep him on ice until I could put him away for safekeeping. "Go ahead. Make it quick."

"I'm out of here today, and I need those papers. They're my insurance policy against Strasser. I work in a high risk business, you know."

Somehow, we had become professional associates. I didn't much care for the association. "No, you can't have them. And no, you don't need them." I felt as if I were reprimanding a willful child. "Not against Strasser in any case. He's out of the picture. Permanently," I added. Karl looked at me with the dawning of respect in his cold eyes, which held an unspoken question. I merely nodded and saw him exhale.

"Who is Strasser to you?" I asked, and he might have answered had not Greta burst into the room, flinging open the door which ricocheted off the wall, hitting her on the rebound, pushing her off balance and glancing off my arm. The gun arm. The gun clattered to the floor and skidded to the middle of the room where for a brief instant we all stared at it, before the mad scramble to grab it. Greta did a fair imitation of a champion diver, launching herself at Karl, arms outstretched, hands clasped together in credible aerodynamic form, tripping him up and causing him to fall forward, the result of which was his head hit the floor with an audible thunk. He was out cold. I winced.

"Hi *Tante* Katrin."

"Hi *Tante* Katrin? You could have been killed. We both could have been killed. "Hi *Tante* Katrin?" I was shaking now at the thought of what could have happened and seemed to have my voice stuck on repeat. "What are you doing here?" I was rapidly flipping through my emotion index, anger having replaced fear, the urge to throttle her within an inch of her life currently ascendant.

"I wanted to help. And I did, sort of. Well, at least after I goofed, I mean," she looked down at the prostrate pastor. "And we did get him after all. That was kind of fun. I like this espionage." She grinned at me. "Now what do we do with him?"

It was a good question. Shooting him dead while he was unconscious did seem rather unsporting. If he could be made to talk, there was much he could tell us. "Get your father," I said. "This is a good time to have the police here."

Greta bounded out of the room, down the stairs, and out the door, which slammed behind her. While I waited for the reinforcements to arrive, I gathered up the stolen documents that Karl had stolen from us and searched the room for any other goodies he might have stockpiled.

A radio codebook lay to the side of the radio, a veritable direction manual for contacting the Reich. It was a nice little find, and I microfilmed it for our guys and added it to the list of supplies I would hand off to John tonight. My skin warmed at the thought of seeing him.

I stepped around the inert form and glanced out the window to see Lars and Greta striding up the front walk to the porch. I went to greet them and get Lars up to speed, although Greta had already done a fair job in that department. I directed Lars upstairs to the bedroom and opened the door. Karl was gone. I shot a glance over at the desk. The keys were gone as well. Karl had slipped through our grasp. I looked stupidly around the room, as if Karl were a misplaced article of clothing - a wayward jacket or a pair of reading glasses. But he had flown the coop, and the open window was the only clue to the avenue of his departure.

At least he'd have a headache, small consolation that it was. I had to admire his resilience and his dexterity. I went to shut the window and glanced down. It was a nasty drop with nothing to break the fall, but there was no body sprawled on the ground below, so he had managed to make good his escape. It was an unsatisfying conclusion but still, I had the documents in my hand, and the radio was on the desk.

"He was here," I gave a final look around the room and turned to Lars, "but he's not here now." The sudden roar of an engine broke the silence and I knew Karl had won this round. I have a marvelous grasp of the obvious, and so with no way of telling where he was headed, for the time being at least, he'd managed to elude capture. With nothing else to occupy us at the parsonage, we headed home.

"Where do you suppose he went?" Greta looked back at the parsonage. We were walking to the house, the bicycle between us and each of us with one hand on a handlebar and the other keeping the radio somewhat in contact with the basket on the handlebars. It was slow going, sort of like escorting an elderly relative. Lars had gone on ahead to tell Inge what had happened.

"I'm not sure. I'm wondering that myself. He was worried about Strasser, he's killed Dagmar, he's been relaying information to the Germans, and he's been exposed. That's quite a bit to juggle."

"Do you think he will still cause us trouble?" Greta's brow was furrowed, but she might just have been concentrating on keeping the bicycle upright.

"I think the Germans are going to cause us more than

enough trouble without worrying about Karl. My bet is that Karl or whatever name he assumes next will show up somewhere else with a new identity, a new assignment, and a new boss. That sort always lands on his feet." He'd better have landed on his feet, I thought, and even at that he might have fractured an ankle or a leg. Checking the hospital, I was positive, wouldn't yield anything of use. He'd drive on until he was back in Deutschland or somewhere else that afforded time to recuperate.

"What about the Colonel, though? She asked. Won't they be looking for him?"

"I'm sure they will. He was a top mucky-muck. But he covered his own trail quite well when he took off on his own to look for Dagmar. That was personal business and he wouldn't have shared his plans with anyone. They'll probably check his route, question anyone along the way, but soon they'll have to let it go. They'll have more urgent matters to deal with and will probably decide he was a traitor or a spy or something of that sort." I glanced at Greta. "That would be ironic, but then nothing is really as it seems at all."

Greta had a blank look on her face, so I explained. "We have a minister who is a spy and one of the good guys. That will be your *Onkel* John. We have a spy who is a minister and one of the bad guys. That would be Karl Mueller. We have a Colonel in the German army they will think is a spy and who is actually dead. That will be Strasser, and a missing file clerk who actually is, or was, a spy of sorts and who is also dead. That is Dagmar."

"So we're safe." It was more a statement than a question.

"In that regard, yes." I smiled at her. "We have other concerns now. In a few hours, our company arrives." We walked the rest of the way home in silence.

Inge greeted us at the front door, and had already exchanged her Easter finery for a housedress and apron. If the flour on her cheek was any indicator, she was working in the kitchen. There was no way we were going to be weak from lack of food today.

"Here's your Easter basket," I said, pointing to the radio. Inge beamed.

"I hope our inventory doesn't slack off when you've gone," she said. "You've been a steady supplier." She appraised the radio with the eye of a professional. "I have decided that I am beginning a new business. I am now in the Reallocation of Supplies."

I burst out laughing and Greta came down with a serious fit of the giggles. We carted our loot into the barn and surveyed our stash. It was looking impressive. Greta left to bring Volmer and Anna up to date on our activities, with a warning from me not to elaborate.

"Just the facts, Greta," I cautioned.

"Yes, ma'am," and she saluted. "Just the facts."

Chapter Thirty-Five

Sankt Peder

Greta was once again seated cross-legged on the floor of Volmer's study, pressing ferns between the pages of her schoolbooks. She was especially fond of her history text for this purpose, as it weighed more than all of her other books combined. It was a way to pass the time while they waited for nightfall, and as she added a few other smaller books to the pile weighting down the plants, she had created a short, lopsided tower while she worked. She now regarded it with a tilt of her head. "I think it looks like the Leaning Tower of Pisa," she said to Volmer.

"More like the Tower of Babel," he replied with a laugh. "I think you are trying to reach heaven itself. It's certainly well on the way."

Greta leaned back and rested her palms on the floor behind her. She considered her little structure and reached forward to coax a book back in line. "Do you think that's really why there are so many languages on earth? The story seems too simple."

"People have always looked for simple answers to complicated problems. Sometimes they're right and sometimes not. And sometimes there are no answers, just more questions."

"Now you're talking riddles," she said.

"No, let me show you." Volmer left her side and fetched the Bible from its stand. He took it to the couch and patted the cushion next to him. Greta accepted the invitation and sat down beside him, folding her legs underneath her.

"Words are marvelously complex. They have layers of meaning, if you know how to seek them out. Listen to this. I want you to think about what is going to happen tonight as I read." And he began.

"In the beginning was the Word, and the Word was with God. In Him was life, and that life was the light of men. And the light shone in the darkness and the darkness grasped it not."

Volmer set the book down on his lap and looked at Greta. "I condensed it a little bit. John has a tendency to repeat himself from time to time, but sometimes it's necessary." He repeated the last line. "And the light shone in the darkness and the darkness grasped it not."

"What word am I supposed to seek? I'm awfully glad you didn't start in on the *Begats*, by the way."

Volmer gave her a gentle scowl. "Another time perhaps. I am going to answer your question with another. Can you find the metaphor?"

It was clear to Greta that Volmer wasn't going to help her find her way out of this one easily. "Let me write it down and work on it. I need a pencil." She stretched over to her books and picked up her writing tablet and pencil and copied down the verse. She cocked her head right and then left and then right again. She closed her eyes and her lips silently repeated the words.

"Okay. Light and darkness, that's good and evil." She opened the eye closest to Volmer and tilted her head up at him. Those are abstract ideas. They could also represent people. Good people and bad people?" The last part was a question.

"Go on," Volmer said.

Greta took this as confirmation. All right, she was on the right track. She studied the rest of the verse and shook her head. "A hint? Just one?"

"It's in the verb."

Greta nodded and studied the words again. "Light shines and darkness can't hold on to it." She was triumphant. "Good will win out over evil."

"There's more. Look deeper."

"More? Really? Then it's got to be in the *grasp* part. Right?" She looked at Volmer. "But I don't think I get it."

"Ah, but you just did. Look," he pointed to the word. "Darkness cannot grasp the light. Not only can it not hold it, it cannot understand it. Evil cannot understand good. That is important. Those who do good will be misunderstood, and they must remain strong in the face of that, if they are to prevail." He searched Greta's face. "Good does not automatically win. There will be a fight. Sometimes a tremendous struggle, but faith and perseverance will eventually triumph if they stay the course."

"Like tonight?'

"Like tonight. This is the beginning, and we must hold onto the light until we have conquered the darkness. We must hold onto each other. That is where we will find our strength." An idea had occurred to Volmer, and he nodded inwardly. The Bible could be an excellent media for communication for the newly formed Resistance. All they needed was a roadmap, and they already had one in the Concordance. He gave a deep chuckle of satisfaction as he returned the Book to its stand.

Greta uncurled her legs and stretched them out in front of her. Her right foot had fallen asleep and was all pins and needles. She stood up and walked across the room to look out the east window. It was the time of day when shadows seemed to have substance. Castel Grunespan, receiving the last rays of the setting sun, was a dark predator swallowing up the remnants of the fading light, as it cast its lengthening shadow across the field behind it. A lonely gull circled high in the darkening sky and a few clouds hovering on the horizon turned from white to gray and finally dark blue as the sun set. They sky looked bruised. Greta now hopped on her right foot, coaxing it to wakefulness. Tonight felt almost like Christmas Eve and the anticipation was almost too much to bear.

"I'll go home now, Uncle Volmer." Greta pushed her schoolbooks against the wall and hopped down the stairs.

"It won't be long now, Greta. I'll be along directly," and Volmer took Greta's place by the window, puffing on his pipe, watching as darkness settled over the land and across the water. He heard her call a goodbye to Anna, who was somewhere in the back of the house, and then the sound of the door closing behind her as she skipped down the porch steps and across the street to home.

Chapter Thirty-Six

Sankt Peder

I was examining Inge's emerald dress with a critical eye and decided it had survived its bicycle jaunt in good shape. Just went to prove the truth of what Mama always said, "Don't buy cheap. You buy cheap, you got cheap and cheap don't last." This dress was quality, and I knew Inge would wear it for many years to come.

Smoothing the fabric with my hand, I adjusted its position on its padded green hanger. I had the hat snug and safe back in its box, and was carrying it to the shelf. Both my arms were occupied when Greta called out to me and I asked her to open the door. She took the hat box and we returned both items to Inge's closet.

"You looked pretty in Mama's dress," said Greta. "Green suits you. I don't like dresses. They get in the way of everything."

I had to agree there, remembering my earlier difficulties trying to get to work without having my skirts billow over my head or worse, be ruined with black grease marks from the spokes and chain. Slacks were the answer. So much more practical. "There's a time and a place for dresses," I said, "and church is one. Bicycles, though. No."

Greta nodded solemnly. She had an ally. We were two of

a kind. My poor sister had her hands full. First me, then the Nazis, and now Greta. But she could handle it. We Nissen women were made from an indestructible mold.

"*Tante* Katrin, can I ask you something?" Greta's voice was serious. She'd plopped herself down on the bed and her lips were pursed.

"Sure, honey. Anything." I sat down beside her.

"Uncle Volmer has the Bible. Of course we all do" she added quickly. "But then Aunt Anna has Gefion, and she's not real. Gefion, I mean, not Aunt Anna."

"Well, Gefion is a legend and legends have their place. They also teach us important lessons." However, this was not what Greta was looking for, so I nodded and waited for the climax. I had an idea where this was headed.

"Who do I have?"

"Hmmm." I considered this for a moment, although this was not as difficult as other questions she could have asked.

"Well, of course you have the Bible, and you also have what Gefion represents. Aunt Anna needed a symbol and Gefion provided that." I had been sitting parallel to Greta and now scooted around so I could see her face. "So you want something that belongs to you alone?

Greta nodded.

"I don't think that is possible, honey. Whatever talisman you select, you must share with others. Do you understand?" I didn't wait for her answer, but pressed on. "When we share something, we become stronger. We cannot do what must be done, alone. So I think you need a protector. Someone strong. Someone who will fight by your side. I studied her face. Do you know the legend of Holger Danske?"

"I remember some of it," Greta said, but it's a fairy tale. It's not real. I want something real."

"This must be your day for stories," I laughed. "Holger Danske was a strong warrior. He was indeed real. He lived many hundreds of years ago, and he fought mightily to protect Denmark. And now he sleeps. But he has promised that should Denmark ever be in mortal danger, he will awaken and once again fight for us."

"Do you believe this, Aunt Katrin?"

"I believe that the spirit of Holger Danske lives in each of us. So yes, Greta, he is very real." I summed up, "Holger Danske is yours. I give him to you." I presented my outstretched hands to Greta, who accepted them with a solemn face and a half bow. "And now you have a responsibility to share him with others who need his help."

"Thanks, *Tante* Katrin. And I do understand. I was kind of hoping to have a woman, but a mighty warrior will work."

"You, my dear, will be the mighty warrior. Holger Danske will be your guide. But right now it is time to eat. If we don't get to the dining room soon, we will both need Holger Danske to protect us from your mother's wrath."

In the face of danger, my sister cooked. I believe she will cater the Last Judgment, and it will be a gala affair. She will be sure everyone has their just desserts. Today Inge's cooking had filled the house with tantalizing aromas. My stomach rumbled, I shrugged, and Greta laughed.

"It's just Sailor's Stew," Inge announced as she carried the soup tureen to the table. "I wanted something simple that would warm us. It's going to be chilly out in the field." My sister doesn't think a meal is anything special unless it consists of eleven courses. There were nearly that many courses in the Stew. Beef, potatoes, onions, ham, spices. I inhaled appreciatively, and fetched the loaf of rye bread from the breadbox on the counter. Presiding over the counter was a wall plaque that admonished: "Kissing don't last. Cooking do." It lost something in the translation. Danish is a difficult language.

The stew was hearty fare, rich and satisfying, and the rye bread, still warm from the oven, and fresh cream butter was exactly the right choice for supper. When Lars finally tossed his napkin on the table, we couldn't have eaten another bite.

So we saved dessert, apple pie, for when we returned.

"We'll need to set out extra plates for the people we'll bring home with us, Mama."

"We will, Greta," her mother replied. "We'll leave the dishes. They'll keep." Lars rose from his chair. It was six-thirty and four lanterns were lined up on the sideboard, waiting.

Inge handed Lars his lantern. "You can help with the dishes when we get back, *Ja*?"

"For sure." Lars had no intention of doing dishes. He knew it and Inge knew it, and I had it on good authority that he had had to ask Inge where she kept the spoons. The man only came into the kitchen to eat. But I knew Inge preferred it that way.

"Did Diogenes ever find his honest man?" Inge asked.

"We're looking for eight honest men, from what Katrin tells me," he said.

"No, seven men and one woman. And they'll be looking for us," I said.

We filed out the back door and down the porch steps, following the cobblestone path that wound past the kitchen garden. At the edge of the garden we left the path and cut across the lower field, ending up at the northern boundary of the farm, where the ocean lapped against the sandy shore. There we stopped, set our lanterns down, and waited.

There was a static charge to the air that was palpable. From all parts of the town, neighbors and friends converged upon Jensen's field, each carrying a lantern. Anna's hymns had done their work.

The lanterns winked on one by one. We were a circle of light, a homing beacon for the plane and a landing perimeter for the parachutists. I looked up at the heavens and waited, my eyes straining to see in the darkness. Then, from the western sky a distant drone, at first faint, but then growing stronger and nearer until the roar filled our ears. The sound passed overhead and faded once again into the darkness. In its wake a silent snowstorm of white silk and gossamer threads drifted earthward. Drifted, that is, until the earth rushed up to greet them.

The silence was punctuated with a series of grunts, gasps, and enthusiastic cussing. The troops had landed. Their movements were efficient as they caught up the billowing fabric in their arms, wrestling it into submission. Inge eyed it greedily, plans for its use already forming in her head.

My heart was racing and my eyes moved rapidly across the crowd, seeking one man. And then there he was. Our eyes met and I raced towards him, arms open wide to embrace him. I launched myself into his arms and wrapped myself around him, burying my face in his chest. I didn't think I would ever let him go and he held me just as tightly. We clung to each other for the longest time and then we kissed. A deep, slow, kiss that set me on fire. We were the only two people on earth. I closed my eyes and felt a longing stirring deep within. It was passion, desire, and ultimately the need for air. We had gotten tangled up in the parachute which was settling down around us, covering our heads and threatening to suffocate us.

We broke apart like two teenaged lovers caught necking on the sofa by papa, and with flailing arms and clawing hands, managed to climb free, but in the process we tripped over the cords and tumbled to the ground. John grinned at me with that lopsided smile and we both burst out laughing. We laughed until the tears came and then we embraced again. Someone collected our parachute, I suspected my sister, and we left for Inge's, arms around each other's waists, holding on for all our might.

I had so much to tell him, but it could wait just a little while. We climbed the stairs to my room and we kissed again. We were making certain, if slow progress towards the bed, and when we finally got close enough, tumbled into it, kissing and groping, and generally acting like two lovers who have been apart for too long. It was good.

"There is someone you need to watch out for," I said an hour or so later, and told John what I had learned about Karl. "I was warned and now I am warning you. He is still out there, and he is dangerous."

"He is very good at what he does," John agreed. "He has a bit of a history and he slips through our grasp just when we are ready to take him in. He covers his tracks well and always manages to land on his feet. You know," he said, "Winston calls him 'The Chameleon.' To others he is Ronin. Either description fits him."

"He is a killer," I said.

"Many of us have killed," John said pointedly.

"No, well yes, but still no. This is different. I think he enjoys killing. He has no remorse and talking with him, I got a strange feeling." I looked at John. "It's like he has no soul. Just an empty place where it should be."

"Maybe he's made a deal with the devil and the department of longevity demons. You know Hitler says the Third Reich will last a thousand years. That's a long time. He's thrown in his lot with that group."

"Maybe." I had my doubts that Karl cared about anything. "It's more like he is exacting revenge. I think down deep he's just plain angry. Just be careful. I don't think you can trust him."

John's eyes were serious. "That's the first rule of the game. I don't trust anyone."

"No one?" I raised an eyebrow at him.

"No one. Especially wanton women." He leered at me and that led to other matters, so it was a bit later when I pursued the former line of conversation.

"Well, what's that supposed to mean? If you think you're just going to say something like that and walk away, you've got another think coming." My face was getting hot. Instead of answering, he kissed me.

"That advice goes for you as well. Be suspicious. Always."

We made love. We slept. We made love again. War is hell. And with the first light of dawn, he held me close and kissed me one last time. Within the hour I was off for Sweden, on a small boat that was part of the fishing fleet heading for open waters. John was bound for Copenhagen to set down the framework by which the small churches throughout Denmark would join together to bring down the enemy in their midst. The pastors and their flocks would be the eyes and ears of the Allies and John, as the Reverend Martin Shoneborger, would walk a dangerous tightrope, passing on their intelligence to headquarters.

By tomorrow night I would be in London, and the night after that, who knew where? I sat in the dinghy, a lonely emigrant with my suitcase beside me, and I held in my hand a small box that John had given me. His instructions were not to open it until I was on the water, so I had forced myself to wait. And now, inside the box, wrapped in tissue paper, I found my wedding band with a note attached by a white ribbon. Three simple words from the man who had said he trusted no one. But the ring gave him the lie, as I read "Nobody but you." I kissed the ring and slipped it on my finger, raised my face to the east and felt the salt spray against my skin as I saw the shores of Sweden come into view.

Postscript

While this is a work of fiction, it is based upon actual historical events. Winston Churchill was First Lord of the Admiralty when WWII broke out. Operation Wilfred was Churchill's plan to mine the waters off the coast of Norway to prevent Germany from transporting iron ore mined in Sweden. The ore was essential to fuel the German war machine. Churchill first proposed Operation Wilfred in September 1939, shortly after Germany invaded Poland. He tried in vain for several months to have his plan acted upon.

Intelligence originating from Denmark did give Churchill the evidence he needed to have Operation Wilfred approved, but the approval came too late. Wilfred was launched on April 8, 1940, but the Germans overran Denmark on their way to Norway in *Operation Weserübung* on April 9.

While Churchill's plan ultimately failed, the credibility he earned as a result of his efforts led to his being named Prime Minister of the United Kingdom upon the resignation of Neville Chamberlain on May 10, 1940. He remained Prime Minister throughout the course of the war, ultimately achieving the victory that mattered.

During WWII, the Danish Resistance was tireless in its efforts. During the German occupation, the Resistance made use of intelligence that was passed on at ladies' church group meetings to sabotage and thwart the Nazis at every turn. The churchwomen of Denmark were the backbone of the Danish Resistance.

World War II remains a watershed time in world history for one fundamental reason. It was a time when good people became heroes, simply by making the moral choice. That so many people did so ultimately led to victory.